INFINITE POSSESSIONS

M. K. Danielson

A Wicked Paranormal Saga:
Part Two

To contact the publisher email: MKEEDanielson@gmail.com

ISBN Paperback: 979-8-9929725-0-4
ISBN Hardcover: 979-8-9929725-1-1

Cover design by: GetCovers

FROM THE AUTHOR

Greetings beloved reader. Welcome to my second novel. This story, and some of the characters you are about to meet, began a number of years ago with a series of mysterious and grisly events that stunned a small community. *INFINITE POSSESSIONS* unites the old and the new under a common goal, even as they struggle with the resurrection of long-buried and distasteful memories.

If you care to explore those original events, I'm happy to share my first novel, *DEADLY POSSESSION* (Copyright © 2023 – All rights reserved). Whichever you decide, I thank you for your interest in my imagination. I hope you enjoy the journey that awaits you.

—M. K. Danielson, Attica, NY

TABLE OF CONTENTS

PROLOGUE

May, 1988

Manny Romero had doubts about his decision to join his friend Mateo in running off from the prison farm, but he had to admit it was exciting. And that was okay until the young man with softly glowing red eyes showed up in the culvert with them.

Leaving the hay field was a breeze. They grabbed two bicycles a pair of teenagers had left along the Tonawanda Creek while they went fishing after school. The men rode quickly along the edge of the hay field, then crossed Route 238, which fortunately had no traffic. Once they turned and followed the railroad tracks, they were quickly out of sight and hoped the hard ballast stones would make them impossible to track.

It was easy going. The original railroad had two main lines. A third siding rail for switching cars used to run for a few miles out of Attica. As the railroad industry declined, usage dropped to a single main line, while the original second line was used as the siding. The third set of rails, torn up years before, made a convenient access road for farmers and maintenance crews. And inmates on the run.

They found an area with thick brush between the tracks and a farmer's field. They ditched the bikes out of sight and began waiting for an eastbound train. They shared visions of returning to their old neighborhoods – East Harlem for Mateo, Newark for Manny. With the western New York spring sunshine warming their faces, they waited and talked of disappearing into the large metro areas they called home – hoping never to be found by the police again.

Unfortunately, the days of trains going by with open-door box cars, just waiting for passengers, were long gone. Jumping on a train in broad daylight seemed like a great way to be spotted. So they waited.

As they stayed hidden throughout the afternoon, it seemed no one had any idea where they were, or where to look. They remained on high alert. But the adrenaline wore off and their initial sense of urgency diminished. Needing to avoid detection, rationality kicked in and they decided to wait until dark before making a move. Another reason, that remained unspoken, was that all the trains were moving much too fast to be able to grab hold and climb aboard. Manny worried about that. But with no other options, they stayed hidden in the brush, near a culvert where they could disappear if they spotted any helicopters or vehicles approaching.

Darkness finally fell and they vowed to jump onto the next eastbound train, no matter what kind of cars it had. Manny still wondered about the speed of the trains but forgot about it as soon as they saw a pair of headlights coming toward them along the tracks. As the vehicle drove around a curve, the driver curiously turned off the headlights. Manny saw it was a pickup truck, not a police cruiser. That offered little comfort, however, as they couldn't afford to be seen by anyone.

"*Vámonos!*" Mateo said and took off from the brush. Manny scrambled behind him, down the embankment and into the culvert.

After the pickup went by overhead, the pair peeked out and watched in the moonlight as the truck pulled into a farmer's field, went over a knoll and disappeared. It all seemed rather odd. But they figured it wouldn't be long before the next eastbound Conrail train came along and they could forget about it.

They waited in silence, wishing they had some cigarettes or food – anything to bide their time. Waiting for nightfall seemed to take forever. Once it arrived, their eagerness to put some miles behind them grew. Manny looked at his friend, his olive skin and brush cut barely visible in the darkness. His dull green prison clothes were almost invisible.

Then Mateo spoke, his accent thick with his Mexican neighborhood dialect. "Let's wait at the other end. I can't imagine who is in the truck, but when the next train comes I'd just as soon be on the opposite side and out of sight when we jump on."

That made sense to Manny. They moved to the other end of the culvert and continued waiting. The culvert had a small amount of water on the floor, so they didn't sit. But at least it was high enough inside that they could stand comfortably. After a few minutes in silence, Manny looked up at his friend again, about to ask a question. Instead, he saw Mateo's eyes widen with terror as he looked over Manny's shoulder.

Manny turned to look behind him. At the far end of the culvert, with only the light of the moon sneaking in, he saw a smallish man with glowing red eyes approaching them. He had no idea what was happening, but running out the end of the culvert seemed like the best option. Mateo needed no convincing and was already moving. Manny followed. But before he looked away, he saw what looked like a pair of long, white fangs hanging over the small man's bottom lip.

They ran out of the culvert and scrambled up the embankment, only to find the creature had somehow gone back out the other end and beat them to the top. Not having a plan, the two decided to keep running. But they started in opposite directions, and neither was inclined to stop.

When Manny looked over his shoulder he saw the creature had gone after Mateo. Showing freakish speed, the creature caught him instantly, grabbing him from behind. It spun Mateo around and their eyes locked. A calm, lustful look came over Manny's friend. Ignoring Manny, the creature went to his knees, gently laying Mateo on the railroad bed, with no resistance.

With his fangs shining in the moonlight, the creature leaned toward Mateo's neck. Manny freaked out in horror. Still, he had to try to help. He ran at them – all six feet and two-hundred forty pounds of him. But as he dove into the creature to try to knock it off Mateo, the small man-creature raised one hand and misdirected Manny with the strength of a dozen men. Manny flew about twenty feet down the roadway, landing roughly on the large ballast stones.

Physically and mentally shaken, he looked back to see the creature already biting at his friend's neck. He couldn't just stand by, so he took another run, only to be sent flying equally as far in the opposite direction.

Sore, but with nothing broken, Manny looked at his partner, lying helplessly – wantingly waiting for the creature to carry on. And it did. Manny started another rush, but the creature pulled away from Mateo's neck. With a trickle of blood running down its chin, the creature hissed at him with a deep, driving guttural sound. Manny stopped short, hopelessly looking at his helpless friend. But he knew he was beat, and nothing good would come from him sticking around.

It hurt, but he forced himself to turn and run along the roadway, distancing himself. As he ran, it seemed odd, but Manny marveled at how the human mind could work. Sprinting away with the monster behind him, he found himself wondering. *Do creatures? . . . Vampires. Face it, Manny, that's what you just saw, a vampire. Never mind that just five minutes ago you wouldn't have believed it. It was a vampire if there ever was one.*

As he ran, Manny couldn't help but wonder, *Do vampires drive pickup trucks?*

Fortunately, his conscious mind returned and told him to keep going. With the rush of adrenaline pumping like never before, he ran.

And ran.

And ran.

When the roadway made by the old siding track ended, Manny kept running between the double tracks. He ran until he couldn't run any longer. Exhausted, he finally stopped to catch his breath – still keeping an eye on his backtrack in case the thing was coming after him.

As he calmed down and his breathing returned to normal, Manny saw a light and heard an eastbound train approaching. He ducked into the brush to hide so the engineer wouldn't see him.

Absently, he wondered why the policymakers in the prison system chose a dull green color for their prison clothes – not that he was complaining.

As the train passed, he noticed there were no box cars. It was made up mostly of hopper cars. The kind with two triangular shapes, narrow at the bottom with a gate for unloading. Because of that shape, there was a natural open area at the front and rear of each car, with plenty of room for a man to sit and have a sort of roof over him.

He also noticed the train wasn't traveling as fast as the previous ones. In fact, after another minute he realized the train was stopping. That would make it easier to board. But he also knew the reason it was stopping. No doubt the monster – *vampire*, he forced himself to admit again – had left Mateo's body lying along the tracks where the engineer had seen and reported it.

Manny didn't know a lot about train protocol. He knew they wouldn't want to keep it stopped for very long. He also knew it wouldn't take long for the cops to identify Mateo. And since they were already looking for Mateo and Manny, he worried they might search the whole train before allowing it to leave.

But he didn't know. He decided to wait in the brush, ready to run if he saw anybody coming from either direction – ready to jump on if the train began to move again. He found a place where he felt hidden but could see fairly well in both directions while he waited.

For the next twenty minutes, Manny grew more nervous. Eventually, he saw and heard a westbound train approaching on the second track. It passed much slower than the previous trains, and he thought maybe it was stopping too. He finally realized it was only going slower because the second track was just a siding, and was only being used so the train could pass. Moving slower, but not stopping.

As he sat there Manny thought about his former life. He had just witnessed an event that would change how he looked at the world forever. And going back to Newark, where he didn't have any friends or even close family, seemed like a good way to get caught. Of course, he told himself, that would be the first place they would look for him.

On the westbound train, there was a long row of auto carrier cars. Empty ones, no doubt headed back to Detroit. They had corrugated steel sides, because when kids like Manny were young they couldn't resist throwing rocks at the shiny new cars. Also, fortunately, there were no roofs. Apparently that wasn't as much of an issue.

He considered what he was doing. Waiting for a stopped, possibly searched train, to go back east to Newark where everyone would be looking for him no longer seemed practical. The problem with going west was that no matter where he went in that direction, he wouldn't return to familiar territory. He would also have to go back through the place where there were no doubt numerous police. And while he doubted the monster – *vampire* – was still around, going back past that scene wasn't a pleasant thought.

Still, the westbound train didn't appear to be stopping. Manny thought if he could stay hidden in a car carrier, he could slide right past the police. He gave one last thought to heading back east and decided it would never work. So he ran as fast as he could along the side of one of the empty cars of the westbound train. When he reached out and grabbed the ladder that ran up the side it felt like his arms would pop out of their sockets. But he managed to stay on and make his way to the top. He climbed over the edge and plopped down onto the convenient, built-in upper deck. He was out of sight behind the steel siding, with an easy climb to get back out when the time came. So far everything was going well.

Before long he saw the emergency lights up ahead. He laid down flat and didn't move. He didn't even breathe until they were well past the death scene. Still, he couldn't help but peek through the slits of siding where he caught one last glimpse of his friend Mateo's body, surrounded by police.

Adrenaline had been pumping furiously for some time, and Manny found it hard to settle down. His mind constantly flashed back to the scene he'd just left, and that didn't help. He stood up and looked back while the distance increased. Long after everything was out of sight, he finally convinced himself the super-human monster wasn't following him, and he laid down.

And the train kept going.

Of course he was unable to sleep. But he was able to rest for a while. After about a half-hour, the train pulled into a switching yard. There were trains and disconnected cars everywhere. And when his train stopped, Manny grew concerned. He wondered if the authorities had second thoughts and decided to search it after all. Looking through the cracks between the siding, he decided they were only switching out sections. He hoped his section would just be sent along to Detroit before long. Unless there was some unknown reason to leave empty auto carriers in . . . he wasn't sure where he was . . . Buffalo, maybe?

He forced himself to stay put. Anxiety was high, but Manny was surprised the whole switching process didn't seem to drag on. Before long they were rolling along at full speed again, heading west. And that was good enough for the time being. He settled back down and tried not to dwell on the red-eyed monster with fangs that attacked and killed his friend Mateo.

A vampire, he reminded himself again. *That's what you saw, and don't ever try to tell yourself you didn't.*

It wasn't easy.

★ ★ ★ ★ ★

The next ride was longer. Manny still couldn't sleep, but he managed to relax and recharge his body and mind despite the chilly night air. As he did, reality settled in. He realized he had been foolish to let Mateo talk him into running off. Did they think they could ride eastbound trains all the way back to Harlem and Newark in prison clothes, without a penny between them?

Unfortunately, heading west with no particular destination wasn't any better. He wondered how much extra prison time he would have to serve for such a boneheaded stunt. And worse, he had time to wonder what he would say to the police who discovered Mateo's body, knowing the two had run off together. That was going to be tough. Manny wasn't even sure what to tell himself about that. Of course, he couldn't tell anybody what he really saw. They'd give him a new home with a straight jacket and padded walls – and probably throw away the key.

Eventually, when the train stopped again, he looked out and guessed he was in the suburbs of Cleveland. Or maybe Toledo. It was hard to tell, but it didn't matter. He knew it was time to get out of the car carrier and face up to things. The sun was hinting at rising, and Manny didn't figure there was any sense in staying on only to show up in Detroit in broad daylight.

Resigned to finding a police car and turning himself in, he climbed out and started walking. In no time he found himself in an older-looking, residential neighborhood. Thankfully, it was still mostly dark and nobody was moving yet. He trudged along a sidewalk between rows of two-story clapboard houses, hoping to find a police officer before anybody looked out their window and reported a guy in prison clothes walking in their neighborhood.

He kept walking until he came to a corner block that was taken up by an old church. There it was, right there amid the houses. It wasn't large, but it had a decent-sized parking lot and a sign in front that read – CUYUHOGA INDEPENDENT CHURCH. Manny figured since he was not only looking for the police, but also running from an evening full of supernatural, super-human forces – with the pains from landing on the stones twice to remind him – he might as well do it in a church.

Then he reminded himself it was early morning on a Wednesday, and told himself that option was probably out. But as he got closer, it appeared there were some lights on inside. And when he got near enough, he saw an old car parked in the lot, near the back entrance. Back in business.

Not wanting to be caught sneaking around, he tried the front doors first. Finding them locked, he went around the side to the rear of the building. The old car was a black, sixty-something Ford Falcon, which Manny thought was pretty cool. Unfortunately, it wasn't the time or place for that.

He looked into the back door window and saw a large kitchen with the lights on. He knocked on the door and waited. Then he knocked and waited again. Finally, with the sun rising and not

10

wanting to be out in the open dressed as he was, he opened the door and peeked his head in.

He called out. "Hello?"

Still nothing. He tried a few more times with no response so he let himself in, surprised at how large the kitchen was – with old wooden cabinets surrounding the appliances, and an island in the center. He moved across the room and through another door that led into another equally large room, sparsely filled with a few couches and chairs.

On the far side was a pair of swinging doors. One was propped open and the lights were on in that room. He made his way toward the light and entered the nave. Rows of pews with burgundy carpet running between them gave it an old-fashioned feel. It was the kind of church you would see in old western movies or small-town settings.

Manny stopped just inside and again said, "Hello?"

A muffled male voice from somewhere responded with a friendly-sounding, "Hello!"

Manny looked around. Not seeing anybody made him quizzical. He had heard people talking about speaking with God, but surely it couldn't be that easy.

After a few seconds, the muffled voice said, "I'll be right with you."

Still not seeing anybody, he looked upward. He shrugged his shoulders and told himself, of course God was busy. He walked past a raised pulpit on his left and stopped at the front row of pews. Upon turning around to sit down he noticed what in Manny's world looked like a raised jury box next to the pulpit. He guessed it was probably a place for the singing choir to sit. In front of that, on the floor level with him, was a piano and an old organ.

11

The organ had been pulled away from the wall in front of the jury box, with a pair of feet sticking out from behind it.

He laughed at himself. Then he heard a muffled thump and a clunk, and what sounded like a couple of curse words. Soon after an older man – about seventy Manny figured, with a balding head of gray hair, blue utility pants, and a short-sleeved, button-down gray shirt – worked his way out and stood up. The old man had a friendly, wrinkled face and gold, wire-rimmed glasses. He gave Manny a once-over – obviously noting his clothes – but didn't seem to judge him.

"What can I do for you?" the man asked.

Manny wasn't exactly sure. Should he ask the guy to call the cops and get it over with? Since his life had been turned upside down by an inhuman monster just a few hours previously, should he ask for help and guidance in the spiritual sense? He was in a church after all.

Finally, he asked quietly, "Are you the preacher?"

"Oh heavens no!" The man replied. "I'm just an old fart trying to get this old organ working long enough to get through another Sunday service."

The man gave Manny another once-over, approached him and stuck out his hand.

"Clyde Wickersham. Everybody calls me Uncle Clyde. Glad to meet you."

Manny took his hand and replied, "Manny Romero."

For the first time, Clyde looked at him dubiously. But Manny was used to that. He continued, "My mother was German-American with blonde hair and blue eyes. I guess I get it from her."

Clyde smiled. "You look like you've had a long night. I'm not the preacher but I'm a good listener. Why don't we go into the

12

kitchen and I'll make you some of my famous French toast? And if you want you can tell me all about it."

That sounded good to Manny. He figured the cops could wait so he followed Clyde into the kitchen and sat at the large island. Clyde started gathering ingredients. Manny was surprised that such a small church had a kitchen full of food. Though he admitted to himself, he didn't know much about churches.

Even as Clyde worked on breakfast with his back to Manny, his friendliness had Manny at ease. Still, he balked when Clyde asked him again if he'd like to talk about anything. Clyde assured him that he'd been through the second World War, and in his seventy-one trips around the Sun he'd seen and heard a lot. So Manny should feel free.

He figured he had to tell somebody someday. It wasn't easy. He started slowly. But Clyde just listened, nodding and assuring him in all the right places. Once Manny got rolling, and Clyde never suggested anything was abnormal, he began to tell the story in full. He laid it all out, including all the details of the vampire with the super-human strength. And how he ran like Hell, caught a train, and wound up sitting there.

When he was done, Clyde said, "That's one Hell of a story." He put a plate filled with French toast, scrambled eggs, and sausage links in front of Manny and said, "Dig in, you deserve it."

Manny laughed at that. But he did dig in, not realizing until then how hungry he was. Clyde went into the other room. Manny couldn't hear, but he knew it was to make a phone call. The only question left was who would show up first, the police or the men in the white coats? By then he didn't care.

He attacked his breakfast. Clyde came back but was silent, cleaning up and doing dishes. After a few minutes, Manny heard a vehicle approaching outside and knew the jig was up.

"I want to thank you for your kindness, sir."

Clyde brightened up. "Think nothing of it."

Then a man walked in. He was average in size, with neatly trimmed brown hair and a beard. He wore a gray suit, which Manny found impressive since it was so early and he had arrived on such short notice. He walked over to Manny and put out his hand. "Hi, I'm Winston Gerrard. I'm pleased to meet you."

Manny took his hand. The man seemed so formal he responded, "Manuel Romero."

Clyde excused himself, saying he had to get the organ working or Mrs. Wickersham would have his ass come Sunday morning.

Winston sat down next to Manny. "Clyde tells me you had an eventful evening."

"That's one way of putting it," he said. Manny was surprised that the man who showed up wasn't a policeman.

Winston kept right at it. "He says you saw a vampire."

Manny was shocked. Flabbergasted. It was not at all what he expected. He couldn't even respond. He just nodded and looked down.

"Congratulations. You're in rare company."

Manny looked back up at the man. Not understanding.

"You're one of the few people in the world who has seen a vampire and lived to tell about it. Tell me, what was your crime?"

Manny was reeling. He had expected an ambulance or a squad car to take him away. And here was a stranger who apparently believed his crazy story and didn't even dwell on it. Changed the subject even. He shook his head, needing a minute.

Winston gestured at Manny's prison clothes and asked, "What were you in for?"

Manny finally caught up. "I was supposed to deliver a trunk load of pot from Newark to a small pub out on Long Island. But when I got there I was caught up in a sting operation. I got possession of marijuana – lots of it – with intent to distribute."

Unfazed, Winston then asked, matter-of-factly, "Did you ever kill anybody?"

"No! Hell no!" Manny was suddenly upset. He had no right to be. But he wondered who the man was to be firing off questions like that. He thought maybe the guy was a cop after all.

Winston changed his demeanor. "I apologize. I got a little excited. And there are things I need to know about you before I can extend an invitation."

Still lost. "Invitation?"

Winston smiled warmly. "Again, my apologies. I belong to an organization called Monkey Beans."

Manny was fit to be tied. Was it supposed to be a joke? Why would a man go out of his way to screw with a man whose head was already screwed with?

"Let me explain," Winston continued. "I belong to a centuries-old, private organization with a long name that comes from Greek and Latin phrases. A part of that name sounds like Monkey Beans, so that's what we usually call it."

Manny burst into a fit of laughter. It was probably a lot bigger fit than was called for. But he had been through a lot and decided to let it roll.

Winston surprised him by joining in. Eventually, they calmed down and he began. "Monkey Beans has been around for ages. We have members from all walks of life, all over the world. We have ridiculous amounts of old money, and all manner of resources at our disposal. We watch, document, chronicle, archive, and whenever possible, eliminate evil supernatural beings. You have encountered one such being – possibly the worst of them all – and lived. I don't have to tell you your life will never be the same."

Manny nodded in agreement. "You mean there are others like him? Like it?"

"Well actually, in this particular case, no. The monster you saw is a special kind of entity. We can talk more about that later. But yes, the world we live in is rife with a population of vampires, werewolves and witches."

Manny didn't know how to respond. He couldn't try to deny it after his encounter. But it was still a lot to absorb.

"I will have to check out your crime history, etc. to make sure you're not too evil yourself. But I've got a good feeling. And if you measure up, I am offering you a chance to leave your old life behind. We're always looking for recruits. And I can tell you, with our resources, you will disappear. You will have a whole new life with a new identity and a full-time purpose. And you will never be bored."

Manny stayed silent. It was a lot to consider. He didn't know what to say.

Winston filled the void. "I must say that if you agree to join us, as a currently wanted man, you will have to forget about ever returning to your old life. You will become a whole new person and a full-time employee of Monkey Beans. But you can never return to your old neighborhood. Never contact anyone from your past. Do you have a wife or any children?"

Manny shook his head no.

"A best friend waiting for you to get out?"

Again he shook his head no. Then added, "The only friend I ever had I left lying with a monster back in Attica last night."

"Well good," Winston said bluntly. "I'll give you some time to think it over. I know it's a lot to take in, just as everything you saw last night was a lot."

There was a bit of silence before Winston added, "Now I don't mean this in any threatening manner. But I guess you know your alternative is to go back to where you just came from. I'll leave you here with Clyde for a while. Go ahead and bounce your thoughts off him. He's a good man with a great head on his shoulders."

They stood and shook hands. Winston headed for the door, saying he would check back in a few hours to see what Manny decided. Then he walked out.

Manny stood there contemplating his future. How could he ever go back to doing time? Answering to the police about what happened to Mateo? Living with the knowledge that the world he once thought he knew was certainly not? He thought about the few people in Newark he used to think were friends. But they weren't. When Manny went away no one came to visit or even wrote a letter. They never missed him at all.

He went to the door. Winston was climbing into a shiny red Cadillac. He called to him.

"Hey, Winston! Wait up."

CHAPTER 1

Thirty-Seven Years Later

County sheriff's investigator Tommy Chandler sat down in his office at his utilitarian metal desk – which was neatly arranged and centered in a sparsely decorated, businesslike room – to look at his afternoon mail. Not that there was much actual mail anymore, with the rise of emails and electronic communications. But there was always something to deal with.

It was Friday evening, closing in on the end of his three-to-eleven shift. He had the weekend off. After spending all afternoon giving grand jury testimony, he was glad to be caught up with his police cases and ready for the shift to be over. Thinking back on his thirty-eight years with the department, he was glad to enjoy the mostly regular day shifts – with only one week of late shifts every month – and the usual weekends off that came with the investigator position.

Toni, his wife of thirty-six years, would be busy running her little country diner all weekend, but he figured they should still be able to find a little time to spend together. The idea of taking a vacation soon had floated around in their recent conversations.

19

Tommy thought that would be fun, and planned on pushing the idea further over the next couple of days. He looked forward to having a nice, western New York, early summer weekend.

After ignoring some typical cop association solicitations and putting a pension statement aside for later, his eyes landed on a plain, white envelope with cursive handwriting. That was an oddity in 2025 for sure. Tommy marveled at the beautifully crafted script, wondering how people could write so neatly when his penmanship had always been barely legible. The letter was addressed to Investigator Chandler at the department address. The return address was Manfred Richter, at a post office box in some Maryland town Tommy didn't think he'd ever heard of. The name, Manfred Richter, didn't ring a bell either. He opened the letter with anticipation. Maybe a little mystery to end the week would give him something to look forward to on Monday.

It only took one sentence to change his outlook. While there was still a bit of mystery, a slew of memories, most of which had been allowed to stay buried and mostly ignored, came rushing back.

Events that weren't just related to Tommy either. Years before, residents of his small community, quaintly referred to as County Line, had been subjected to a whirlwind of events. Mysterious, grisly murders that, even though they thankfully ceased soon after they began, were hard to forget. Repressed for sure, but not forgotten. Tommy thought about Toni. Those events had reached into her life too. That made the letter more disturbing, even after only reading one sentence.

There had been many unanswered questions. But with a nominal amount of evidence pointing to a guy named Bud Rogers, who had also left a suicide note and confessed to all the killings, most everyone was content to let it go away and be mostly forgotten. Or at least rarely ever mentioned. Somehow, reading the first sentence, Tommy had a sinking feeling that was about to change.

Dear Investigator Chandler,
Allow me to introduce myself. My name is Manfred Richter, although you will probably remember me as Manuel Romero.

Tommy couldn't bring himself to read any further. "Manuel fucking Romero," he said out loud.

Layla, the second shift dispatcher, was walking by his door on her way back from one of about thirty daily trips to the restroom. She stopped and said, "Who?"

Tommy looked up at her young, round face and blond curls. "Nobody you would know," he said quickly, and truthfully enough. Manuel Romero had been quietly missing and wanted by the law for more years than Layla had been alive. Tommy smiled, hoping she wouldn't inquire any further. It worked. She shrugged and shuffled off.

He silently mouthed the words again. Slowly. "Manuel . . . Romero." Before Mr. Romero went missing all those years before, he and a companion named Mateo Martinez had walked off the prison farm in Attica. Later that evening, Mr. Martinez showed up dead under mysterious circumstances, while Manuel Romero, presumed to be present at that time of that death, vanished without a trace and was never heard from again.

Until now, Tommy thought.

21

On another day, in another town, under other circumstances, a cop would be excited to hear from a fugitive that disappeared for over three decades. But visions of dead bodies drained of blood returned. One named George Lewis, was found decomposed deep in the woods. Cause of death determined as loss of blood (oh, and don't forget, the closest thing his wife, Toni, ever had to a father). One, Martinez, discovered freshly after being killed (and don't forget the unnerving puncture wounds in the neck, and again, loss of blood as the cause of death). How did the missing Mr. Romero fit in with that? And yet another body of a man they had all known and liked – Jimmy T – had his bones run through a homemade, diesel-powered corn shredder after having his soft parts fed to a farrow of pigs.

All the deaths were supposedly perpetrated by Bud Rogers, a young man they had also all known and liked. Many questions about how Bud could have done all the things he confessed, along with his reference to a "madman spirit" in the suicide note, left a lasting emptiness to accompany the uneasiness caused by those events.

In the end, however, overwhelming evidence tying Bud to the scenes, along with a full confession with details in his last written words, combined with an abrupt end to the grisly crimes once Bud died, allowed the entire community – and the police – to let it all fade silently into the past. Tommy realized right then that all that uneasiness was undoubtedly the reason nobody ever tried too hard to find Manuel Romero. Letting it go to rest seemed to be everybody's preference.

Those events had shaken County Line to its core and then some – thirty-seven years before – when Tommy was just a rookie deputy. And somehow, seeing that Manuel Romero had been right in the middle of it, Tommy didn't feel the rest of the letter would be a sudden, epiphanic plea for atonement and redemption. No, it was going to be more. A lot more. Tommy admitted that he had secretly, silently expected this past to come rushing back someday. There was just too much . . . strangeness, was the only way he could describe it, in those events. There were too many disturbing and unanswered questions.

That time had come. Right there on a Friday evening in the early summer, thirty-seven years later. Though he still didn't know exactly what to expect, Tommy read the rest of the letter under a shroud of dread. It continued—

Yes, I am the man whom you may or may not have been searching for all these years. And no, this isn't going to be a redemption request or a turning of myself in. But I believe if you give me a chance, you will find there is a whole lot more to this world than you have ever seen, even though you were somewhat exposed to it all those years ago. I believe the research of my life's mission will convince you to assist me in a once-in-a-lifetime chance to rid the world of an incredibly evil, murdering entity that is, and also is not, a part of this world as we know it.

I know that sounds like a lot of hooey, and by now you're thinking I'm a nut job who is playing a cruel joke using events from the past. But I assure you, while it sounds like so much inter-dimensional mumbo jumbo, my research, my volumes of facts resulting from my quest, and the pending request I will be extending to you and your wife, Toni, will all be backed by undeniable facts. Yes, I have it on good authority that your wife has also been touched by this monster. And I will be extending my invitation to her as well.

Tommy had tried to prepare himself by not expecting a simple letter asking for Manuel Romero to be allowed to turn himself in. He wasn't disappointed in that regard. On one hand, he wanted to be incensed that the possible nut job would dare to include his wife. As far as Tommy was concerned, she was the sweetest woman God ever created, and he didn't like her name being brought up one bit. Unfortunately, the guy was right. She had been touched by . . . something. Still, that didn't assuage the haunted, empty feelings of the past. And while uncomfortable, knowing about her involvement did add credibility to the man who called himself Mr. Richter. Tommy had to admit, maybe the guy wasn't a nut job. Or at least a total nut job. He continued reading—

And yes, it is far out there. I don't pretend for a minute that I'm asking you to believe the kind of stuff you have always believed. I'm asking you to believe in a supernatural entity that exists in and out of our world. One that also kills humans around the world on average about once a week. And this evil spirit has been doing this for over 50 years. That's right, this pure evil monster has killed well over 2,500 people since the late 1960s – including the three people from your area back in 1988. I know, I was there when my friend Mateo Martinez was killed by this monster.

But I have found a way, possibly, to put an end to it. Admittedly, it probably doesn't have a very good chance of success. But this monster is practically unstoppable, and I believe with all my heart that even though it may be unlikely to succeed, we (if you will join me) or I at least have to try. I see this as a one-time only, ever, for the rest of time, opportunity to put an end to it all.

So I'll leave you with this. I implore you, no matter how difficult and uncomfortable it is, to sit down with your wife and dredge up the events from the past. Discuss them openly and tell each other exactly what you remember without holding back. And after you do that, if you don't agree that there are things in this world beyond what we can normally explain – and therefore it's possible I'm not crazy – you have my word I will once again disappear and never bother you again.

Sadly, there have been more than 2,500 dead souls over the past 50-plus years. And there will be countless more into eternity if we don't grasp this limited opportunity to stop it. I ask you to at least meet with me and let me convince you that my mission is far more important than anything you have ever been involved with in your lives. Please, have an honest conversation with your wife. And then if you will, have a conversation with me. I'll be waiting for your call at the number below so we can meet. But please don't wait too long. Unfortunately, time is a short but crucial factor.

With hopeful anticipation,
Manny Richter (Romero)

Friday night became a whole lot more interesting. Not that Tommy thought of that as a good thing. But the thing that kept digging at him was the part about other-worldly forces being involved. The events of the past had been smothered. That didn't mean they had never been talked about or completely forgotten. Tommy knew from previous conversations that Toni would have no trouble believing in a certain amount of that so-called inter-dimensional mumbo jumbo. That made it impossible to file the letter into the trash can. He would never be able to forget about it. Or even keep it smothered any more. The box had been opened and it had to be looked into.

So it seemed Tommy would be spending the rest of his shift looking into the background of a person known as Manfred Richter – formerly Manuel Romero. Then he would need to go home and have a very long talk with his wife. She would already be sleeping, having to open the diner in the morning. He decided to hold off on the talk until Saturday when she would be home

26

fairly early. They planned on having a nice dinner in Batavia or East Aurora, but that no longer seemed like a great idea. He decided to tell Toni he would be grilling chicken Saturday night. It was their favorite stay-at-home meal, and he didn't think she would object.

With that in mind, he opened his laptop and began accessing FBI files and other things only police can access. He decided to do a little refresher first, so he typed in "Manuel Romero." To no surprise, he didn't find anything he didn't already know. Mr. Romero had been convicted of possession of marijuana – lots of it – with intent to distribute, in 1987. He subsequently escaped from the Wyoming Correctional Facility in Attica, New York – the town next to where Tommy lived and part of the County Line community. The other person who escaped at the same time, Mateo Martinez, had been found dead several hours later. After that, Mr. Romero disappeared from the face of the earth.

Until now, Tommy told himself again.

Typing in "Manfred Richter" didn't provide much either. Any addresses for the man came back to a corporation based in Maryland – which seemed odd. That aside, the man with the assumed identity showed up as a fourth-generation German-American, with a full history and an uneventful past. The cop in Tommy made a note that if he ever decided to meet Mr. Richter, he would ask him how that was possible. The cop in him also considered meeting with Mr. Richter to bring him in as a fugitive. That would make a nice feather in the cap of a thirty-eight-year career. But the points made in the letter were already taking hold.

Somehow, Tommy had the feeling it was a lot bigger than that.

CHAPTER 2

The big man named Henry pulled his shiny, black, jacked-up three-quarter-ton pickup truck off Main Street and into the parking lot of Joe's Junction. It was an old two-story house that had been converted into a restaurant and bar years before. One of Gorham's lesser-known hot spots that was frequented by more residents than tourists. The neon lights in the windows contrasted the old, white, painted clapboard siding.

As a construction worker in northern New Hampshire, Henry had to work on Saturday while the June weather was good. But Friday was payday, and being a healthy young male in his late twenties meant Henry could pound down a few and still recover in the morning.

The parking spots on the side of the building were all full, so he headed around the back to find a place. It wasn't crowded yet, so he pulled into one of the spots near the front of the back lot. The radio played a Judas Priest classic – rather loudly. As Henry shifted the truck into park he suddenly heard—

WHY DON'T YOU PARK IN THE BACK ROW? THE FLOOD LIGHT IS OUT AND IT'S NICE AND DARK BACK THERE.

Henry froze, wondering where the voice was coming from. He looked around frantically, but there was no one else around.

The voice continued. *TRUST ME. YOU WILL BE GLAD YOU DID.*

Still glancing around, confused, he turned the radio down to eliminate some of what he was hearing. That did nothing to ease his mind as the voice went on.

THANK YOU. WE CAN TALK NOW WITHOUT SO MUCH DISTRACTION. AND I CAN'T SAY I SHARE YOUR TASTE IN MUSIC.

Still confused and on edge, Henry said out loud, "Who the Hell are you? And how did you hijack my sound system?"

The voice laughed and said, *MY NAME IS JASPER CZYMIAK* – Henry heard it pronounced as Shimmy-ack – *AND I ASSURE YOU, I HAVEN'T HIJACKED YOUR SOUND SYSTEM. I'M COMMUNICATING WITH YOU TELEPATHICALLY. I HAVE TEMPORARILY, PARTIALLY INSERTED MY SPIRITUAL PRESENCE INTO YOUR PHYSICAL BODY. WE'RE GOING TO—*

"Fuck you! I don't know who or what you— OUCH! OW! OW! OW!" Henry had the feeling someone was inside his head banging on the back of his skull with a pointed hammer. "OOOOOWWWWCH! STOP IT! STOP IT! THAT HURTS!!!"

The pain stopped. The voice did not. *LOOK, HENRY, I KNOW IT'S A LOT FOR YOU TO ABSORB. BUT LET'S GET ONE THING STRAIGHT, I'M IN CHARGE. WHAT I SAY GOES. AS SOON AS YOU UNDERSTAND THAT, WE WILL GET ALONG MUCH BETTER.*

Henry wasn't used to having pain inflicted on him. Or to being intimidated in any way by anyone. But he couldn't deny he had met his match. Confused and disoriented, he wasn't about to attempt any more intimidation. He didn't know what to do. His mind raced, trying to catch up and understand what was happening. He wasn't sure what to say next – or if he should say anything.

I KNOW, I KNOW. A THOUSAND QUESTIONS. BUT FIRST, WHY

DON'T YOU PULL THIS MONSTROSITY AROUND TO THE BACK ROW OF THE LOT? THEN WE CAN BE ALONE WHILE WE TALK.

Henry was flabbergasted. Lost. He kept looking around as though there would be somebody, or at least something, that would explain what was going on. He sat motionless, trying to understand.

Until the voice added, with an impatient tone, *NOW.*

The recent memory of the pain in his skull was enough to compel him to move. While still beside himself, he managed to shift to drive and do as he was instructed. He pulled the truck to the back of the lot where the blacktop gave way to a woods, with a trail for ATVs and snowmobiles. With the driver's side facing the rear of the lot, he looked out the window and stared into the darkness of the woods – afraid to say or do anything.

THAT'S BETTER. NOW, LET'S GET TO KNOW EACH OTHER, SHALL WE?

Henry stayed silent.

IT'S OKAY, I UNDERSTAND. BUT SINCE I ALREADY KNOW EVERYTHING ABOUT YOU, IT'S ONLY FAIR FOR ME TO TELL YOU A BIT ABOUT MYSELF, AND EXPLAIN WHAT IS HAPPENING THIS EVENING. AS I SAID, MY NAME IS JASPER. THIS MAY BE HARD FOR YOU TO BELIEVE, BUT WHAT I'M ABOUT TO SHARE WITH YOU IS REAL, EVEN THOUGH YOU'VE LIKELY LIVED YOUR WHOLE LIFE NOT BELIEVING IN SUCH THINGS.

I KNOW YOU'RE ANXIOUS TO GET INSIDE AND CAVORT WITH YOUR BUDDIES, SO I WON'T BORE YOU WITH A LOT OF INTRICATE DETAILS. HERE IT IS IN A NUTSHELL. I AM A UNIQUE SPIRIT, EXISTING IN A REALM ALL TO MYSELF, THOUGH I USED TO BE HUMAN, JUST LIKE YOU. DUE TO A RATHER ODD CHAIN OF EVENTS, WHILE I WAS FIGHTING FOR DEMOCRACY IN VIETNAM

BACK IN NINETEEN SIXTY-SEVEN, I BECAME SOMETHING OF AN
ODDITY, AS MY SOUL WAS MADE IMMORTAL, BUT MY WOUNDED
HUMAN BODY WAS DESTROYED. AND WHILE I CAN EMBODY
HUMANS IN SUCH A WAY AS I'M DOING NOW – AND EVEN TO A
HIGHER LEVEL WHEN NEEDED – I'M NOT LIKE A DEMON SPIRIT
THAT CAN EMBODY HUMANS FOR LONG PERIODS. MY SPIRITUAL
MAKEUP IS NOT OF THAT REALM. AS SUCH, I CAN ONLY EMBODY
HUMANS FOR RELATIVELY SHORT PERIODS WITHOUT CAUSING
THEM HARM ON A SUBATOMIC LEVEL. ARE YOU WITH ME SO FAR?

Henry couldn't believe what he was hearing. He didn't know
what to do or how to answer. He finally spoke – out loud – which
for some reason seemed better, "I don't know. I mean, that display
of pain in my head was impressive. But it's still hard for me to
grasp all this. You're saying you can take me over, like some body-
snatcher, but only for short periods. That sounds kind of far out
for me. Giving me a psychosomatic pain is one thing, but—"

Instantly Henry found himself slapping his face. First with
one hand, then the other. It wasn't him doing it, but he couldn't
stop. It continued for five slaps with each hand.

DOES THAT CONVINCE YOU? OR SHALL I GIVE YOU A BETTER
DEMONSTRATION?

Henry knew he was beat. He didn't like being beat one bit. It
went against everything he'd ever experienced. But there was no
denying it. "Okay, you win. But I still have a million questions."

OF COURSE. AND I'LL TRY NOT TO HIT YOU WITH TOO MUCH
ALL AT ONCE. JUST KNOW THAT I HAVE CERTAIN NEEDS RELATED
TO MY ONCE HUMAN, BUT NOW SPIRITED CONDITION, THAT
REQUIRE ME TO OCCASIONALLY EMBODY HUMANS IN ORDER TO
FULFILL THOSE NEEDS. REST ASSURED, I COULD EMBODY YOU AND
DO WHAT I NEED WITHOUT TELLING YOU ABOUT IT, OR EVEN

INTRODUCING MYSELF. BUT I KNOW THAT WOULD PROBABLY SEND YOU OVER THE EDGE. SO I TRY TO EXPLAIN MYSELF IN ADVANCE. I ALSO WANT TO SHOW YOU THAT I'M NOT ENTIRELY A MONSTER. I HAVE GIVEN YOU A LOT TO ABSORB FOR NOW. I WILL RETURN AT SOME POINT WITH A GIFT FOR YOU, TO HELP YOU UNDERSTAND THAT, WHILE WHAT WE'RE EVENTUALLY GOING TO DO TOGETHER IS NOT NEGOTIABLE, I TRY TO EASE MY PARTNERS INTO THINGS. YOU'LL UNDERSTAND MORE AS TIME GOES BY AND WE INTERACT. AND IN TIME I WILL TELL YOU ALL ABOUT WHAT I'LL BE USING YOU FOR. FOR NOW, I'LL SAY GOODBYE. IT'S BEEN NICE GETTING TO KNOW YOU.

Just like that, the presence was gone. Henry felt it leave. It left behind a healthy, euphoric feeling which, while refreshing, didn't do much to diminish his confusion and fear over everything he'd just been through.

He thought about going home but figured that wouldn't make much difference. He decided if he was losing his mind, he might as well do it with his friends and some beer. Still, he sat in the truck staring at nothing for several minutes before heading inside where he would be in the company of friends.

CHAPTER 5

Toni Chandler pulled into the driveway at a little past six. Saturdays were a slow day at the diner. She called Tommy earlier and told him when she'd be home. Patty, her number one employee for over three decades, stayed late to handle the remaining crowd and cleanup. Toni took a moment to look at their house. It was a cozy, ranch-style log home that Tommy had rented when they first started dating. They eventually purchased it not long after their wedding.

She took a moment to appreciate her life, remembering how she had almost gone down a different path in her younger days. Between the guidance of George Lewis, her father figure, and falling in love with Tommy, she got it together before it was too late. Toni felt blessed to have such a happy life as she neared sixty.

As she made her way up the steps onto the spacious front porch, Tommy came out with a bowl of marinating chicken. Chicken on the grill was their long-time favorite dish. She noticed Tommy had fired up some charcoal instead of the gas grill. That was more time-consuming, and generally reserved for special events. It made her curious, but she wasn't complaining.

She took a moment to appreciate his face as he bent to kiss her. A handsome man, still holding strong features, with a full head of hair that only recently turned salt-and-pepper brown, even though he was two years her elder.

"Hi Honey," she said. "Chicken dinner, yum yum." She kissed him again and said, "Good, you haven't started yet. I need a shower. I smell like cheeseburgers and onions."

Tommy smiled his killer smile. "Take your time. I'll cook it nice and slow."

She went into their country home, down the hallway, into their bedroom. Peeling off her clothes, she checked herself in the full-length mirror on the closet door. *Not bad for an old broad*, she chuckled to herself. She went into the master bath. Having no children, many years before they converted the third bedroom into an extra large bathroom with a tiled, walk-in shower and a large, seductive bathtub.

One look at the tub stopped her in her tracks. It was filled with water and a generous heap of lavender bubbles. A candle burned at each end, and a glass of white wine waited on the edge. Toni wasn't expecting anything special. She reminded herself she had the best husband ever. And she believed it, even though her curiosity light was flashing on high. It wasn't a typical Saturday night, and she wondered what Tommy was up to.

She settled into the bubbles and took a sip of wine – Tommy's homemade Riesling – also her favorite. Letting the warm water do its thing, she closed her eyes and tried to relax. She did relax, but she couldn't help but try to figure out what prompted Tommy to give her the all-out queen treatment. They had been discussing a vacation. Something they rarely did as their careers often got in each other's way. She hoped that's what it was about. Lately, a vacation seemed like a good idea.

With that thought somewhat settling her mind, she took another sip of wine and put her head back, enjoying the fine things her life had to offer.

✦ ✦ ✦ ✦ ✦

Some time later she woke with a start as Tommy poked his head in. "Chicken's almost done, Hon."

She wondered how long she had been asleep. The water was cooler, but she felt clean and refreshed as she climbed out and dried herself off. Staying home for dinner had benefits. She threw on some comfy sweatpants and a loose shirt with no bra.

After the treatment she had received thus far, she half expected the dining room table to be set with a tablecloth and candles. But Tommy, ever the enigma, had brought the dinnerware out to the porch, where it waited on a square table along with the rest of the bottle of Riesling. It was a beautiful evening, and Tommy had lit a pair of tiki torches to keep the mosquitoes away.

Toni gave him another kiss and sat down. Curiosity drove her crazy, but she knew he'd get around to it. She let herself enjoy the perfectly cooked chicken, garlic rice, and lemon-flavored broccoli.

They ate in relative silence. The conversation centered mostly on current local events or whose kids were getting married. What they didn't talk about was taking a vacation or anything that had to do with what she was sure Tommy had in mind. As the food disappeared, Tommy asked about her day. She told him, but it had been mostly uneventful. Then there was silence. It seemed they both knew it was time.

Toni couldn't take it any longer. She finally asked, "And how was your day?"

Tommy stared at his plate for a moment. Toni felt bad. She realized he was uncomfortable and grew certain he wouldn't bring up any vacation talk. Still, she didn't prod. She let him do it in his own way. Before long he looked up, into her eyes.

"I got a letter." After a pause, "An old-fashioned, hand-written letter from a man named Manny Richter."

That didn't mean anything to Toni, but she sensed she was supposed to speak next. "And who is Manny Richter?"

Another pause, longer than before. Finally, Tommy spoke. "Manny Richter used to be Manuel Romero."

That name didn't register with Toni at first either. As she began to put it all together, Tommy confirmed, "He was the inmate that escaped on the same day as Mateo Martinez."

Then it was both of them who went silent. It lasted a while as each of them waited for something from the other. Eventually, Toni said, "Something tells me it wasn't a letter saying he wanted to turn himself in after all these years, was it?"

Tommy shook his head and rubbed his arms. The sun was setting and it suddenly seemed chilly. He said softly, "Why don't we go inside and sit by the fireplace? We need to talk."

Toni gave the dishes a quick rinse and put them in the washer while Tommy started a fire. He opened a second bottle of wine and poured them each a glass, not stopping until they were full to the rim. They both seemed to know they were stalling, but eventually settled in on the black leather couch and got down to business.

Tommy pulled out two pieces of paper. He set one down on the coffee table and handed her the other. Toni looked at it, then at him. He nodded that she should read it. She unfolded the letter and read everything Tommy had read the night before. As she did, she was overwrought with waves of emotion. Tears began to flow, but she kept reading until the end, with Tommy snuggled up to her, hugging and reassuring. By the time she finished, they were holding each other and weeping. The cork had been popped and the past overflowed.

They stayed there, hugging and crying for some time – letting emotions run their course. After a while, Tommy got up, poked the coals, and put another log on the fire. When he returned to the couch Toni had dried her puffy eyes and showed a determined look. After Tommy sat back down she said, "This is probably long overdue. We both had ideas of what happened back then, but it was so uncomfortable and ended so abruptly, it has just been easier to keep it buried. We probably should bare our souls, so to speak."

Tommy didn't seem so sure and looked at her quizzically. But Toni was adamant. "Look, I know you saw some things that made you wonder. But what happened to me, well, let's say I have no trouble believing in a supernatural force. So I'll start."

Tommy didn't argue the point. They leaned back and held hands while sitting tight together. Then she started. "It was a long time ago, but some things you never forget. Late one night, after I finished playing my guitar and singing at Jed's Tavern, I decided to go for a drive in the country to wind down. It was late, but it was a beautiful night. I drove up around the old loop and then back into Picton. I was heading up Route 98, but when I tried to turn left onto Route 35, I couldn't do it. No matter how hard I tried, it was as if someone else had taken over my body. I just kept driving straight up 98."

They both knew what was coming next. Tommy tried to say something but Toni shushed him. "I have to do this now." He nodded grudgingly, and she went on. "After I went a little farther, scared out of my wits but unable to control myself, I . . . we . . .whatever it was, made me turn into Bud Rogers' driveway. I remember all his lights were off – it was late after all. Then I remember walking up his driveway and to his front door. You remember how our small, tight community was back then. Nobody locked their doors. We never felt the need to, and Bud was no exception. I remember reaching for the doorknob."

Toni's hand was tightly locked onto Tommy's. But she finished before he could try speaking again. "Then I blacked out and don't remember anything until I woke up in Bud's bed with him singing in the shower." The tears started again but she wasn't about to quit. "I don't remember it, but I know what happened. Whatever was inside me forced me into Bud's house and we had sex. I didn't want to acknowledge it or even think about it. I just got the Hell out of there before Bud came out of the shower."

By then the tears were gushing. Tommy again tried to speak, but Toni was unstoppable. "No," she cried. "I have to finish this now or I never will. Even though you know the rest, I have to say it." He let her pause until she finally let go. "I ran into you the next day. You broke up with Lisa and I had a huge crush on you. We started seeing each other, and I didn't want to tell you about what happened because, how could I ever have expected you to believe me?"

"Then as we became a couple and you started filling me in on some of the details of your investigations into the killings, Bud Rogers' name started popping up. And I swore I would tell you if anything abnormal happened. But I still couldn't do it. I couldn't bring myself because we were so happy together. And you were so good to me after George was killed, and I was madly in love and didn't want to wreck it. And I knew I couldn't expect you to believe a story like that. Then a while later I had a late-night conversation with Tanya."

Tanya Lambert worked as a bartender at Jed's Tavern back in those days. Tommy knew that, so Toni kept going.

"She seemed out of sorts and started telling me a story. I found myself astonished at the similarities. Our conversation went on until we realized, not only did the same thing happen to us both, but both times it was with Bud Rogers."

It didn't seem possible, but the hand squeeze tightened even more. By then Toni was gushing tears and emotions. She finished with a run-on sentence as though she didn't dare stop again. "So then I had to tell you because you were mentioning strange things too and Bud's name was popping up all over and so I told you and you were skeptical but also admitted to a lot of strange things happening and then Bud killed himself and confessed to everything and we were all finally able to put it all behind us but oh Tommy I've always wondered through all these years if you ever really believed me I swear to God I was powerless to help myself!"

She rolled into him and collapsed, sobbing but mostly cried out of any more tears. Tommy held her and let her weep, then finally tilted her head up so he could look into her eyes. "Toni, I've been the happiest man on Earth since the day you agreed to go out with me. Never, ever have I had any reason to doubt you or not to trust you. Of course I believe you. And don't you ever give it another thought."

✦ ✦ ✦ ✦ ✦

41

They held each other on the couch for a while. Eventually, it was Tommy's turn to begin. They composed themselves and poured even more wine until Tommy started in, remembering when he was a rookie road deputy.

"Well," he hesitated knowing his story would be painful for Toni too. But she knew that much already, so she urged him on. "Though I didn't know it at the time, for me it started when Phil Waters found your . . . friend, George's body out in the woods while playing a Bigfoot hoax."

Toni squeezed him but that was all. "I was on duty that night so I had to go secure the scene. Over the next few days, we were able to determine the cause of death as loss of blood. That didn't seem too out of whack, even though there was no blood at the site in the woods or George's house, or the last place he'd been seen – that old bar called the Silver Nickel."

Toni nodded. Reassuring that she knew all that.

"Then, just as we thought things might be getting back to normal, one of two escaped inmates was found along the railroad tracks. That's when it got weird. Again it was loss of blood. And again, there was no blood anywhere near the scene. At least not more than a couple of drops. No real sign of a struggle. But also no indication of how the body got there – if it was killed there or moved. Though with no blood on the ground, it was our assumption the body had been moved. But if that were the case, why would the killer leave it in such an easy place to be found? I mean, we were lucky we found George's body in a relatively short time thanks to Phil and his Bigfoot stunt. But at least that time the killer tried to hide George's body deep in the woods."

Toni knew the rest. It wasn't like they had never talked about it. Just very little over the years. Tommy hesitated, but she nudged him, "And?"

He gave her a look. He knew she knew. But he could tell she knew it was important to spell it all out and bring it back to the surface. So he went on, "Well, as you know," he emphasized that part. She punched his arm. "As you know, with the body being so fresh, the medical examiner was able to determine the loss of blood was facilitated by two pencil-sized puncture wounds in the jugular vein."

He waited for a response again but Toni remained quiet until he added, "That's not natural."

He searched her eyes for a reaction. She looked like she was contemplating what she would say next. Finally, Toni asked, "Would you say it was supernatural, then?"

Tommy didn't answer so she pushed on, "Because that's what this Manny Richter, or whatever, is currently, after all these years, asking us to believe."

Tommy couldn't answer. It was still too much for him to admit to the evidence in front of him. He sat and thought for a bit. Finally, he picked up the other piece of paper he had brought and unfolded it. He started to read but realized he was being unfair. He leaned over so Toni could see it too.

It was a copy of the suicide note left by Bud Rogers so many years ago. Tommy knew Toni had seen it once before. Right after Bud killed himself he'd brought it home and shared it with her. Not that it answered any questions at the time. But it contained mysterious passages that, looking at them anew, may have made sense. That is if a person could get by the paranormal aspect.

To all,
I am sorry. To help solve the riddle, it was

43

me. I was the one who killed George Lewis,
Jimmy T, and the escaped inmate. More
specifically, it was the result of my deadly
possession by a madman spirit named
Jasper Shimmy-ack, but his horrendous
deeds were carried out through me, and for
that I am eternally sorry. I wish to apologize
to Jimmy T's wife Dawn, Toni Birch, Tanya
Lambert and anyone else I've harmed.
Please believe me, I was powerless to stop.

As Tommy read that first paragraph, two things stood out.
Bud Rogers took responsibility, but went on to say it was the result of a possession by a madman spirit. Nobody in County Line
would have ever suspected Bud of being a serial killer. The idea of
spirit possession was generally passed off as a well-disguised mental illness. Manny Richter's note gave it a more ominous feel.

Tommy also remembered that the Jasper Shimmy-ack listed
in the note was likely, as far as anyone could tell, a man from Buffalo named Jasper Czymiak, who had gone missing in action in
Vietnam in 1967. But if that were the case, how would Bud
Rogers know anything about him over twenty years later if he was
just crazy in the head? Tommy had to acknowledge it was another
point toward supernatural legitimacy.

Bud Rogers also specifically apologized to Toni in the letter,
and to Tanya Lambert – the girl Toni mentioned earlier. Both of
them had experienced embodiment by an unknown force.

Possessed by a madman spirit? Tommy asked himself. There
didn't seem to be any other logical explanation. Yet another point
for supernatural.

44

After the two spent some time rehashing the note, they once again sat in silence. Tommy wanted to speak but didn't know what to say. Toni broke the ice when she finally said, "Listen."

Tommy had been married long enough to know that meant whatever she said next, she would damned sure be serious about. And although she was small in stature, Toni never had any trouble standing strong. He wasn't too surprised when she continued.

"I understand this is all hard for you to jump in head first and believe. You just showed me a letter from a man who claims to have documented proof that a supernatural being has not only killed thousands of people over the years but is also the son of a bitch that killed George. And I was there too. You can see the personal apology in Bud's note. And I'm telling you right now, I don't have any trouble believing Mr. Richter's story. I've spent well over half of my almost sixty years never having doubted that what happened to me – and to Tanya don't forget – and Hell, likely Bud too, was the product of a supernatural force . . . or being, or whatever."

Tommy didn't know what to say.

"Mr. Richter is asking us to believe in a supernatural entity. An evil one. You can check me off that list. I believe it. I've always believed it. And Mr. Richter says there's a small chance, but he seems to have a plan that we can help rid the world of that monster. The same monster that killed George. And if we don't at least try, this evil spirit will likely go on killing forever. I can't just sit around the rest of my life knowing I could have done something and didn't. He wants us to call and have a meeting. We can give him that. And if you don't want to – if you want to live the rest of your life with the knowledge you didn't try – that's up to you. But I'm going to meet him, with or without you."

Tommy was shocked. He couldn't remember more than a couple of times in all their years together when Toni spoke in ultimatums. But she was making a good point. And when he looked at her, the determination he saw was just one of the many reasons he had fallen in love with her. There was no longer any question. He grabbed his phone and dialed.

To say Manny Richter was pleased to hear from them would be an understatement. But they knew they had much to discuss. With a quick conversation, they made plans to meet for dinner at 8 o'clock the next Tuesday night in Batavia, at a swanky place called Skeeter's Surf 'n' Steak. A couple of cordial goodbyes and that was it.

Tommy hung up and took a deep breath, wondering what he'd gotten into. Their after-dinner talk had dragged on, and it was getting late. But Toni seemed pleased to have him on board. Although Tommy admitted, in hindsight, there was never really any question. He sighed and asked, "So what do we do now?"

Toni grabbed him by the chin and gave him a mischievous grin. "Well, I've come to realize over the years that whenever my husband draws me a hot bubble bath with candles and homemade wine, then cooks me a charcoal-grilled chicken dinner, it usually means he's trying to get laid."

Tommy smiled and they laughed. He picked her up and she wrapped her legs around him as he carried her to the bedroom.

CHAPTER 4

oe's Junction was filled to its normal Saturday night capacity. Almost all the occupants were local residents and regulars. Every bar stool was full, and most tables had couples seated – some just drinking while others dined on pub burgers and fries.

Henry hadn't slept a wink the night before. He worked all day but decided since he probably wouldn't sleep for a while – and since Saturday was the only day he had when he didn't have to work the next morning – that he would go out. As time passed, thoughts of the previous night's strange events faded. But only slightly.

He sat at a table in the corner with a couple of friends, taking turns trying to beat whoever had won the previous pool game. Annie, a good-looking, dusty-blonde waitress in her mid-thirties came by with a round of beer. She gave Henry a friendly glance, with just enough behind it to remind them both they had once had a little fling. But that was all in the past.

Henry contemplated that for a bit. Hanging with the regulars at the Junction was a great time, but it wasn't much in the way of meeting any new women. But he was exhausted even though he didn't feel like sitting home alone. He looked around and decided

47

a night with his friends was good enough.

One of those friends was currently the table champion. Jenny Bosko could shoot pool as well as any of them. And she could rock an outfit like no other woman in town. She wore a tight-fitting, low-cut black shirt over a black pleated skirt that matched her jet-black hair. Beneath that, her well-defined bare legs gave way to a pair of green cowboy boots that matched her eyes.

Henry laughed when she missed her eight-ball shot and said, "Shitballs!"

Jenny Bosko could also curse like a sailor and, to the disappointment of most of the guys that hung out at Joe's, was truly one of the boys.

Oh, they tried their best over the years to take her out on dates or take her fishing, bowling, sky diving, and many other things. They tried just about everything to spend individual time with her. But to Henry's knowledge, none had ever succeeded – including himself. It was generally regarded that Jenny had a "friend" in the next town over who she visited whenever the mood struck her.

But they all got along. And while she was a knock-out to look at, none of the guys considered her an actual tease because she never pretended she was going home with any of them, or led any of them on. She just showed up looking great, shot the breeze, drank beer, and played pool. Just like the rest of them.

Joe, the fifty-something year old owner, walked past her on his way to make the easy eight-ball shot Jenny had left him. On his way by she gave a fake jab at his privates with the blunt end of the pool cue. He jumped back and yelled, "Oh, you bitch!"

She returned his compliment. "Prick."

The rest of the guys at the corner table laughed. Henry decided a night with the boys and Jenny Bosko would be good enough for now. She did catch him staring at her cleavage as she slid past him to grab a seat. They both laughed when she flipped him off.

And that's how the evening went. Henry finally beat the champ and won three games in a row, eventually losing to Jenny. He cursed her for making it impossible to concentrate on his shots when she had those damned fine legs on display. She promptly told him to piss off.

The back and forth between the gang continued for a couple of hours. Somebody ordered a big pile of hot Buffalo wings for the table. The beers flowed freely for most of them, though Henry didn't hit them too hard. He was tired and didn't feel like drinking too much.

Eventually, around eleven o'clock, the fatigue caught up with him. Henry said his goodbyes and decided to call it a night. He paid his tab with Annie and left a bigger tip than his bill called for. He wasn't sure why. Maybe he still harbored feelings for her. Anyway, it was payday.

He said some more goodbyes as he made his way out the back door and walked across the dark parking lot to the back. He suddenly became unnerved. The distractions of the evening had helped him forget about his encounter with whatever it was inside his head. Having to park in the back of the lot again, and seeing his truck there as he walked out, brought it all back.

With no other choice, he kept walking, finally going around to the driver's door on the far side. As he reached for his keys he was startled by a movement near the back of his truck. He jumped higher than he normally would have – still on edge remembering that guy in his head. Regaining himself, he saw the movement was none other than Jenny Bosko.

Henry had trouble catching up. His encounter the night before came flooding back. Since then things were almost back to normal. But not anymore. It was odd enough for Jenny Bosko to follow him to his truck. The fact that her eyes had a soft, red glow made things even weirder.

There was nothing normal about what was happening. Jenny – with a stoic look that seemed to look right through Henry, even with the red glow – reached out and began undoing his belt. His mind and heart raced.

What the Hell is going on here? He asked himself. The girl's odd behavior and the other crazy stuff from the night before had to be related. It was all a mystery but he didn't care. As the normally elusive Jenny Bosko worked him up, his focus narrowed.

Once she had his full attention, the eerie form before him stepped back. She reached up under her skirt and peeled off a thin pair of what would barely be described as panties. She let them drop and kicked them off, leaving her cowboy boots on. Her red eyes looked into Henry's eyes, and the lust washed over him like a spell had been cast.

Jenny Bosko threw her arms over his shoulders, jumped up, and wrapped her legs around him so tightly he thought something might break. With her head next to his, eye contact was broken. For a brief moment, Henry considered trying to stop it. Somewhere inside he knew it was all related to the earlier events, and that doing what they were doing was probably not a good idea – even though it was her who followed and came onto him.

But twenty-eight-year-old male hormones have a way of casting rational thought to the side. In no time Henry found himself inside the object of every man in Gorham's desire. His buddies would never believe he was banging Jenny Bosko up against the side of his pickup truck in the darkness of Joe's parking lot. But that didn't matter. Nothing mattered in that moment except pure physical pleasure.

As he moved within her she started making noises. Loud noises that could probably be heard by anyone if they were outside. Fortunately, it didn't last long. They were both in a frenzy and it ended quickly. She shuddered and gave him a squeeze with her arms and legs so powerful Henry was unable to do anything but come deep inside.

Then it was over. He let her down and, just as before, without a word, she walked back around the truck – stoic expression, red eyes and all. Henry was left in wonder. Satisfied in one way, but very confused.

Eventually, he gathered up the souvenir panties left behind and drove home. As he did he thought how ironic it was. Normally a tune-up before bedtime would have him sleeping like a baby. Somehow Henry doubted he would be drifting off peacefully any time soon.

Oh boy, Henry, What have you gotten yourself into?

CHAPTER 5

Henry barely slept Saturday night. He somehow nodded off for a while, probably due to being so exhausted. But his mind wouldn't calm down. Too many things had happened. He spent most of the night lying in his bed while his mind raced and whirled from one crazy thing to another.

Eventually, he got up for the day and tried to stay busy. He spent some time tidying up his house. He vacuumed and dusted and kept himself occupied doing different chores until it was almost dark. Then he decided, tired or not, he was going out. Unable to sleep anyway, he reasoned there was no sense in hanging around being miserable.

He took a long, hot shower and tried to rest his mind. It didn't work. He knew he had to go out and get some distractions. He wasn't sure if he would return to Joe's or not. Usually laying eyes on Jenny Bosko was a pleasure. But Henry wasn't sure what, or how much she knew of what had happened. Not that he knew a whole lot more himself, but he didn't think dealing with that uncertainty was the distraction he needed.

But there were other places to hang out. So he threw on his jeans and grabbed a light blue T-shirt. As he did he felt the presence and heard—

WHY DON'T YOU WEAR SOMETHING DARKER?

Henry froze. That guy in his head – Jasper something – said he'd be back and was going to use Henry's human body for something. Since then he had been able to push those thoughts away – having plenty of other issues.

WE'RE GOING OUT INTO THE NIGHT, AND YOU PROBABLY WANT TO AVOID BEING SEEN.

Not knowing what else to do, Henry said, "Hello, Jasper."

IT'S TIME. I HOPE YOU ENJOYED YOURSELF LAST NIGHT. I KNOW I DID. THAT JENNY BOSKO IS A REAL SPECIMEN. MAKING LOVE TO YOU WITH HER BODY WAS A SPECIAL TREAT.

Henry shook his head. "So that was your doing?" Even though he already knew the answer. "I was nailing you in the parking lot?"

IN A MANNER OF SPEAKING, YES. BUT DON'T WORRY. I FULLY EMBODIED HER SO SHE WON'T REMEMBER HOW IT HAPPENED OR WITH WHOM.

Henry was shocked. He had never been a great person. In fact, many people would describe him as a total asshole. But he would never do anything like that.

"Holy shit! I can't believe you would use somebody like that. Not to mention I probably have her knocked up now. You're the biggest piece of sh— ouch. OUCH! OOOOWWW . . . Okay I'm sorry."

The pain in his head almost sent Henry to his knees. And it didn't stop when he asked it to.

"I'm sorry. I'm sorry! Okay, you win. Stop it, oh please STOP IT!"

The pain finally ended. Henry held his head in his hands, though it didn't help.

I TRY TO BE NICE. THIS IS HOW I'M TREATED. VERY DISAPPOINTING, HENRY. BUT I GUESS YOU'VE BEEN REMINDED WHO'S IN CHARGE, AND THERE WILL BE NO FURTHER DEBATE.

As with the previous night, Henry was humbled into not being the bully in control. He hated it. But he was beaten.

"Yes sir. Whatever you say."

THAT'S BETTER. NOW IT'S TIME FOR US TO GO. I SUGGEST YOU PUT ON SOME DARK CLOTHES. AND YOU MIGHT WANT TO GRAB SOME GLOVES AND A FLASHLIGHT.

Henry did what he was told without another word. As he started the truck he dared to ask, "Where to? And please don't think I'm being out of line, but I would like to know exactly what we're about to do." He braced himself just in case.

MAKE YOUR WAY SOUTH ON ROUTE SIXTEEN, LIKE YOU'RE GOING TO VISIT MOUNT WASHINGTON. I'LL FILL YOU IN ON THE WAY.

Henry lived on the opposite side of town from where Route 16 headed south. They would have some time. Resigned to his fate, he pulled out of the driveway and said, "Not a very good night for sightseeing. It's dark and cloudy, and there's a new moon besides."

WE'RE NOT GOING SIGHT-SEEING. BUT I SUPPOSE YOU DO NEED TO KNOW WHAT'S GOING ON. I'LL TRY NOT TO DRAG IT OUT WITH TOO MANY DETAILS. ARE YOU READY? THIS MAY ALL BE A BIT SHOCKING TO YOU.

"Uhh, I've been shocked ever since you came along. Are you saying it's going to get worse?"

A MATTER OF OPINION I SUPPOSE. NEVERTHELESS, HERE GOES. I WAS AN ORPHANED CHILD BORN IN BUFFALO, NEW YORK. WHEN I REACHED MY TEENS I WAS SUMMONED TO FIGHT FOR

DEMOCRACY IN VIETNAM. ONE NIGHT I WAS BLOWN UP BY A ROCKET-PROPELLED GRENADE. I WAS PARALYZED AND BLIND. LEFT FOR DEAD ON THE JUNGLE FLOOR AS OUR ENTIRE UNIT WAS WIPED OUT.

I WAS IN TERRIBLE PAIN AND UNABLE TO MOVE, WITH BUGS AND JUNGLE ANIMALS ALL AROUND ME. TO MY JOY, OR SO I THOUGHT AT THE TIME, A MAN NAMED WILLIAM CAME BY. NOT REALLY A MAN, THOUGH. WILLIAM WAS A VAMPIRE LIVING IN CAMBODIA, AND HE COMMUNICATED WITH ME TELEPATHICALLY, JUST LIKE I DO WITH YOU. UNDERSTAND?

"I guess so. But I don't like the sounds of this one bit."

REGARDLESS, WILLIAM OFFERED TO TAKE MY PAIN AWAY. I JUMPED AT THE CHANCE AND PLEADED WITH HIM TO DO SO. HE TOLD ME IT WOULD INVOLVE MAKING ME A VAMPIRE LIKE HIMSELF. THE PAIN WAS HORRIBLE AND I WASN'T THINKING STRAIGHT, SO I AGREED.

NOW JUST SO YOU KNOW, WHEN A VAMPIRE FEEDS ON A HUMAN, THE HUMAN DIES. THEY DON'T AUTOMATICALLY BECOME VAMPIRES THEMSELVES. IF THAT WERE THE CASE, THE ENTIRE WORLD WOULD HAVE BEEN CONVERTED INTO VAMPIRES CENTURIES AGO. TO CREATE A VAMPIRE THERE'S A PROCESS INVOLVED THAT REQUIRES THE EXCHANGE OF HUMAN BLOOD WITH UNDEAD BLOOD. THE PROCESS TAKES A FEW DAYS. STILL WITH ME?

"Yeah, but I think I'm gonna be sick."

HANG IN THERE. ANYWAY, WILLIAM BEGAN THE PROCESS ON THAT FIRST NIGHT. THANKFULLY MY PAIN WENT AWAY. THEN WILLIAM SAID HE WOULD RETURN THE NEXT TWO NIGHTS, AFTER WHICH, I WOULD BE ABLE TO WALK, TALK AND EXIST AS HE DID. AND HE DID RETURN THE FOLLOWING NIGHT

FOR ANOTHER UNDEAD TRANSFER. BUT ON THE LAST NIGHT, HE NEVER SHOWED UP. IT TURNS OUT HE HAD BEEN DISCOVERED AND DISPOSED OF BY A GROUP OF HUMAN VAMPIRE HUNTERS.

WHILE THAT WAS BAD FOR WILLIAM, IT WASN'T GOOD FOR ME, EITHER. I WAS UNABLE TO FINISH THE UNDEAD TRANSFER, SO MY BODY WASN'T PREPARED FOR ETERNITY. YET MY MIND AND— SOUL, FOR LACK OF A BETTER WORD, WERE THAT OF A FULL- FLEDGED VAMPIRE. AS MY BODY CONTINUED TO FAIL, AND JUST BEFORE THE NVA DUMPED ME INTO A MASS GRAVE, I ROSE FROM MY HUMAN BODY, NEVER TO RETURN. NOW I EXIST AS A SPIRIT VAMPIRE, FOREVER IN NEED OF STEALING HUMAN BLOOD, BUT UNABLE TO OCCUPY HUMAN BODIES FOR ANY EXTENDED LENGTH. I AM TRULY ONE-OF-A-KIND.

Henry did start to feel sick. Fortunately, he had been looking forward to a cheeseburger and fries and hadn't eaten anything yet. He couldn't think of anything to say. He drove in silence, horrified at what he'd just heard, but unable to do anything about it.

AND HERE WE ARE. I'VE CHOSEN YOU TO HELP ME GET TONIGHT'S MEAL. TURN RIGHT, DOWN THAT DRIVEWAY. IT LEADS TO A PARKING AREA FOR A HIKING TRAIL. THERE WON'T BE ANYONE AROUND TONIGHT, AND WE CAN GET OFF THE MAIN ROAD.

Henry did as he was told, following the driveway into the forest until it ended. Jasper was speaking in a friendly tone, but Henry knew better. They were into some serious business. Part of him held out hope that he was losing his marbles. If what Jasper said they were about to do was true, a trip to the funny farm would be a welcome alternative.

"I don't want to do this,"

WE'VE BEEN THROUGH THIS. YOU DON'T HAVE A CHOICE.

PLEASE DON'T BECOME DIFFICULT, HENRY.

"But why me? All the people in the world and you chose me. Why?"

BECAUSE I DON'T LIKE HOW YOU'VE ACTED AS A BULLY ALL YOUR LIFE. DO YOU RECALL THE TIME YOU MADE TEDDY BRONSON EAT DOG POOP? OF COURSE YOU DO. YOU THOUGHT IT WAS FUNNY. AND YOU'VE LIVED YOUR LIFE DOING SIMILAR THINGS TO OTHERS, NEVER HAVING BEEN CHALLENGED BECAUSE OF YOUR PHYSICAL STATURE. WELL, IT'S TIME YOU LEARNED WHAT IT'S LIKE TO BE PICKED ON. I'M SURE WHEN WE'RE FINISHED YOU WILL HAVE A WHOLE NEW OUTLOOK ON YOUR LIFE AND HOW TO TREAT YOUR FELLOW MAN.

"Well okay, I can see your point. I guess I have been a dick all my life. But how do I know you're real? Maybe I'm just crazy and all I have to do is take control of this situation. Tell the voice in my head to shut up and then just turn around and go home. What would you do?"

YOU ALREADY KNOW WHAT I WILL DO. DON'T MAKE ME DO IT AGAIN. NOW LET'S GET GOING. THE WOMAN WE'RE AFTER IS CAMPING SOME DISTANCE OFF THE TRAIL, ALONG THE PEABODY RIVER. THE SOONER WE GET THIS OVER, THE SOONER YOU CAN HIDE THE BODY AND GO HOME.

Henry's natural tendency to not be bullied kicked back in. He had no desire to do what Jasper said they were about to do. He was afraid it would hurt, but he had to try to defy Jasper one last time.

"No."

NO?

"No. I don't believe you can turn me into a temporary vampire, make me suck the blood out of some poor woman, and then just leave me as though nothing happened. It can't be. I don't believe this is really happening."

FIRST OF ALL, I ASSURE YOU IT IS REALLY HAPPENING. AND THE POOR WOMAN YOU'RE SUDDENLY CONCERNED ABOUT MAKES HER MEAGER LIVING BY SELLING FENTANYL-LACED NARCOTICS ALL OVER NEW HAMPSHIRE, RESULTING IN THE DEATHS OF DOZENS OF YOUR FELLOW CITIZENS. SHE DESERVES WHAT SHE GETS. NOW STOP ARGUING AND GET MOVING.

"No. I'm not going to play this game any—ouch. Ouch! OUCH!"

There it was again.

ENOUGH ALREADY. GET MOVING.

Henry gave it one last try. "No. You can't be real. I refuse to play this—OOOOWWWWW! Oh my God! OW! OW! OW! OOOHHHH!" The pain was unbearable. Henry grabbed at the back of his head but it was pointless. It was worse than before, and it didn't stop. "Okay okay OUCH! Okay please stop! Please, please! Oh my God! Jasper, please stop it! OOOOHHHH! OOOOHHHH! OOOOOOOOOHHHHHHHHHH!"

Finally, the pain subsided.

ARE YOU DONE NOW? CAN WE GET ON WITH IT?

"Yes." He whimpered. Never had he experienced such pain. "Yes. I'm sorry. Oh God, I'm sorry. Please don't do that anymore."

GOOD. NOW GET MOVING. SHE'S CAMPING ALONE. WE SHOULD BE ABLE TO WALK RIGHT IN ON HER AND FINISH OUR BUSINESS.

"Is there going to be a big bloody mess?" Henry was almost crying.

NO, THERE SHOULDN'T BE ANY BLOOD. THERE IS A REACTION THAT HAPPENS WITH THE BLOOD BETWEEN OUR DIMENSIONS.

YOU WON'T FEEL FULL. YOU WON'T EVEN REMEMBER IT HAPPENING. WHEN THE TIME COMES AND I FULLY EMBODY YOU, YOU WILL BLACK OUT. NOW LET'S GO. AND BE QUIET.

"Sure. Okay." Full compliance. He got out of the car and closed the door gently. It was early summer but still warm for a northern New Hampshire night. With only a crescent moon he could see Mount Washington plain enough, but the trail into the woods wasn't lit very well. He was done arguing so he walked into the darkness.

They walked silently for several hundred yards – stumbling occasionally and getting poked in the face with unseen tree twigs. Finally, Henry saw the flickering of a campfire off to his left.

YOU'RE DOING GOOD. NOW BE AS QUIET AS YOU CAN, AND SLOWLY MAKE OUR WAY TOWARD THAT FIRE. WE'RE ALMOST DONE.

Henry, shaking with fear, begrudgingly did as he was told. As they neared the fire, he felt his incisors lengthen. Filled with horror, he didn't know how he'd be able to carry on. Fortunately, Jasper was right, and he blacked out.

* * * * *

When Henry came back he was looking at the corpse of an unkempt woman with shaggy hair and baggy, torn clothing. She also smelled like she hadn't showered in a month.

THANK YOU, HENRY. THAT WAS A GOOD MEAL.

Henry was speechless. He couldn't believe what had transpired. It was Sunday night. He should be back in Gorham playing pool at some bar.

"So what happens now?" He realized he was still shaking with fear.

WELL, I DON'T KNOW ABOUT YOU, BUT AFTER A BIG MEAL, I LIKE TO TAKE A NAP.

"But . . . what am I supposed to do? Just leave her here?"

I DON'T KNOW. BUT ANY EVIDENCE IS GOING TO POINT TO YOU. FOOTPRINTS. TIRE TRACKS. CLOTHING FIBERS. YOU COULD TRY TO HIDE THE BODY. MAYBE DRAG HER BACK TO YOUR CAR AND DISPOSE OF HER SOMEPLACE. MAYBE DRAG HER DEEPER INTO THE WOODS. OR THROW HER INTO THE RIVER AND HOPE NOBODY FINDS HER FOR A LONG TIME. THEN GET RID OF THE TENT AND ALL HER GEAR. SHE PROBABLY HITCHED A RIDE OUT HERE WITH A LONG-GONE TOURIST, SO IT'S UNLIKELY ANYBODY KNOWS WHERE SHE IS OR THAT SHE WILL BE REPORTED AS MISSING. WHATEVER YOU DECIDE, I WISH YOU ALL THE BEST. I'VE ENJOYED OUR TIME TOGETHER. WHO KNOWS? I MAY CALL ON YOU AGAIN SOMETIME IN THE FUTURE. MAYBE I'LL BRING YOU ANOTHER PRESENT LIKE THAT BOSKO GIRL. THAT WAS FUN. IN THE MEANTIME, TRY TO BE A LITTLE NICER TO PEOPLE FROM NOW ON, WON'T YOU?

Before Henry could answer, he felt Jasper's presence leave. The warm, healthy feeling washed over him, mixing strangely with the sense of fear that bathed him. He covered his face with his hands, as though maybe he could wish it all away. Of course that didn't work, and when he opened his eyes he was met with the same fate.

He was lost. All his life Henry bullied and bossed people around. But there in the woods he stood beleaguered – not knowing what to do. He didn't want to drag the stinking woman's corpse all the way to his car and take her any place. From what he could see in the darkness, the river wasn't all that deep and wouldn't do much to hide her. Should he drag her into the woods as Jasper suggested? That seemed like the best plan, so he started. He soon found out the dead weight of a human – even a smallish woman – is a lot harder to move than expected.

Plus it was dark and he kept tripping. After a few hundred yards, getting tired, Henry was overcome with all that had happened. It grew heavy in his mind as he tripped on another tree root. Falling backward, he landed on his buttocks and it all came out. The big man, the big bully, began sobbing. Grief and despair emptied into the middle of the dark woods on a Saturday night. Through the cries of misery, the animals of the night heard him asking, over and over, "Ooooh God! What did I do? What have I done? What have I done?"

Eventually, as he sat there thinking about what he'd done – what he'd done to Jenny Bosko and to the wretch in front of him – being subjected to realities he never believed existed, Henry's whole world turned upside down. It was too much, and he didn't see how he could go on living with it. He'd never be able to hide the body and go on with his life like nothing ever happened. It would be impossible.

He sat there in the darkness, certain if he had a gun or a knife he would end it all right then and there. Instead, the big bully of a man sat and cried like a baby.

CHAPTER 6

Toni and Tommy got a little more dressed up than usual. A blue dress for Toni and a button-down shirt and slacks for Tommy. Skeeter's Surf 'n' Steak was more swanky than their usual hangouts.

As it turned out, they needn't have bothered. The hostess led them to a small, private room in the back, decorated with ornate china and paintings of lobster boats and cattle drives. They were greeted there by Manny Richter wearing blue jeans and a black golf shirt. They shook hands and settled into the table. Drinks were ordered, with Manny ordering a bottle of red and another of white – covering the pairings for both the surf and the steak.

Sensing Toni was staring, Manny said, "You seem surprised."

Looking embarrassed, she stammered, "Well it's just . . . I . . . uhh—"

"Was expecting someone a little more Latino looking?"

She didn't speak but gave an affirmative shrug.

"My father was Puerto Rican. Hence the last name Romero. But my mother was a fourth-generation German-American, with blonde hair and blue eyes. I guess I take after her. It made it easier to become Manfred Richter. I could still let people call me Manny so the transition was smoother."

Toni gave an understanding, yet still nervous-sounding laugh. "Oh, I see."

A moment of awkward silence followed. It finally ended when Tommy said, "Speaking of which, you're under arrest."

The silence was deafening for a few moments until Tommy's poker face finally cracked a smile. The ice had been broken and it seemed they all felt better.

The drinks came along with stuffed mushrooms. None were there to eat, but Manny reminded them they would probably be there for some time, and doggie bags were free. The food was bound to be delicious. And of course, it was on him. So they all ordered prime rib and lobster platters.

When the waitress left Manny started in. "Let me tell you about what I've been up to. But first, I need to know for sure. Are we all on board? Do we all fully believe there are supernatural beings that live in our world?"

Toni nodded and said yes immediately. Tommy hesitated, but facts were facts and he'd been convinced – at least for that much, so he finally said yes.

"Good. My new life began on that fateful night in 1988."

Manny went on to tell the whole story of his train ride and meeting first with Clyde, and then Winston. When he got to the part about his organization being called Monkey Beans, they lost their seriousness and laughed.

The main course showed up. They dug in while Manny continued. "So Winston gave me a new life and a career. Monkey Beans is a centuries-old association that has been at war with the peenos throughout the ages."

"Peenos?" Toni asked as Tommy also looked questioningly.

"Oh, sorry. Peenos is our shortened word for paranormal beings. Like P-normal becomes peeno. Which makes me, and all Monkey Beans members, peeno hunters. Dedicated to the extinction of all peenos, be it vampires, witches, or werewolves."

"Werewolves?" Tommy jumped in. "Really?"

"Yes, they do exist. Though it's doubtful you have ever or will ever see one. But don't go cold on me now. And there are witches and warlocks. Not your typical self-proclaimed Wiccans – humans practiced in the art – though they can extract and deliver a certain amount of witchery. But real witches, whose entire biological makeup is fundamentally different from humans. There are also demons, but we don't deal with them. They are impossible to kill, and there are too many of them. We leave demons to the Catholic church and their fifty-thousand exorcisms around the world every year."

Manny paused as though he expected that number would seem high to them. When he got skeptical looks from both, he went on. "It's true. You can look it up. All other religions have their forms of exorcism too. There are peenos everywhere, but even we don't pretend to be able to deal with demons."

He went on. "Monkey Beans has ridiculous amounts of old money. And we have a huge amount of other resources at our disposal too. We're based in Maryland but have members everywhere. They range from basic observers, who report anything they see we might be interested in, to full-fledged peeno hunters, who go to war with peenos whenever possible. I was accepted by the group right away, almost as a celebrity. It seems there are very few people in the world who get to see a vampire in the wild and live to tell about it. And believe it or not, I've spent the last thirty-seven years studying one thing – Jasper Czymiak."

At the mention of his name, Toni tensed up. She put her fork down and Tommy could see goosebumps forming. He reached over and grabbed her hand.

Manny slowed down. "Apologies. I get carried away and sometimes forget to be sensitive. I should know better. I have a good idea of what you experienced years ago and I know it's not something anyone would want to carry around. Again, I apologize."

Toni surprised them both when she adopted a determined look. "Don't worry about me. I'll be fine. You say you have a plan to kill the son of a bitch that killed George Lewis. Let's get on with it." There was an awkward silence, so she added, "But just how the Hell do you think you know what I went through?"

Manny, trying to be careful, finally started up again. "Well, over the years I've met with hundreds of people who have had dealings with Jasper. It's not always easy to gain information from them. Many times, as in the case of your neighbor Bud Rogers, Jasper's subjects can't take the guilt and do themselves in before I can get to them. Just as often they wind up in asylums, which makes it hard to gain access or information. But thirty-seven years is a long time. And other people who have had encounters similar to yours will sometimes open up. I knew about the cases in your town. But I've studied hundreds more. Anyway, sometimes it takes a person on their deathbed to open up. In this case, about five years ago I talked to a woman you used to know, Tanya Lambert."

Both Toni and Tommy seemed surprised. Tanya left County Line shortly after the Bud Rogers and Jasper business faded. It was rumored she had gone to Texas, but all contact with her was lost and it seemed nobody ever heard from her again.

It was Tommy's turn to speak. "Okay, but how on Earth did

you ever know to talk to her? I can't imagine she went around telling anybody about her experience, knowing what I know about what it was like for Toni."

Manny nodded, understanding how they would question that. "As I said, we have people – observers – everywhere. One day in 1989 a woman gave birth in Texarkana. The child was born with a caul. That's when a section of the placenta covers the face and or head. It's not usually an issue, but cultures all around the world often look at it as a sign of something special. Well, we have observers everywhere, and when a caul birth happens we watch and study everyone involved. In this case, I was made aware that the woman in Texarkana, Miss Lambert, was a resident of your community during Jasper's reign of terror there. We've kept an eye on things ever since. Over the years I attempted to contact Miss Lambert several times, hoping for an interview. I was always met with resistance. That, of course, fueled my belief over the years that she had some connection with Jasper Czymiak."

"About five years ago our observers informed us that she was terminally ill with lung cancer. That's sad, but I feel my research is important, so I again made contact all those years later. And to my surprise, she agreed to meet with me. She didn't think her story was important. And she didn't think anybody would believe it, so she never told anyone. But once she understood that I did believe her and that I had a lot of information on the thing that had invaded and abused her, she poured it all out to me." Nodding at Toni. "Including the fact that she knew about a similar occurrence in your case."

Manny paused to fill everyone's wine glasses. The red was gone and they were onto the white.

Tommy asked, "So Tanya Lambert has passed away?"

"Yes, about four years ago."

More silence. Then Toni said, "That's sad. She was a great girl, and we became quite friendly after our common-themed encounter. It was sad when she disappeared, but I can understand it." After a short pause, she switched gears. "It sounds like you know a lot about this Jasper guy. It's uncomfortable, but I'm interested in knowing more. I've never been able to understand much of what happened."

Manny nodded. "Well, I've put together quite a story over the years. So let me back up and tell you what I know." Neither objected, so he started in again, first looking at Tommy. "You probably know that Jasper Czymiak was born in Buffalo, orphaned, and eventually listed as missing in action in Vietnam in 1967. It was there that his odyssey began. The following has been pieced together, much of it from seemingly rambling insane people who have previously been used as Jasper's subjects. It seems he likes to tell his story to those he's using. But let me get to it. Jasper was injured by an explosion during an assault on his unit's firebase near the Cambodian border. It was a total loss and the area was overrun, so there was no recovery made by his allies."

Manny related the pieced-together story of how Jasper came to be and how the odd situation left Jasper in a sort of inter-dimensional limbo. He had the metaphysical spirit of a vampire, but his physical body was dying.

"At some point, Jasper left his dying body behind and began to exist as a spirit-vampire. One who has the never-ending need to suck human blood, but without a physical body. He needs to use human bodies to get his bloody fix. But unlike a demon, his makeup is different, and he can only embody humans for relatively short periods without causing them harm. So he's stuck in a

68

conflicted state of being."

Manny paused to let that sink in. They were covering a lot of ground in a short time. They took sips of wine and played with their food.

Toni finally spoke. "Okay, that explains why he killed George and the inmate . . . your friend. Sorry, now I'm being insensitive." Manny waived it off so she continued. "But what does any of that have to do with what he did to me? And to Tanya?"

Manny took another sip of wine and cleared his throat. "Well, there are a couple of things at play. It seems Jasper often talks to his subjects and gets to know them, so to speak. He doesn't need to. It just seems that he has no one else to talk to. He's an evil, one-of-a-kind spirit, and none of the other peenos want anything to do with him. They would rather he ceased to exist just as much as we would."

"Anyway, Jasper winds up telling his subjects what they're going to be used for – sucking blood. Understandably they have a hard time with it. So, in a very condescending way, he pretends to be benevolent. He tries to give the subjects something in hopes it may soften their natural resistance to being used. I don't know how much it helps. It's hard to believe, but in your case, and Miss Lambert's, Jasper would have told Bud Rogers he was giving him a gift."

"But there's more to it. Unlike all other spirits, who were created as spirits and have always been as such, Jasper was once human. His only forms of pleasure, including his blood-sucking, come in the form of human interactions. So while I hate to say this . . . I really hate to say it . . . even though I'm sure you don't have an actual memory of what happened – blacking out happens when Jasper fully overtakes a body – you can be certain that through you, Jasper was enjoying every minute of his and your time with Bud Rogers."

Toni stared at the table. Tommy felt helpless. They had learned a lot, but he was sure there was more ahead of them.

It was Toni who got things moving again, sounding more determined than ever. "So you have a plan, somehow, to kill this bastard spirit? Let's hear it."

Manny ran a hand through his blondish-gray hair. "Here's where things get a little complicated. I have a plan, but it involves a perfect amount of coordination by multiple people. And as strange as this may sound, I have to ask you to trust me. I'll ask you to meet with me again, along with another man, at which time everything will be explained and hopefully, we can pull it off. I hate to be so vague but I believe it's best to do it this way. Also, I know it's not only asking a lot for you to trust me, but the timeline is important too."

Tommy looked skeptical while Toni seemed unfazed. But with her it was on a personal level he'd never understand.

Manny kept on. "If you can, I will ask you to meet us at the Mountain View Conference and Resort Center, located just outside Saranac Lake in the Adirondack mountains. And I need you there next Thursday afternoon. I know that's only nine days from now. But it's the only way the plan can ever work. So if you can, I'm asking you please, with all my heart, to say you will trust me and that you will be there. Everything will be paid for. And we can give you spending money if needed as well. This is a limited opportunity that will almost certainly never happen again. So we'll happily do whatever it takes to accommodate you if you agree to help."

Tommy didn't like the secrecy. But before he could object,

Toni said, "I can get Patty to run the place for a few days. That's not a problem." Then she looked at Tommy, expectantly.

The ambiguity of the plan was killing him. But he had to admit, Manny had come well-prepared and full of more knowledge than he ever expected. Furthermore, looking at Toni, he got that same feeling from the night before, where he could tell she was all in. She was getting ready to go into ultimatum mode again. And what's more, he believed her. So grudgingly he said, "Well the department isn't going to like the short notice. But I have a boatload of vacation time coming. And my cases are all caught up." Putting on some bravado for his wife's sake, he added, "And if they don't like it, well Hell, I've been there too long anyway. I'll just quit."

Manny smiled and Toni beamed.

"Wonderful" Manny was ecstatic. "I'll give you directions. You have my number. I'll see you a week from Thursday. I don't know how to thank you." Then, before they asked for their doggie bags, he added, "Do you have any questions?"

Tommy had lots of questions. But only one that just occurred to him to ask. "You say you've studied hundreds of cases involving murders by Jasper. I'm curious, out of all the people you could have chosen, why us?"

Manny took on a serious look again. "Yes, I should have mentioned this earlier. Apologies again as I get excited and we were covering a lot. As I mentioned in my letter to you, Jasper Czymiak has killed over twenty-five hundred people. I chose you to help me based on the fact that you both have first-hand knowledge. You're a police detective with certain experience that will be helpful. But more importantly, you don't have any children, and neither of you have any parents or siblings. And while it goes without saying, what we're planning is probably dangerous."

71

CHAPTER 7

Between Lake Placid and Saranac Lake, in the heart of New York's Adirondack mountains, in a hamlet called Ray Brook, is a federal correctional facility. It lies near the old bed of what was once the New York Central Railroad. Next to that facility is an unassuming dirt road that leads south, alongside another old, abandoned railroad bed, through a mixture of conifers and deciduous trees with intermittent views of Scarface Mountain to the east.

After nearly a mile, nestled in isolation, lies a small collection of around twenty houses, leftover from the days of an iron ore mining operation in the early nineteen hundreds. While not an incorporated village, the hamlet is known as Ferro. Residents commute to their jobs in Ray Brook and other neighboring towns. Recently, their community added a conference center and a snowmobile rental company, both taking advantage of winter visitors to the mountains. The newer buildings contrast the century-old houses. But progress is progress, and any business thriving in the area is welcome. The recent growth has even sparked discussions of getting the road paved at some point.

For another half-mile beyond the hamlet of Ferro, the old iron rails remain in place while the road bends away through the woods. Eventually, the road meets back with the rails at the end of the line, at the base of a smaller peak, unofficially but affectionately called Peckerneck Mountain.

At the base of Peckerneck Mountain lies a small house – converted from a depot many years before – occupied by an elderly black gentleman. Very elderly, most people would say.

Max Beauregard sat in a well-worn leather recliner, deciding what to watch on TV. His choices were limited. There was no cable, and Peckerneck Mountain blocked the sight line to any satellites. But Max didn't care. He had digital channels that came in from Saranac Lake and Lake Placid. And there was still a place to rent movies in Saranac Lake when he felt like it.

He sat with a glass of blended Canadian whiskey on a stand near his right hand that held the remote. Cradled in his left arm was a brown chihuahua named Little Whiskey, who patiently waited for Max to settle on a show to watch so he could resume scratching between his tiny ears. He nudged Max's belly, showing his displeasure.

"Hold your horses, little one," he said in a low, gravelly voice. Little Whiskey curled up as if to ignore Max while pouting. Max smiled. He loved his little dog's personality. Finally, they settled on an old western rerun. Sipping his whiskey with one hand and scratching his Whiskey with the other.

There was a fire in the old stone fireplace. Flickering flames danced over them, casting light and shadows on the sparsely furnished living room and its old log walls. Max reflected on his long life, thinking about all the good things he'd experienced. And also the bad. There was the war in Korea. Nasty times for sure. But his life had been mostly good for a long stretch. He had a wonderful wife for many years, and her memories remained vivid. But she was gone, and Max knew he wouldn't be far behind. Still, things had been good until a few years ago, when the evil of the world reared its ugly head once again.

Max didn't know if it was a coincidence, but he felt the presence of a familiar monster named Jasper Czymiak enter his body. At the same time, Little Whiskey hissed and growled, then jumped out of Max's lap. He paced back and forth in front of the television, looking up at Max and protesting with a high-pitched bark.

Yip! Yip! Yip! Yip!

Then Max heard in his head, *HELLO, OLD-TIMER. HOW HAVE YOU BEEN?*

"Jasper, what on earth are you doing here? You're not due for another week and a half."

Max spoke out loud. It was possible to communicate with his thoughts, but talking out loud seemed to keep a psychological distance. And any distance kept from Jasper was welcome, no matter how small.

Little Whiskey kept up his protest. Growling and yipping.

Yip! Yip! Yip!

The situation was not good, and Max was worried. Jasper's arrival meant he would be used for some evil business. He could deal with that, no matter how detestable it was. But Jasper wasn't supposed to be there.

Max knew from experience that Jasper could tell what he was thinking. Recently, Max had hatched a plan with an acquaintance, Manny Richter, to hopefully end Jasper's existence. Max was expecting Jasper to visit in ten days. The plan included a way for Max to have no memory of the plan during the visit so Jasper wouldn't read his thoughts and be tipped off. Unfortunately, that part of the plan had yet to be initiated, as Manny had to jump through some hoops to pull it off.

Yip! Yip! Yip!

SERIOUSLY, MAX. CAN'T YOU CONTROL THAT VICIOUS MUTT? HE'S VERY ANNOYING.

Max scrambled. He hoped maybe if he kept talking, he could somehow not think about the plan to kill Jasper. It seemed unlikely, but with no other choice, he went on. "I guess he just doesn't like you. Speaking of annoying, what is it you want?"

The question triggered a flash of pain to the back of Max's skull. He knew he was pushing the limits, but it helped him forget about his plan, or so he hoped. The first time they met, Max learned the hard way about Jasper's ability to inflict pain to force compliance. The little jab was a reminder that no matter how friendly he may seem, Jasper was always in charge.

Yip! Yip! Yip!

Max already knew all that from past experiences. Yet sometimes, Jasper would let him slide. He thought Jasper may have even considered him a friend. Something Max was sure Jasper had very few of, if any. The monster had a way of acting friendly but would also get very high-handed if Max dared to question his evil deeds or his existence. He was also overly condescending. But in the end, the pain in the back of the head won every time. And Jasper always got what he wanted.

Pretending to ignore the jolt, Max asked, "I don't suppose there's any point in asking what it is you're here for?"

Sometimes Jasper just liked to talk. But ultimately, his arrival always meant mealtime was near. Jasper had explained it once. And Max's friend Manny, who had studied Jasper from afar for many years, summarized it as inter-dimensional mumbo jumbo.

Max didn't like it and never really knew why Jasper had selected him. Regardless, there was no stopping it. Of that he was sure.

YOU KNOW WHY I'M HERE. BUT NOT TONIGHT. AND DON'T WORRY, I'LL BE BACK FOR OUR ANNUAL DATE NEXT WEEK. BUT FOR TONIGHT, I JUST WANTED TO ASK IF THERE'S ANYTHING OR ANYONE I CAN BRING YOU. YOU KNOW I LIKE TO BE GENEROUS TO THOSE I CHOOSE. CAN I BRING YOU A WOMAN? THERE ARE SOME FINE SPECIMENS OUT THERE. YOU CAN HAVE YOUR CHOICE.

Max laughed. He was in his seventies when his wife had passed on twenty years before. Being with a woman was still nice to think about, but he would just rather sit at home with his dog.

Yip! Yip! Yip!

"I'll pass, thanks."

OKAY THEN. I JUST THOUGHT I'D CHECK IN AND SEE. LET ME KNOW IF THERE'S ANYTHING YOU THINK I CAN DO FOR YOU. OH, AND DON'T MAKE ANY PLANS FOR FRIDAY NIGHT. I'LL BE BACK.

Max started to speak, but just as quickly as Jasper had appeared, he was gone. A warm, healthy feeling washed over him. It always did whenever Jasper came and went. Unfortunately, between worrying about whether Jasper had discovered the plan to assassinate him, and knowing Jasper would be back in two nights to turn Max into a proxy bloodsucker, he didn't figure he'd be getting much sleep between then and Friday.

He stoked up the fire and went to the kitchen to get more whiskey, filling his glass to the top. When he sat back down, Little Whiskey jumped into his lap. Max scratched his ears and said, "Don't worry, little one. We'll get through it. We always do."

CHAPTER 8

The big man named Henry didn't understand why they kept asking the same questions. Of course his story was incredible, but he kept telling the truth, no matter how crazy it made him sound.

And maybe that's where he was headed. Sitting in an empty room handcuffed to a stainless steel table. A paper cup of coffee in front of him, and a two-way mirror. He had to admit, his story sounded crazy even to him. This time around there were two men across from him, neither of whom was a police officer.

The first man was older with a mix of blond and gray hair. He said his name was Manny. He sat silently, listening with a blank expression. The second man – who introduced himself as Dr. Ten Eyck – claimed to be some kind of doctor. He was friendly looking, with soft eyes and a fatherly look about him. But Henry didn't feel like going down the same road of questioning the cops had already put him through. They tried the good cop routine and the bad cop routine. And various other routines. In the end, it was always the same questions. And Henry kept giving the same answers.

The Doctor began with a soft, friendly voice. "I know you've been through this several times, Henry. But I hope you understand, I'm willing to believe you."

Henry rolled his eyes and looked skeptical.

Gesturing toward the mirror he said, "Remember, it's their job to find out exactly what's happened. And I'm sure you can admit your story doesn't make sense to them. They like everything to be nice and easy. Cut and dried, so they can fill out their forms and be home for dinner. I won't try to fool you by saying I don't think your story is incredible. I've read the transcripts, and I'll be the first to admit it's hard to believe. But that doesn't mean I think you're lying. And believe it or not, I'm on your side. So as much as I know it likely pains you, I'd like to go through it again. Okay?"

Henry had to admit, the doctor at least sounded more like a friend than even the good cop actors did. And with not much else on his schedule, he shrugged, looked at Manny for a second, who remained stoic, and said, "Why not?" Then looking back at Dr. Ten Eyck he added with a sarcastic smile, "I'm not going anywhere anyway."

Dr. Ten Eyck began. "I'm sure you know this is all being recorded, but I don't want that to bother you. Let's be frank, you know I'm a doctor and you know why I'm here. But I want you to be as honest as you can, and I don't want you to feel intimidated or concerned any time you might see me taking notes. So I won't take any notes. I'll just ask you to tell your story. Fair enough?"

"Yeah." Henry appreciated the doctor's honesty. But the other man, Manny, was still a mystery and Henry wanted to know more. He tried to spread his arms in a questioning gesture, but the chain kept that from happening. "What's your story? Are you a doctor too? Or are you another cop just working undercover?"

Manny smiled warmly. "I'm not a police officer. I belong to a

80

group of people who watch and listen to people with stories similar to yours. I'm not here to judge you or to interrogate you. I'm just here to listen and try to understand."

Henry gave an eye roll as though he wasn't sure he believed Manny.

Manny added, calmly, "And while this may seem hard for you to accept, I'm leaning towards believing your story. That's why I'm here. To hear it first-hand from you. But I promise, I will make no judgments or have any influence on any of the police, or even Dr. Ten Eyck here. I want to listen to your story rather than just read the transcripts. If it were possible I would ask you to pretend I'm not even here."

With a nod, Manny indicated he was finished and sent it back to Dr. Ten Eyck.

"Great. Now, let's go back to the beginning. Did things get started on the night you wound up in the forest with . . ." he quickly checked a small notepad . . . "the woman identified as Miss Clairemont?"

Henry shook his head. "No. It started a couple days before then. I had just pulled into the parking lot of Joe's Junction when I heard a voice in my head." Henry stopped there for a second. The doctor may have looked and acted all friendly, but it was the point where the questioning always headed south.

"Go on. It's all right. I'm listening."

Henry proceeded to tell his story. He stopped frequently as he had in the beginning, expecting objections of disbelief like he'd gotten previously from the police detectives. To his surprise, neither man seemed interested in stopping him or questioning his unbelievable story. He kept on, growing more comfortable as he went.

81

When he got to the part about Jenny Bosko coming onto him the next night, he hesitated again, not knowing how much detail they were looking for. Dr. Ten Eyck assured Henry that they would listen to as much detail as he could give them. When he told them about how hard and tight the woman's grasp on him was, he offered to show them the bruises left behind, as they were still there.

"No need," the doctor said reassuringly. "It's been part of your story all along, and the police have the photos. We believe you."

So Henry kept going. "Well, that was pretty much it. I couldn't pull out so I came hard and deep inside her. She finally let me go, and without a word she walked around the back of my truck and disappeared. Though she still had that eerie red glow in her eyes. Instead of having the awesome feeling I should have had after a surprise quickie, I was filled with dread. I knew somehow it was all related to that same weird shit from the night before, and that Jasper fucker was behind it."

Henry took a break then. He straightened his back to stretch the muscles and laughed as he said, "So you think I'm cuckoo don't you?"

The doctor gave him the same warm, friendly smile. "I haven't finished evaluating yet. Why don't you finish? What happened then? You went home?"

Henry had to appreciate the doctor. He was good. But without much else to do, he proceeded. "Yeah. I went home but barely slept again. I was miserable, let me tell you. Crazy shit going on and let's face it, it's not the kind of thing where you can call up your buddies and get a bunch of beer and spill your guts. I was alone with my thoughts. I was getting crazier by the minute thinking about the whole thing non-stop. I made it through Sunday by staying busy with chores. Laundry and stuff."

Manny stayed quiet while Dr. Ten Eyck nodded to go on.

"Then that night he came back. That Jasper fucker told me all about how he enjoyed himself, fucking me through the body of Jenny Bosko. And how grateful I should be to him for the opportunity. I couldn't believe the way he was spinning things. I ain't no saint, but damn that's a Hell of a thing to do to a woman. That poor girl. Imagine her coming to after blacking out, knowing what happened but not who with or anything. She probably thought she'd been roofied. I even worried about that. But she followed me out, so that would make it hard for her to accuse me, I guess. Still, that's rotten business. And we were unprotected. I tell you, that Jasper guy tries to sell himself as a nice guy, but he's a real shithead. Evil fucker if you ask me."

Henry stopped again, shaking his head. "Who am I bullshitting. There ain't no way you guys believe this any more than the cops did."

The doctor reassured him again. "It's okay, Please, go on."

"Well eventually, after telling me how wonderful he was, Jasper told me it was time, and that I should wear some dark clothes and gloves. I tried to protest but he reminded me of what a bad idea that was." He attempted to reach up and point to the back of his head, but again the chains stopped him. Then he told the rest of the story, winding up with him becoming overwhelmed with guilt and emotions and calling the police.

At the end of the story, Henry felt the need to sum it all up again, as if trying to justify, or somehow rationalize it all. Uncomfortably, he started rambling and running on. "I mean, this guy in my head told me this big, long story about how he was wounded in Vietnam and left for dead and then was about to be transformed into a vampire but something happened halfway through and it left him as a vampire but without a body. And that he had to use human bodies to do his necessary blood sucking but due to his metaphysical nature or some bullshit he couldn't just take over a body for too long or the person would die. And he chose me because I've been an asshole all my life and he wanted to teach me a lesson."

"I tried to put a stop to it. I tried objecting and telling him he wasn't real. I wasn't going to go through with it, and if I turned around and drove home Jasper would just disappear. Then he hit me with the pain in my head again. It was unbearable. Horrible. It turned me into a whining baby. Something I've never thought was possible."

He kept going, repeating the rest of the story only in short form. He told them again how he went into the forest and then blacked out when the murder took place. Then when he came to, Jasper left him on his own, and how he broke down in the middle of the night in the middle of the woods while dragging the dead body of a woman he had killed. Unwillingly, but killed just the same.

Dr. Ten Eyck calmly urged the rest of it out.

It took a few moments but Henry finally finished. "So I just left the body there and went home. I don't mind telling you, I was a mess. I picked up a bottle and drank until I passed out in my chair. I drank until I blacked out. When I came to in the morning with my head killing me, I wanted so bad for it to all have been a dream. I struggled to find anything at all that would explain it away. Anything that would allow me to believe I hadn't killed a woman the night before. But as I sat there feeling miserable, I smelled that poor, unwashed woman's stink on my clothes, and I was forced to admit it was all too real."

The doctor remained quiet. Henry leaned forward, the chains from his handcuffs rattling. "I decided I couldn't live with it. There was no way I could spend my life knowing I killed a woman and left her in the forest. Even if she was never found and I could live scot-free the rest of my life, it would be too much to bear. Hell, it was too much to bear after one night. So, hoping for absolution, or atonement, or whatever the words are, I dialed nine one one."

"It's okay." Dr. Ten Eyck was just as calm and friendly as when they began. "You did the right thing. That's all for now. We'll talk some more in the future."

* * * * *

Manny and the doctor left the cold room, stepping aside as a deputy entered to escort Henry out. They were met by two plain-clothes policemen who had watched and listened through the two-way mirror.

The shorter one with a mustache asked, "Well, what do you think?"

"I think he's sincere," the doctor said.

The taller, older cop looked incredulous. "Don't tell me you believe that story?"

"Of course I don't believe the story. But I can say with certainty that it's not an act. That man fully believes everything he just told me."

The shorter cop again. "So you're saying he's nuts?"

The doctor sighed, visibly annoyed. "I'm saying I will be reviewing the tape of our conversation. But when I'm finished, I have no doubt my determination will be the man has mental issues. Deep ones for sure. But unmistakably present."

Tall cop. "But what about the cause of death? Loss of blood? Two puncture wounds on the neck but no blood present anywhere near the body? And his only explanation is that he was overcome by a spirit vampire, blacked out, and doesn't remember? So where is the blood? Where did he kill her? He has no answers for any of that. Come on."

"I don't know the actual explanation. Physical forensics is not my field. All I can tell you is the man believes what he's saying, one hundred percent."

With that, Dr. Ten Eyck shook Manny's hand and walked away, down the hallway, leaving both cops shaking their heads in wonder.

Then the older, taller cop looked at Manny. "Don't tell me you believe it too. And for that matter, who the Hell even are you? You're not a cop. Not a doctor. You're a civilian who gets to join in on an interview? What are you, writing a book? You must have some serious pull to sit in there."

Yes, serious pull, Manny thought to himself. *Monkey Beans is far and wide.*

For the first time, Manny spoke. "Me? I don't get to have an opinion. I'm just a casual observer."

Both cops looked disgusted. They already knew Manny had connections or he wouldn't have been there. They stayed silent as he walked away.

Once outside, Manny drew a deep breath and enjoyed the sunshine as he walked toward his car. His day was about done but it was still early afternoon. He turned on his phone to check in with Monkey Beans.

Jerry, his main contact, had called three times in the past half-hour. That meant something was important and he needed to talk rather than leave a message. He called Jerry's cell phone number rather than go through the switchboard and the secret covers he would have to navigate.

When Jerry answered in his low, New Jersey voice, Manny got right to the point. "What's up?"

"Hey, how did your interview go?"

"More of the same. We need to stop Jasper somehow. So tell me, what's up?"

"It seems your plan has gained traction. The bigwigs here have made a truce and a deal with some peeno bigwigs, and have set up a meeting between yourself and the powerful Witch Of The Catskills."

That was good news. Manny and his friend Max had a plan, but it was full of holes. One of the biggest holes was how to keep Max from thinking about the plan and tipping Jasper off while Jasper was inside him. The only solution was to hope the peenos didn't like Jasper either and to get a witch to cast a spell on Max that would keep his mind clear of their plan. This was a big step.

"That's awesome news. Where's the meeting?"

"It's at the home of the witch, in the Catskills."

"Okay. When?"

"She expects you there in time for dinner."

"Tomorrow?"

"No, today."

"Do those bigwigs know I'm in northern New Hampshire? And there aren't exactly any direct routes between here and there.

Do they know how long it's going to take me to get to the southern part of New York State?"

"It seems it was the only way. They explained that you would likely push dinner back to eight or nine o'clock. But the plan is set. And the Witch Of The Catskills is supposedly supreme, so it's on you to get there as soon as possible. I'll send you an address pin. Good luck."

"Yeah, thanks."

Manny had seen an interesting barbecue place on the main drag of Gorham, and was thinking about it all day. But duty calls. He headed for his car, looking forward to nothing more than a drive-thru coffee and about six hours of road time with a rumbling stomach. Then he would meet with a witch – something he'd never done. Monkey Beans was Hell-bent on eliminating peenos, not meeting with them.

But it was all for a good cause. The best cause. He was excited because his plan needed all the help it could get. Meeting with a witch is what he would do.

He just hoped she was a good cook.

CHAPTER 9

Manny followed his GPS directions and turned right onto Route 28, near Pine Hill in the heart of New York's Catskill mountains. He drove about a mile until he came to an unassuming dirt road with a sign saying: PRIVATE – KEEP OUT.

The road led to the home of Saavi, the powerful good Witch Of The Catskills. Over the past few years, Monkey Beans learned that members of the paranormal community were just as displeased with Jasper Czymiak as humans were. Manny went to them with a somewhat viable plan to finally put Jasper out of business. They liked the idea, and the elders were able to work out a truce with Saavi – hoping she and Manny could work together toward their common goal.

It was after dark and Manny was glad to reach his destination. Getting older had drawbacks. He hated driving at night and only did so when necessary. He carefully made his way in the darkness, through several turns while climbing uphill. At last, he came to what could only be described as an ancient Gothic mansion. He supposed it was the kind of place where one would expect a witch to live.

As he went around the circular drive and parked in front,

Manny was surprised to find himself a bit nervous. He had seen much over the years, but the place was imposing to say the least. As he approached the large, double wooden doors, one of them opened. A gentle-looking man in a blue suit, about Manny's age, smiled and welcomed him inside.

"You will be Mr. Richter.

Manny nodded. "That's right."

"My name is Donovan. I am at your service for whatever you require."

Manny nodded again and looked around. The inside was as grand and Gothic as the outside. High ceilings covered a stairway that curved up and away from the great room they were in. An old chandelier hung down, illuminating different decorations ranging from African-looking ceremonial masks to full suits of armor. The furniture was made of dark wood.

Donovan spoke again. "I see you're traveling lightly. If you follow me, you can refresh yourself. Then Miss Saavi will see you. It's late, but she insisted we hold dinner until your arrival. I hope you haven't eaten."

That sounded good to Manny. He had been scrambling for days, traveling to see Investigator Chandler and his wife, meeting with Henry, making arrangements for the upcoming meeting, and planning for the week ahead. He happily entered the large bathroom full of ornate brass and marble fixtures. He cleaned himself up while Donovan waited outside.

Feeling refreshed, he went out, prepared for an all-important meeting with the powerful good witch. Donovan led him down a hallway to another large room, no less grand and decorated than the rest. There, standing at a wooden table, he was greeted by a beautiful woman with straight, long black hair and features that made Manny think she must be of Indian descent – or possibly some other area of South Asia. She wore a black dress that highlighted her breasts and finely shaped body.

"Greetings, Mr. Richter. Welcome to my home."

Her voice was pleasant enough, but Manny noticed she didn't smile or show any emotion. "You can call me Manny," he said, attempting to soften her up.

"I'm afraid not. While we have a common goal and a truce is in place, ultimately, you and I are at odds. No?"

So much for softening her up. He nodded and said, "Yes, I suppose that's true."

She gestured and asked, "Won't you be seated? We have a long night ahead of us."

Manny wasn't sure what she meant by that. He was under the impression he was there to detail the parameters of a spell he required and that would be it. Monkey Beans had told him everything was in place for that to happen and Saavi agreed. Still, he made the gesture of pushing Saavi's chair in as she sat before him. He figured it wouldn't hurt, though she still showed no emotion.

Donovan appeared out of nowhere and filled their wine glasses. He was immediately followed by a slim, elderly, East-Asian-looking man who brought a serving tray loaded with shrimp scampi and homemade bread. Manny dug in, not realizing just how hungry he was. Eventually, looking over at his dinner companion and noticing her pecking at her food like a bird, he realized he was probably making a hog of himself. He sat back, determined to present himself better moving forward. Saavi, typically, made no indication of any sort and continued pecking.

They remained silent until the main course arrived. Manny looked down at a beautifully cooked salmon filet under a gorgeous-looking sauce. It came garnished with lemon slices on the side, roasted broccoli, and small red potatoes. He had to restrain himself from diving in head first. Especially once he got a taste.

Saavi finally spoke as they ate. "As you know, much like you and your people, our people have no use for Jasper Czymiak and his evil ways. We would also like to see him vanquished. My understanding is that you have a plan, but it will require a spell applied to a man up north, on the Saturday following the next one. Is that correct?"

"Yes." Manny was glad to be getting down to business. "I admit it probably has a slim chance of working. But as long as there's a chance I feel we need to pursue it. The problem is that Jasper can tell what a person is thinking while he's inside them. And the only way the plan can work is to have him inside the man, Max, while we execute it. So we need for Max to be completely unaware of the plan on the day of the event. Is that something you can do?"

Saavi didn't hesitate. "I can. But you should know, that kind of spell and the distance involved will require a lot of energy. It will be expensive."

Manny shrugged. Monkey Beans had money coming out of their wazoo. That was a non-issue as far as he was concerned. "Not a problem."

Saavi remained stone-faced. "Then we shall finish our dinner and begin the ritual payment."

Manny was confused. The elders at Monkey Beans told him everything was in place and all he had to do was show up and inform the witch what was needed. But he figured eventually she would let him know what she meant. He concentrated on filling up with salmon without looking too gluttonous. Declining dessert, while wondering what delectable dish it would be, he finally put down his fork and looked at Saavi. He noticed how she was not just beautiful, but also really put together. Put together like a brick shithouse, his grandfather would have said.

With the meal finished he stated, "I assumed the payment was taken care of. I do have a credit card, and our credit is impeccable. If you need cash I will have to arrange for it."

Saavi remained stone-faced as ever, and said, "I don't think you understand. I'm not interested in your money. Payment from a mortal to a witch is made in an age-old manner, which is not to be altered in any way."

Manny grew nervous and wondered where the conversation was headed. He had been helping Monkey Beans hunt witches for years, but had never dealt with one in a business sense. Was she requesting a child sacrifice? Or something else of an evil, peeno nature? Or was it . . . then he felt foolish as understanding set in. He couldn't help but smile while making a note to remember to give the elders Hell for having kept him in the dark. *Good one, guys.*

Saavi continued, "You have traveled and no doubt will like to freshen yourself. Donovan will show you to your quarters. It's late, but nothing we can't overcome. I shall visit you in your quarters at eleven of the clock. Please don't disappoint me."

And with that, the beautiful, powerful, good Witch Of The Catskills excused herself. Donovan appeared again and escorted Manny up the curved staircase to an unsurprisingly large bedroom – complete with a fireplace with a fire, a huge bed, a bathroom, and a set of French doors with a private balcony. The room was similarly decorated with ancient-looking artifacts. Swords and daggers were the theme.

"Do you require anything else, sir?"

Manny reached down and tapped his front pocket to be sure

his tiny box of little pills was with him. It was, of course. He never left home without them. Working with Monkey Beans, there were often different surprises. And while this was a surprise, he was determined to see it through, despite her being less than half his age. If a little pill would help ensure success in this mission, his sixty-five-year-old ass wasn't going to let a bit of pride ruin it.

"No, thank you," he said to Donovan, who smirked before nodding and letting himself out.

Looking around, Manny noticed his small travel bag had been brought from his car. He took a shower and prepared himself for the night ahead. Not knowing how involved it would get, but vowing to see the job done.

After he dried himself he looked at the old clock on the mantle, coming up on twenty minutes to eleven. It was time for a pill, after which, he let himself out onto the balcony and let the cool, night air dry his hair. Looking down the hill he could see lights from a town and what he thought might be the Hudson River in the distance.

He returned inside just as his door opened. In walked the powerful good witch. Her black gown had been traded for a blue, satin sash with a slit skirt that revealed a dark-skinned, finely sculpted leg as she entered. Still stone-faced, Saavi glided toward the large bed, dropped the sash, and laid herself down. He looked at her masterpiece of a body, and with the backing of his little pill there was no need of any convincing. It was game time and he was ready.

Ahh, the things I do for my fellow man.

He let his towel drop and settled in next to her. Not sure how she might like to proceed, he cautiously put a hand on her belly and she shuddered. And as he ran his hand up to cup her breast, the stone-faced witch, who had previously shown no emotion, transformed into a sensual beast, softly moaning with pleasure at every touch and caress. The hard-nosed businesswoman seemed to enjoy any stimulation he offered. His fingers caressed and probed. His lips nibbled. And while for the time being it was certainly all about her, Manny was enjoying himself.

CHAPTER 10

With Little Whiskey in his left arm and a glass of whiskey in his right hand, Max stared at the television, nervously awaiting Jasper's arrival. Jasper said he'd be back on Friday, but didn't say what time. The only thing Max knew was he wouldn't be getting to bed early. He worried that Jasper would catch him thinking about his plan to kill him. Manny had a plan to deal with that when the time came. But neither of them expected Jasper to be around a whole week early.

Previous encounters with Jasper had taught Max that resistance was futile – and very unpleasant. So he waited, resigned to his fate. He drained his drink and took in an ice cube to crunch on. As he was about to get up and get a refill, Little Whiskey announced Jasper's arrival by jumping to the floor and starting with his little bark.

Yip! Yip! Yip!

I SEE YOUR DOG STILL DOESN'T LIKE ME.

"Jasper, how ya doin'? Long time no see." Max spoke out loud, as he almost always did when talking to the voice in his head. He laughed at his little joke. Jasper seemed unimpressed.

VERY FUNNY. DO YOU THINK I HAVEN'T HEARD THAT ONE BEFORE?

"Whatever. Always so humdrum." Max tried to appear casual. Inside he was dealing with a mountain of of anxiety. At ninety-two years of age, anxiety wasn't something he let bother him much anymore. But knowing what he and Jasper were heading out to do, and worrying about Jasper discovering his plan was stressful, to say the least. Without much choice, he hoped his facade would work.

Yip! Yip! Yip!

"So where are we off to?" Getting to the point. "It's too soon for our annual reunion."

IS THAT OLD TRUCK OF YOURS GASSED UP? WE'RE GOING FOR A BIT OF A DRIVE TONIGHT.

"Of course it is. I've lived in these mountains long enough to know you have to prepare for any emergency. Keeping the tank full is at the top of the list."

GOOD. I SEE YOU'RE DRESSED IN PLAIN, DARK CLOTHES. THAT'S ALWAYS A PLUS. AND YOUR SHOES ARE ON. LET'S GET GOING.

As Max grabbed his keys and cell phone, he reassured Little Whiskey that he'd be back soon. "It's okay, Little One. I won't be gone long."

Little Whiskey wasn't buying it. *Yip! Yip! Yip!*

CAN'T YOU CONTROL THAT LITTLE RAT?

Max tried to ignore him – but ignoring Jasper was difficult – and headed for the door.

YOU WILL PROBABLY WANT TO LEAVE THE CELL PHONE.

Max stopped, confused. "Didn't you just hear my sage advice about being prepared? Now we're going for a drive at night and you want me to leave my phone at home?"

ARE YOU GOING TO BE DIFFICULT?

"No. Of course not." Being difficult in previous encounters incurred Jasper's pain and wasn't something he wanted any part of. "It just seems a little strange. Sheesh. Pardon me for asking."

Jasper assumed a condescending tone – something he was very good at.

IT'S JUST A SUGGESTION. I HAVE A PLAN. AND I UNDERSTAND AT YOUR AGE, EVEN THOUGH YOU GET AROUND QUITE WELL, DISPOSING OF A BODY CAN BE A CHALLENGE. SO I'M GOING TO ASSIST YOU WHEN THE TIME COMES. BUT FRANKLY, SHOULD ANYTHING GO WRONG, THE ONLY EVIDENCE WILL POINT TO YOU, AND YOU ALONE. IF ANYONE SHOULD BEGIN TO SUSPECT YOU FOR ANY REASON, IT WILL BE A GOOD THING THAT YOUR TRUCK IS OLD ENOUGH THAT THE GPS AND WHATEVER OTHER PROGRAMS MODERN VEHICLES HAVE, WON'T BE PINGING OFF ANY TOWERS AND THEREBY PROVING YOUR LOCATION AT A GIVEN POINT IN TIME. YOUR CELL PHONE WOULD ALSO CONNECT WITH DIFFERENT TOWERS AS WE MOVE AROUND. POLICE HAVE MANY WAYS TO PUT YOU AT A CERTAIN LOCATION. LEAVING YOUR PHONE AT HOME WILL MINIMIZE THAT IF SOMETHING GOES WRONG. AND YOU'LL BE ABLE TO SAY YOU WERE HOME ALL EVENING.

Max had to admit that Jasper made sense. "Why didn't you just say so in the first place?" He had found that Jasper would tolerate a certain amount of kidding, though his demeanor was usually boring when not condescending.

IT'S YOUR CHOICE. I'M NOT THE ONE WHO WILL GO TO PRISON. CAN WE GET GOING NOW?

"Buzz kill," Max muttered as he set his phone down. He gave Little Whiskey one last round of reassurance and headed out the door.

It was a nice night, but dark with just a crescent moon. He started up the old Chevy and asked, "Where to?"

HEAD UP NEAR PAUL SMITHS.

The college town of Paul Smiths was about fifteen miles to the north. Max couldn't imagine what – or who – they would find there. Regardless, he drove down the long driveway, past the Ferro hamlet, and onto Route 86. The conversation was minimal. The radio played softly, but Max wasn't listening. He tried concentrating on the task at hand. And on the road ahead. Anything he could do to keep himself from thinking about his upcoming plan to kill Jasper. He had no idea if it was working, but there was no alternative.

After going through the village of Saranac Lake, the road turned dark. They continued in silence for a few miles. Just before they got to Harrietstown, Jasper told him to turn left onto Route 186.

That seemed odd. The road they were on led straight to Paul Smiths. Heading west on 186 would take them to Lake Clear, where they would then have to take Route 30 north. Max knew better than to argue, but he figured some conversation wouldn't hurt.

"That seems like the long way around."

YOU SHOULD KNOW I HAVE MY REASONS.

Jasper could often be quite chatty. But he seemed contrite – hardly his normal, high-handed, condescending self.

I'M HUNGRY. IT'S BEEN A WHILE.

So that was it. Understandable, Max thought. But a darker thought occurred. He hadn't said anything out loud about Jasper's demeanor. That meant Jasper knew what he was thinking. And that wasn't good for a man who had been thinking of a way to kill Jasper for the past three months. Nervously, he started a conversation, hoping to distract himself from his thoughts. "Ahhh, so you're hangry?"

I SAID HUNGRY. WHAT IS HANGRY?

"It's a new term made up by youngsters. It means you're angry because you're hungry. They usually resolve it with tacos. But of course in your case . . ." He trailed off, wishing he hadn't started with that thought.

I SEE. I SUPPOSE BEING AWAY FROM YOUR SOCIETY FOR THE LAST FIFTY YEARS SOMETIMES LEAVES ME SOMEWHAT IGNORANT OF THE TIMES. THANK YOU FOR THE UPDATE.

Max almost believed Jasper was sincere. Almost. He had come to know Jasper as a perpetual liar. An evil one at that. But with that settled, they continued in silence again, turning north onto Route 30 without being told. Eventually, they came to the town of Paul Smiths. Calling it a town was an exaggeration. The place was nothing more than a college campus with a few houses for faculty and staff and a tiny post office in the middle.

As they passed the town on their left, Max expected Jasper to tell him to turn into the campus. To his surprise, they let the town pass until they came to the intersection of Route 86.

TURN RIGHT HERE.

Max did as he was told, turning right onto 86 and heading back toward Saranac Lake.

"You know, when I was in the army we would call this a circle jerk."

YOU'RE NOT IN THE ARMY.

"It sure feels like it. Following orders without question. Driving around in circles. You know that in less than ten miles we'll be right back in Harrietstown, right?"

101

IT SEEMS TO ME YOU ASK A LOT OF QUESTIONS. AND OF COURSE I KNOW.

Jasper was still being curt. Max shrugged his shoulders and drove into the darkness, away from town. He felt Jasper leave him for a short time. Just long enough to give a false hope that maybe they would call the whole thing off. But after only another mile, he felt him return.

I SUPPOSE YOU NEED TO KNOW OUR PLAN. IN ANOTHER MILE OR SO WE'RE GOING TO PICK UP A HITCHHIKER. IT WOULDN'T DO US MUCH GOOD TO TRY TO PICK UP A HITCHHIKER IF WE WERE TRAVELING IN THE WRONG DIRECTION, WOULD IT?

"There you go making sense again. But come on, a hitchhiker? Nobody hitches anymore. I haven't seen a hitchhiker in twenty years. Certainly not in the middle of nowhere after dark. People realize it's dangerous and just don't do it anymore."

NONETHELESS, THERE WILL BE A STUDENT FROM THE COLLEGE HITCHHIKING TONIGHT. YOUNG MEN FROM THE CITY WHO COME TO COLLEGE TO LEARN HOW TO BE LUMBERJACKS TEND TO FEEL INVINCIBLE. AND HE'S HEADING TO TOWN TO SEE A GIRL HE THINKS LIKES HIM. NEVER UNDERESTIMATE THE POWER OF A HORNY YOUNG MALE TO DO FOOLISH THINGS.

Max laughed, but it didn't last long. Sure enough, up ahead there was a young man in a blue windbreaker, blue jeans and white sneakers, standing there with his thumb out.

JUST MAKE CONVERSATION UNTIL WE GET TO A PLACE BETWEEN HARRIETSTOWN AND 186. DO YOU KNOW WHERE THE FARMER'S MARKET IS?

"Sure, but I think it's closed at this time of night."

OF COURSE IT'S CLOSED, THAT'S THE POINT. WHEN YOU GET THERE, PULL OFF INTO THE PARKING AREA. YOUR PASSENGER

WILL PROBABLY GET SUSPICIOUS, BUT I'LL TAKE OVER FROM THERE. ONCE HE LOOKS INTO OUR EYES HE'LL WELCOME HIS FATE. THERE WON'T BE ANY STRUGGLE.

Max knew all that from previous encounters, but arguing with Jasper was out. "Whatever you say."

Max slowed to a stop to take on the passenger. A teenager with acne opened the door and climbed in. Max smiled and asked, "Where ya headed?

"Saranac Lake," the young man said in a high voice that sounded like he hadn't hit puberty yet.

"Good deal. Me too." He started driving again. "Going to see a girl?"

The young man brightened. "Yeah. I met her last week. She works at that diner on Forest Hill. Hope she's as friendly tonight as she was last time."

"Nice. I hope she is too." He laughed and added, "Don't forget to wear a rubber. You're too young to be tying yourself down for the next twenty years."

The young man smiled. "Got a whole box full. Be prepared is my motto."

"Good boy."

They drove in silence then. It was only about two miles to the closed farmer's market. As they approached, Max slowed down and said, "Man, I gotta piss like a racehorse. One thing about getting old, it seems like ya gotta piss every hour."

The young man laughed. Max pulled into the parking lot and drove behind the building. He didn't have a chance to see if the young man grew suspicious because, as promised, Jasper took over and Max blacked out.

CHAPTER 11

Max returned to the world of consciousness and found himself standing at the back of his pickup truck. The body of the young man Jasper had recently killed lay sprawled in the bed, having been shoved – with Jasper's help of course – under the tonneau cover.

YOU DID A FINE JOB, MAX. I FEEL REFRESHED AS A DAISY IN THE SPRINGTIME.

Max wasn't in any mood to be pumped up. They had just committed murder. Something Jasper used him for on several previous occasions. As far as Max was concerned, the sooner they finished their business the better.

"Why are we loading up the body? Can't we leave it here?"

WE COULD LEAVE IT HERE. BUT THEN IT WOULD BE DISCOVERED BY TOMORROW, AND WHERE WOULD THAT LEAVE US? I DOUBT ANYONE COULD TRACE THIS TO YOU, BUT YOU NEVER KNOW. THERE AREN'T ANY CAMERAS HERE, BUT POLICE HAVE MANY TOOLS AT THEIR DISPOSAL THESE DAYS AND ARE VERY ADEPT AT FINDING CLUES AND TRACKING THEM DOWN. AND DON'T FORGET WE HAVE A DATE NEXT SATURDAY. I DON'T WANT YOU GETTING LOCKED UP.

Max didn't want to get locked up either. But it was late. And at his age, he didn't think he'd be doing much dead weight lifting.

"So what's the plan? I don't think using our regular method is a good idea with another . . . job coming up next week. You just going to leave me now to dispose of this guy on my own while you go take a nap?"

IT'S TRUE, I USUALLY TAKE A NAP RIGHT AFTER A BIG MEAL. BUT YOU'RE A SPECIAL CASE, MAX. YOU'RE THE ONLY ONE OF MY SUBJECTS WHO HASN'T GONE BONKERS AFTER ONE OR TWO MISSIONS. I'M LOOKING FORWARD TO NEXT WEEK. SO IN YOUR CASE, I'M MAKING AN EXCEPTION. I HAVE A NEW PLACE IN MIND WHERE I'M CERTAIN THIS BODY WILL NEVER BE FOUND. BUT IT WILL REQUIRE TAKING YOU OVER AGAIN WHEN THE TIME COMES. I KNOW YOU'D NEVER BE ABLE TO DO THE WORK REQUIRED AT YOUR AGE WITHOUT ME. NO OFFENSE.

Max was irritated. But as much as he wanted to give Jasper a piece of his mind, he knew better. The condescending voice with the friendly tone had a way of rearing its ugly, evil, invisible head. Incredible pain wasn't something Max wanted to deal with, especially not there and then.

"Okay, so where are we headed?"

KEEP HEADING BACK DOWN 86 TOWARDS YOUR HOME. I'LL BE GONE FOR A WHILE BUT WILL RETURN WHEN THE TIME COMES.

Just like that, he left. Max felt the Jasper hangover envelop him. As distasteful as everything else about the night was, the healthy feeling that washed over him from the inside out was welcome. With a heavy sigh of surrender, he closed the tailgate, started the truck, and turned out the driveway onto Route 86.

Harrietstown was only another mile or so. He passed through its sleepy ambiance without much fanfare. Just as they were almost to the intersection of Route 186 – where they had turned off previously to circle up to Paul Smiths – he saw a host of flashing red and blue lights.

It was time to panic, as it was likely a DUI checkpoint by the state police. Max was all about law and order and respected good police officers. But these types of intrusions rubbed him the wrong way big time. Years before, he'd been sent to Korea in the name of freedom and democracy. Yet there he was, many years later being stopped from traveling freely on a public highway by members of the police state. Once there, they would bombard him with questions like where was he going? Where was he coming from? Where did he live, and what was he doing out so late? The correct answer to all those questions was none of anybody's business. But under the mantra of "this day and age," police use a legalized DUI stop as an opportunity to interrogate people without probable cause. Especially annoying were the gung-ho pissants who couldn't just see you weren't drunk and let you go. They had to keep up with the questions, trying to turn your refusal to answer against you – as though you must be guilty of something if you don't like being stopped for no reason and subjected to questions you don't have to answer.

Even if you answer their questions, the answers are never good enough. They continue, trying to twist your answers and question your actions until they can justify the pretextual nature of their ultimate goal – getting you out and searching your vehicle. And don't dare use a cuss word or they'll accuse you of being argumentative and combative, then suggest maybe you're hiding something. Or that you're under the influence of alcohol or narcotics. Don't dare try to laugh and joke innocently. That will get you the same treatment. They'll ask you why you're laughing and suggest it makes you appear nervous and again accuse you of hiding something. Then they'll say they need to pull you out of the vehicle for officer safety. They keep going until they feel they've had their way with you long enough.

Max hated every bit of that type of behavior. His general response when entering such situations was to make that sentiment well known. Normally he wasn't afraid to start right off with the none of your damned business response, then see which way the officer wanted to play it.

But things were different. He had a dead body under cover in the back. Even if the overzealous cops violated every right in the books, finding a corpse in the back would make for a lot of trouble Max would rather avoid. He slowed down and stopped with his window down, already forming his opinion of the snot-nosed trooper who stuck his head into the truck. Then, with a friendly but condescending tone that reminded him of Jasper, it began.

"Good evening sir. Where are you coming from tonight?"

Max was boiling inside – his hatred for the intrusion fighting a huge battle with his instinct for self-preservation. He hesitated, telling himself to play the game while staring at the word PLESHETTE on the trooper's name tag. Then something told him the best way to get through it would be to act naturally instead of pretending to be something he wasn't.

With that settled, and before he could change his mind, Max looked Trooper Pleshette in the eyes and said, "None of your damned business, Sonny Boy."

Trooper Pleshette backed his head out of the window, eyes wide. Then the questions began. "What's with the attitude?

"Last time I checked, this was a public highway. And I didn't risk getting my balls blown off in Korea years ago just so some member of the police state could force me to stop with no reason whatsoever, just to ask me where I'm coming from. So while we're at it, I'm also not telling you where I'm going, where I live, or what my name is. Can I go now?"

Trooper Pleshette acquired an attitude of his own. "No, you may not. I have the right to stop you and engage you. This is a lawful sobriety checkpoint—"

"Yes, it is lawful. So let's keep it that way. The law says I have to stop for this bullshit, and that's all it says. It doesn't say I'm required to answer your questions or tell you anything. And I sure as Hell am not going to get out of the truck and do tricks for you on the side of the road like some dog in a pony show. You have the right to stop me and see if I'm drunk. You figured out in the first ten seconds when you stuck your head inside my vehicle that I'm not. So where do we go from here? Are you going to act all butt hurt because I'm not intimidated by you? Are you going to start in with your bullshit of twisting everything I say just to show me who's the boss?"

Emotions inside Max clashed big time. He'd been through the same type of conversation before and normally didn't care which direction it went. But he kept reminding himself he had some fresh meat in the back. So he stared at Trooper Pleshette, hoping to appear normal and wondering if it was working.

After a pause, trooper Pleshette started in with, "I have a job to do, and the fact that you're being uncooperative makes me think maybe you've got something to hide. Is there anything in the vehicle that would concern me? Any weapons?"

Max didn't like the way it was going. Trooper Pleshette was more interested in scoring points with his boss than he was in letting an obviously sober motorist pass.

The trooper continued with, "How about narcotics? You don't look like the type but—"

Just then a different, slightly older trooper named FRANCIS appeared over Pleshette's shoulder, and said, "Hey, It's Mr. Beauregard! How ya doing this evening, sir?"

Max felt instant relief. Trooper Pleshette looked irritated and turned toward Francis questioningly.

Francis gestured back toward Max. "This is Max Beauregard, the hero of the blizzard of nineteen-seventy. A bona fide celebrity in these parts."

Pleshette looked back at Max. Recognition set in and his demeanor changed. "Oh hey! Yeah, okay. The guy with the train." Suddenly smiling from ear to ear. "That's a Hell of a party you guys throw over there in Ferro every year. I'm looking forward to it next week."

"Don't you have to work?" Francis asked.

"Yeah, but I'm off at eleven. It'll still be going strong then."

"Ha ha, rookie."

Max cleared his throat. Turning their attention back to him, Francis asked, in a much friendlier and curious tone than Pleshette had used, "What are you doing running around out here at this time of night, Mr. Beauregard? Cruising chicks?"

Max laughed. It was time to lighten up. Smiling, he joked, "I got a load of crystal meth in the back. Gonna deliver it down to Albany. Then blow all my money on cocaine and hookers."

They all shared a laugh. Francis said to have a good night. Then Pleshette added, I'll see you next Saturday at the party."

Max just smiled. "Not if you don't get there 'til eleven you won't. That's long past my time for a glass of warm milk and a blanket."

110

Pleshette laughed again. "Take care."

Max drove away, wondering if he would need to change his underwear. Still not knowing the plan, but awash in indescribable relief, he drove on toward his home as Jasper had said. In less than ten minutes he was back in Saranac Lake. Driving through and almost to the turn-off road to get to Ferro and then home beyond, he wondered if Jasper actually meant to go all the way home. What was the plan? Dig a hole and then plant flowers over the top of the corpse? Max didn't think he liked that idea.

With no further direction, he turned down the road to Ferro just as he felt Jasper return.

INTERESTING STRATEGY YOU USED THERE, MAX. HOW DID YOU KNOW IT WOULD WORK?

"I didn't know it would work. And if you were a human we'd be settling this the old-fashioned way right now. That was a rotten trick." He hoped he wasn't overstepping. But he'd come to know Jasper as more forgiving after his meals.

WHY WHATEVER DO YOU MEAN? I'M JUST AS GLAD AS YOU ARE THAT YOU MADE IT OUT OF THERE.

"Oh, I'm sure you are. But don't pretend you didn't know about the checkpoint. I know better."

MAX. ARE YOU INSINUATING I WOULD SUBJECT YOU TO SOMETHING LIKE THAT ON PURPOSE?

Lying. Condescending. Max hated everything about Jasper. "I don't have to insinuate. Every time we've . . . worked together . . . you've always known everything about the victims. Tonight you knew there would be a hitchhiker at a certain place at a certain time. You even knew he'd be chasing a skirt. You knew the farmer's market didn't have any cameras. And you knew damned —" he caught himself. Jasper didn't like swearing. "—darned well

I was driving head first into a bunch of cops with a dead body in my truck. Don't piss on my boot and tell me it's raining."

FORTUNATELY, I DON'T HAVE TO ANSWER TO YOU. BUT YOU WERE REMARKABLE, SO LET'S BE CIVIL, SHALL WE?

Max didn't have any choice so he let it go. "Just what is your plan? I have no desire to start a boneyard on my land."

KEEP DRIVING. WHEN YOU GET TO YOUR PLACE CONTINUE ON PAST. RIGHT BEFORE YOU GET TO THE BASE OF WHAT YOU CALL PECKERNECK MOUNTAIN, TURN LEFT INTO THE FOREST. IT MAY BE TOUGH TO SEE, BUT THERE'S AN OLD ROAD THAT GOES OFF TO THE EAST. I ASSUME THE FOUR-WHEEL DRIVE IN THIS OLD TRUCK STILL WORKS?

Max had lived there most of his life. He was familiar with the old road Jasper was talking about. Old was an understatement. "What you're referring to as an old road may have been a road a hundred and fifty years ago. The only thing traveling it would have been a horse with maybe a buggy or a cart. The story goes it used to swing around to the south of Scarface Mountain and connect with Averyville. But man, you gotta be kidding to think I can drive this old truck through there now."

HAVE A LITTLE FAITH, MAX. DIDN'T YOU JUST GET DONE LAUDING ME FOR MY ALL-KNOWING SENSES?

"Lauding is not how I would describe it."

But arguing with Jasper was a no-go. He shrugged and when he got to the base of the hill where old Peckerneck once lived, he turned left into the forest just as he'd been instructed. Surprisingly, he was forced to admit, with just his headlights and with almost no moonlight casting shadows from above, it looked different than ever before. He could make out the path of the old road to Averyville. The tall pine trees were as old as the hills, and there was never much sunlight filtering through. Much like the rest of the forest in the area, there was hardly any undergrowth and no new sapling growth in his way.

Still, the ground was covered with hundreds of years of pine needles. The back wheels began to spin in the softness. Shifting into four-wheel drive made the difference, and he continued – hating that Jasper was right.

They plodded on in the dark. "So where is it we're going? I can tell you from years of living around here and having walked in this forest many times while hunting in my younger days, we are quickly approaching the proverbial middle of nowhere. I mean, we could dump the body here and there's a good chance the coyotes, foxes, and Mother Nature would dispose of it long before anybody found it."

POSSIBLY. BUT OVER THE YEARS I'VE SEEN NUMEROUS EXAMPLES OF TIMES WHEN MY SUBJECTS THOUGHT THEY HAD A GREAT DISPOSAL PLAN THAT DIDN'T GO SO WELL. NOW, I UNDERSTAND YOUR PHYSICAL SHORTCOMINGS BECAUSE OF YOUR AGE, NO OFFENSE.

"None taken."

BUT YOU'RE ALSO MY MOST DEPENDABLE. YOU'RE THE ONLY MAN I'VE MET WHO DOESN'T GO CRAZY AFTER HELPING ME ONCE OR TWICE. I ALSO ENJOY OUR ANNUAL OUTING AND LOOK FORWARD TO THAT NEXT WEEK. SO I DON'T MIND HELPING TO DISPOSE OF THIS BODY. IT DOES REQUIRE ME TO USE A LOT MORE ENERGY. BUT TO ME, YOU'RE WORTH IT. AND I BELIEVE IN DOING A JOB RIGHT. SO I CAN ASSURE YOU, WHEN WE'RE DONE HERE, NO ONE WILL EVER FIND THIS BODY.

"Gee, thanks."

I KNOW, IT'S NOT MUCH IN THE GRAND SCHEME OF THINGS

FROM YOUR POINT OF VIEW. BUT IT'S IMPORTANT TO ME. AND THEREFORE, BY DEFAULT, IT'S IMPORTANT TO YOU TOO. SO NOW IT'S TIME FOR A LITTLE HISTORY LESSON. THERE WAS AN OLD IRON ORE MINE ON THE BACK SIDE OF SCARFACE MOUNTAIN BACK IN THE EARLY EIGHTEEN HUNDREDS – A HUNDRED YEARS BEFORE EVEN YOU WERE BORN. IT STARTED AROUND THE SAME TIME AS THE LARGER MINE OVER IN TAHAWUS, BUT IT NEVER AMOUNTED TO MUCH. WITH THE DISCOVERY OF IRON ORE IN PECKERNECK MOUNTAIN, WHICH WAS FURTHER FROM AVERYVILLE BUT CLOSER TO THE GROWING COMMUNITIES TO THE NORTH, THE MINE WAS ABANDONED SHORTLY AFTER IT BEGAN. VERY FEW PEOPLE ALIVE ARE AWARE IT EVER EXISTED.

THE OWNERS BLASTED THE ENTRANCE AND SEALED IT SHUT BACK IN THE EIGHTEEN FIFTIES. WHAT THEY DIDN'T DO WAS SEAL OFF THE VENTILATION SHAFT THAT COMES OUT A FEW HUNDRED YARDS UP ON THE SOUTH FACE OF THE MOUNTAIN. IT'S A ROCKY AREA THAT HUNTERS AND HIKERS HAVE NO INTEREST IN, AND HAS REMAINED HIDDEN. WE'RE GOING TO DROP THE BODY DOWN THAT HOLE WHERE IT WILL NEVER BE DISCOVERED.

"You mean if we don't get stuck in these pine needles? This is not the place to get stuck. Nobody knows we're here. And remember, I don't even have a phone with me." Max figured they'd gone maybe a mile, though it could have just seemed that way with the slow going.

STOP WORRYING. WE'LL BE FINE.

Max hated it. But that always seemed to be true whenever Jasper said it.

IT'S JUST A LITTLE FURTHER ANYWAY.

Sure enough, a few minutes later they came to a natural opening. Max stopped where Jasper indicated and looked up in the darkness at the seldom-seen, rocky, back side of Scarface Mountain. Without being told, Max shut the truck off and went to the back. He opened the tailgate and looked at their prize. He knew there was no way his old frame would be able to haul that body up the hill. He suspected that Jasper could do extraordinary things inside a human that no human could do on his own. But since complete embodiment by Jasper always caused a blackout, he couldn't say he'd ever seen it firsthand.

Not knowing what to do, he said, "There's a rope behind the seat if you think we need it."

NONSENSE. I'LL TAKE OVER AND WE'LL HAVE HIM UP THERE IN NO TIME.

* * * * *

The next thing Max knew, he was teetering on the side of Scarface Mountain, struggling to stand on the smooth, slanted, rocky face. There wasn't much light, but he could make out a hole where one section of rock jutted up a couple of feet higher than the section he was on. The body was presumably long gone down the hole.

Standing on the side hill in the darkness was uncomfortable. At his age, Max wasn't all that steady on his feet anyway. Between the slope and the darkness, he was afraid to move.

THERE. ALL DONE. YOU DID A WONDERFUL JOB TONIGHT, MAX. I WANT TO THANK YOU.

"Whoa whoa whoa. We're not done here. You aren't leaving me here all alone. Max didn't usually plead with Jasper, but he found himself doing just that. "Please don't say you're leaving me

115

on this rocky hillside. Even you aren't that mean."

BUT MAX, I'VE ALREADY USED A LOT OF ENERGY HELPING YOU OUT. IT TOOK A LOT MORE ENERGY THAN I EXPECTED. IF I DON'T GET MY NAP SOON I'LL HAVE TO COME BACK TO FEED AGAIN BEFORE OUR DATE NEXT WEEK. YOU DON'T WANT THAT, DO YOU?

Max knew from experience that despite the friendly tone and occasional, supposedly benevolent gestures, Jasper was pure evil. But this was a rotten trick to top them all. "No. No no no! You can't do this." He hated being at Jasper's mercy, but he had to try. "Please, man. Come on. I don't think I can make it. And I don't even have a phone." A tear of fear began to trickle down. Max couldn't remember the last time he cried. Though he figured it was probably due to Jasper then too.

YOU'LL BE FINE. JUST BE CAREFUL. AND DON'T WORRY, NEXT WEEK WE'LL GO BACK TO THE OLD SYSTEM THAT WORKS SO WELL. I'LL SEE YOU SOON.

And with that, he was gone.

It didn't take long for resolve to set in. Max was livid. He was barely standing on the side of a rocky slope, in the dark in the middle of nowhere, with no cell phone and no idea if he would ever make it home. He decided more than ever to find a way. He would get home, make his plan work, and rid the world of that evil bastard forever.

In the meantime, he had to use his head. *Get your shriveled-up ass back down this hill in one piece. Back to Peckerneck Mountain. Back to Little Whiskey.* And oh yeah, he told himself, when he finally got back, he was going to enjoy an extra big whiskey too.

A slight breeze almost blew him over. In the darkness, Max could barely see the outline of his truck below. He told himself it was only a few hundred yards, though almost all of it was bare rock with no trees or anything to hold onto.

No time for heroes. Before another gust blew him down Max sat down on his butt and began to make his way down the hill. Using the healthy feeling that accompanied Jasper's departure to his advantage, he extended his feet, then skittered his butt towards them while bending his knees up. *Like an ass-backward inchworm.* He tried not to think of negative things like what he would do if the truck wouldn't start. Or whether Jasper had read his mind and become aware of his assassination plan.

He concentrated on getting down the hill. Accomplishing his goal, one scoot at a time. Working toward a reunion with Whiskey and whiskey. More determined than ever. All the while muttering, "No good dirty-rotten, thin-skinned, evil, murdering bastard. Son of a bitching piss-poor excuse for a ghost . . ."

CHAPTER 12

Tmmy lay sleeping on his back, snoring softly. But that didn't bother her. The sound was a constant reminder that he was near. Toni lay on her side with her butt backed up to her companion. Her lover and protector. Her lifelong friend. She let the steady drone of the ceiling fan lull her until she finally drifted off and—

* * * * *

—walked up the driveway and the steps to Bud Rogers' old farmhouse. Something inside of her controlled her body, and she was horrified at not being able to stop herself.

She walked through the house until she came to Bud's bedroom. Opening the door, she saw he was awake. He said something but she couldn't hear. She continued – against her will and unable to stop – to undress in front of him. She noticed his look when he finally recognized her in the dim light. He said something else. But again she couldn't hear.

As Toni dropped her skirt and panties, she became aroused.

119

Horrified, but aroused nonetheless. She saw herself pulling off the blanket and peeling off his shorts. It seemed the force inside her figured a blow job wouldn't hurt, and Bud wasn't arguing. Before long the desire inside her grew and she mounted him. Filled with terror, yet she realized at that point she didn't want it to stop. Riding him for all she was worth, she rose to the top of her roller coaster – to the brink. She heard herself let out a moan that she eerily didn't think came from the force within. And finally she—

* * * * *

—woke with a start. Sweat poured off her as Tommy held her tightly, alarm in his eyes. "What's wrong?"

Toni took a deep breath. She thought back to the time Jasper had forced her onto Bud Rogers. For a long time, she never remembered anything past the drive to the house and the walk up the drive. Everything was a total blackout. But eventually, over time, she discovered she could remember if she tried.

She never tried. It was a long time ago, and it was best kept buried. She hadn't had the dream in over twenty years. But recently, with their agreement to involve themselves once again in past events, she wasn't surprised. The horror she felt faded in the comfort of Tommy's arms. The rest of the feelings remained.

"I'll tell you later." She pushed him back onto the bed and reached into his boxers. Tommy, obviously concerned, attempted to slow her down. But she wasn't slowing down, and he quickly came around.

Getting on top wasn't something Toni usually did. She was

normally happy to let her man be on top and in charge. But the dream had left her horny, and there was an eerie compulsion to see it through the same way. So she did. Out of character, but on top and in charge, she gave Tommy a ride for the ages. She worked herself up over and over until she was finally satisfied. Tommy patiently waited until she was ready, and then let himself go. Then she rolled off and they lay there in silence.

Tommy finally reached over and put his hand on her thigh. "You had the dream again?"

"Yeah. I thought we were long past that."

"Well, there's no doubt our upcoming . . . adventure . . . is weighing heavily on our minds. It's not that surprising. I've been dredging up a lot of the old memories too. Of course . . ." he drifted off, not needing to remind Toni that her involvement had been personal, while he was more of an outsider.

Sweating since before she jumped his bones, she said, "I need a shower," and headed for the bathroom.

When she returned, Tommy had prepared two cups of chamomile tea with a small plate of sliced Parmesan cheese and strawberries. He sat on the bed sipping his tea. Toni threw on one of his V-neck cop tee shirts and sat facing him, cross-legged.

"That was pretty awesome," he said with a smile.

Toni took a sip of tea and grabbed a slice of cheese. Then she laughed. "Don't get used to it."

They sat, sipped, and snacked in silence until Tommy finally spoke. "Jasper Czymiak. It's pretty much all I can think of. I imagine you too?" He looked questioningly. When she nodded, he added, "Why don't we just leave tomorrow?"

"It's only Monday. Mr. Richter doesn't want us there until Thursday, and it's only about 350 miles. We could leave in the morning and be there by afternoon. I doubt he has our rooms reserved for us before then anyway."

"So we'll take our time. We'll take the back roads. Stop in the Finger Lakes and taste some wines. Maybe go to the casino. Visit the little craft shops we find along the way. Our thoughts will be stuck on where we're going for the next few days anyway. If we start heading in that direction, it might sit better in our minds. Even if we only travel a hundred miles or so each day. I've already got the whole week off. And you know Patty can run the diner for you. She loves it when you go away. Gives her a break from your totalitarian rule."

She knew he was kidding, of course. Toni didn't argue. And it had been a while since they'd done anything together. A mini vacation on their way might be just what they needed. She smiled and nodded, "Okay, good idea."

"Great. We should go over to Horizon's and rent a little motor home. Then we can stop anywhere we get the urge."

After some thought he added, "And there will be plenty of room for you to bring your guitar. You can sing songs to me while we travel. Just like old times."

At that point, Toni was hooked. When they first met she used to have a steady gig at a local tavern. She always loved playing and singing for Tommy. He would listen to the old classics, and all the new songs she wrote, with equal enthusiasm. It was a great idea, and just what they needed.

"Okay, I'm in."

"Cool. We'll head to Horizon's in the morning and be off before noon."

"You go. I'll get to the diner early and make sure Patty has everything she needs."

122

"Don't you want to help decide which custom ride we should choose?" He seemed surprised.

Toni thought about his question. Her answer was simple enough, but it carried a much deeper meaning when she said it.

"No. I trust you."

CHAPTER 13

Max looked at the old steam locomotive housed in the shop. There were lights, of course, but he used a flashlight to check all the plumbing fittings. He walked around the side and looked fondly at the words *"Candy's Carriage,"* written in fancy letters on the cab. Flooded with memories of his wife, he took his old, gold railroad watch from its pocket. He flipped open the cover and looked for a few moments at an old picture.

Then he spoke to both the steam engine and his wife, "Just one more trip old girl. One more trip and it will all be over."

The iron rails leading out from the shop used to run about a mile and a half – to the main line in Ray Brook. They were abandoned and mostly torn up years ago. All that remained was roughly a half-mile section running from the shop near Max's house to the edge of the Ferro hamlet. Long since retired, Max had rescued the steam engine from the scrap yard by convincing the folding mining company to let him keep it –along with the short section of tracks. Throughout the years Max maintained the old engine as a hobby.

Then, during the summer of 2020 when COVID had a stranglehold on the world, a spontaneous celebration took place that had since turned into an annual event. The whole thing was blown out of proportion. Max chalked it up to young kids looking for a reason to have a party. Still, it was fun to fire up the old girl and run the half-mile section once a year. He thought about the upcoming trip in less than a week and reminded himself it would be the last one.

Rather than let that bring him down, he smiled to himself, as Little Whiskey tugged on his pant leg.

"I know little one. I know."

He bent down and picked up the small dog, cradling him in his left arm where he seemed a natural fit. As he walked toward the door, Max looked back fondly once more. Then he turned off the lights and went to the house.

He set Little Whiskey down in the old leather recliner while he stoked up the fire. Then he went to the kitchen and ladled himself a bowl of sausage and beans from the slow cooker – a late Sunday night treat he'd been enjoying for ages. After toasting a slice of sourdough bread and filling up his whiskey glass, he took the whole works into the living room where Little Whiskey looked on anxiously.

He settled in and turned on the television, changing channels until he found a weekly, north country news program. Dipping his bread into the beans and enjoying himself, Max watched as the anchorman related a bizarre story about a man in New Hampshire. The story went on that the man had called authorities and reported a homicide, which he claimed to have committed.

Max thought that story had Jasper's fingerprints all over it. It prompted him to reflect on the ugly things Jasper had forced him to do. He did his best to keep it buried. But his upcoming date with Jasper, along with his and Manny's plan to eliminate the fiend, made it hard not to think about.

Little Whiskey, annoyed by being ignored, poked his nose into Max's belly a few times and then stared at him, waiting. Max smiled at his little friend. "Okay okay." He took a hunk of sausage and set it on a napkin on the arm of the chair. Little Whiskey gobbled it down in two seconds, turned around, and demanded more.

"Sorry, little one. You should have taken time to appreciate the fine things in life."

Little Whiskey looked unimpressed and kept staring. Max regained interest in the television show, as the anchor began talking about how the authorities had questions the suspect couldn't seem to answer. And the suspect's story contained some rather unbelievable aspects that led them to think he might not have acted alone. Max could relate to that, considering some of the things he'd been through. He couldn't imagine trying to explain it to anyone. No one would believe him if he tried.

Except for Manny. Manny seemed to know more about Jasper than anybody, including Max. And thinking about that reminded Max that Manny hadn't returned his phone calls. He hadn't spoken to Manny since late in the past week. He decided to try again after eating, even though it was getting late. It wasn't like Manny to disappear, and that was concerning.

Little Whiskey prodded for another snack. But when Max looked down at his bowl, there was no more sausage.

"Sorry little one," he laughed. "No beans for you. I'm not putting up with Chihuahua farts all night."

Little Whiskey curled up and looked away – his way of pouting. Meanwhile, the television anchor went on about the bizarre murder. The more he talked, the more Max was convinced it was a Jasper killing. It sounded similar to his experiences, and also a lot like the stories Manny shared. Max sighed and changed the channel where he found a local news story about a college student who had been missing since Thursday. They showed his picture and Max had to close his eyes. He wanted to be angry. He was angry. But he knew lashing out to no one except Little Whiskey wouldn't resolve anything.

He tried not to think about the young man's family and friends. He tried not to think about the young man's body lying all alone at the bottom of a mountain, and how that would leave his loved ones to wonder what happened for the rest of their lives. If there was any remaining inclination to back out of his plan to eliminate Jasper, it was gone. Max was determined to see it through.

He set Little Whiskey on the chair arm and returned to the kitchen. As he rinsed his bowl in the sink, he swore he could feel Little Whiskey's daggers in his back. He fished out another hunk of sausage, returned to his chair, and watched his little dog hog it down in one gulp – once again looking up for more. Max laughed and scratched between his tiny ears, saying softly, "One more week little one. One more week and we'll get the bastard."

CHAPTER 14

Manny stood on the balcony, enjoying the fresh air and growing anxious. It was almost time for Saavi's after-lunch visit – which normally wasn't a problem.

In the beginning, it was a lot of sexual satisfaction for her, and he was up to the task. But she kept coming back for more – morning, noon, or night didn't matter. They were on day five, and he wondered if she was trying to put him through all the positions of the Kama Sutra. Time was growing short. There were plenty of arrangements to make and he wasn't sure how much more of Saavi's traditional payment he could handle.

Making matters worse, he was all out of little pills. He figured he could manage the old-fashioned way, but he was no spring chicken. And securing her spell was paramount. Keeping his end of the bargain was too important to leave to chance. Left with no option, he went inside just as Saavi opened his door. He noticed her typical sash was missing. Instead, she wore an elegant dress, similar to the one she had on when they met. She stopped just inside without closing the door.

Stone-faced as usual, she spoke. "You have fulfilled your part. Your account is current. I will grant the spell on the man called Beauregard one week from this Saturday, beginning at twelve of the noon clock. The spell will remain until the Sunday sunrise. Do you have questions?"

Manny was relieved, to put it mildly. Filled with stories to tell the guys at Monkey Beans, but relieved nonetheless.

"No, I don't believe so." He couldn't think of anything else to say, though some thoughts came to mind like, *Thanks for the incredible five days of being your sex slave.*

"Very well. Your kind and mine are still at odds. But we wish to see Jasper Czymiak vanquished as much as you. There is nothing good for either of us in his existence, but he has proven rather difficult to pin down. We wish you success. In that regard, I have arranged for the Oracle Of The Champlain to visit you and your party. You will do well to heed his advice. He is one of the most all-seeing oracles in the world. He will visit and read for you, free of charge."

Manny wasn't sure, but he thought he almost saw a smile when she said that. And it was a good thing. After his recent transaction, he didn't want to entertain what kind of payment a powerful oracle might require. Especially a male oracle – not his type.

"Appreciated. When will he arrive? Time is of the essence. And will he require a room?"

"No room. He will be there on Thursday at nine of the clock in the evening. He requires to be served *Petite Frimousse* from two-thousand fifteen. And that is a strict requirement. You can accommodate?"

Manny didn't know what that was. He thought it might be French, but it didn't matter. Monkey Beans had resources everywhere. This was probably the only chance they would ever have to wipe out Jasper Czymiak. He was number one on the list. The

Oracle could order iced tea made with moon rocks and Manny had no doubt Monkey Beans would come through.

"No problem. And thank you for everything."

"Do not thank me." Stone-faced. "Do not forget, our kind and yours are at odds. We wish you success and will aid you as we can, but only because it serves our purpose. Also, should you desire to remove the spell from the one called Beauregard, you must make eye contact and repeat the words, pretty-hippie-gypsy, three times in succession. Do you understand?"

Pretty hippie gypsy three times. Got it."

"And do you remember our agreement?"

He smiled. "I remember."

"Very well. You may leave."

With that said, she turned and walked away. Manny had a thousand things to do, but he took a moment to watch her as she walked down the hallway. He may have been sixty-five and wrung out like an old dish rag, but he could still appreciate the way her dress swished over her curves as she moved.

Donovan appeared out of nowhere with Manny's phone, which hadn't been checked in five days. Not nearly as stone-faced as Saavi, he grinned and said, "I hope you have enjoyed your stay, sir. You may see yourself out."

Manny laughed. A good, hearty laugh, which was much needed. Donovan disappeared without another word. Manny wondered if he was supposed to tip him. But it was a private residence, not a hotel, so he figured it was a no. Then again, it certainly wasn't your typical private residence. But Donovan was already gone, and Manny had things to do. He made a note to run it by the experts at the office and they could send something if they felt they should.

He gathered his belongings and made his way back out the same way he came in. It took some remembering. Except for the balcony, he hadn't been outside his room since Thursday. A sex slave if there ever was one. *Ahh, the things I do for my fellow man.*

Unsurprisingly, his car was waiting out front. He threw his meager belongings onto the passenger seat, plugged his phone in, and checked his messages. Tommy Chandler had called twice. Manny hoped there were no issues there, he needed Tommy. There were a few other voicemails that could wait or be ignored. Max had called numerous times. Manny figured they would have much to discuss. He would call him last.

He noticed, conspicuously, that there were no messages from anyone at Monkey Beans. Five days was a long time for him not to check in, especially given the importance of his mission. It was almost as if they knew he wouldn't be available for a while. He would call them too. Not just to give them Hell for the sex slave surprise, but he needed to order a beverage, special delivery.

There was also one short message from Bianca Lambert   the girl from Texas born with a caul. *Hey, Manny. Just returning your call. You seemed very cryptic, but if you have a plan to get rid of that evil bastard, I'm on board. Get back at me when ya can.*

Manny checked his watch. It was going on two-thirty. Plenty of time to get from the Catskills to the Adirondacks. That pleased him, not only because he needed to get there as soon as possible, but he didn't want to have to drive at night. He fired up the Cadillac and headed out the circular driveway, winding down to the road.

As soon as he got a good signal, he called Bianca, even though he wasn't sure what part she could play in the plan. A fiery redhead from Texas, she was one of the few people in the world who was aware of Jasper and his evilness, had met Manny, and, though it seemed too much like a coincidence, had also previously attended the upcoming party known as the Hero of Seventy Bash. He figured the more people on the team the better, and wanted to leave no stone unturned.

Her message was five days old, and things have a way of changing when people feel they're being ignored. To his surprise, she answered on the first ring – her voice oozing Texas. "Manfred! It's about time you got back to me. I was starting to think you don't love me anymore."

She also loved to flirt. "Hey there Red, my apologies, I was unavoidably tied up for a few days."

"I hope she was cute."

If she only knew. Still, he figured a little truth couldn't hurt. "Of course she was," he said, and they laughed. "So tell me, are you still on? I know it's late notice, but I can send a plane if you need one."

"Send a plane! Oh! Em! Geeee!!! Send a freakin' plane!" More laughter. "Where the Hell you been all my life you rich bastard?"

"Well I just thought—"

"No need, but you can owe me. I'm already on my way. Driving up in my new red Mustang. Only got one ticket so far. But yeah, I'll be there. Those mountain folks really know how to put on a shindig. And I'm just dying to hear of this plan you have for that fuckin' . . . oops, potty mouth . . . ghost. Let's nail that rotten bastard once and for all. When's the big pow-wow, Thursday you said?"

Encouraged by her enthusiasm, he answered, "Yes, I'm hoping to have everybody there by Thursday afternoon so we can get introduced and finalize the plan."

"Count me in. I'll see you soon."

"All right then. Looking forward to it."

"Me too. Buh-bye now."

So far so good. He made the turn to head north on Route 42 and called Tommy Chandler, thankful for hands-free calling and hoping to hear more good news.

"Hello."

"Hello Mr. Chandler, how have you been? I hope you and Mrs. Chandler are doing well. And let me apologize for my lack of access for the past few days. I hate to make excuses but sometimes this crazy Monkey Beans business throws us curve balls. I was un-avoidably and unexpectedly off the grid. I do hope you haven't changed your minds about joining me on Thursday."

"No, we're still in. And it's Tommy and Toni, not Mr. and Mrs. Though I have to admit, I wish I knew a few more details."

Manny delighted in hearing that Tommy seemed to be in good spirits, even as he heard Toni in the background telling Tommy to trust him. "I know. And I understand. It's just best. But I promise, by the time we're done on Thursday evening you will have the whole plan laid out. You have my word. And if there's anything you can think of you need, please don't hesitate to call. I will answer the phone from now on, for sure."

"Nah I think we're good. We're actually sort of on the way. We decided to take some time away from our jobs and meander our way north. Take the scenic route and stop to smell the roses, so to speak."

Manny was two for two and getting excited. "Great idea. I'll see you guys soon. Give my best to Mrs. . . . . I mean Toni."

"Will do. Talk to you later."

"Yessir."

He disconnected and told his car to dial the Monkey Beans main office. A professional-sounding woman answered. "Jackson Investments, how can I help you?"

"Is Jerry there?"

"I'm sorry sir, you have reached Jackson Investments. There is no one named Jerry here."

Monkey Beans, being a secret society, had to keep a good cover even though their number was unlisted. "Hey Jessica, it's Manny. Is Jerry around?"

"Oh hey, Manny! Nice to hear from you. You've been rather quiet lately. Let me put you through."

He was pretty sure he heard her giggling. No doubt the whole office knew about his recent mission. Monkey Beans was like a small town where secrets were few. He waited until he heard Jerry's low voice and New Jersey accent.

"Manny, nice to hear from you. Where ya been? Last we knew you were going to visit that witch in the Catskills. We were about to send out a search party. Nice to hear you've made it out of there alive."

"Very funny. You know damn well where I've been." But he had to laugh.

"Oh, the things you do for your fellow man, right?" Jerry was laughing too. And probably jealous.

"Right. But listen, I'm running short on time. You guys have to hook me up with a special delivery of some kind of beverage. I think it's a wine called Patty Free Moose."

"Patty Free Moose? Never heard of it. Can you give us a little more info?"

I don't know much. It sounded French when the witch said it. It's what the Oracle of Lake Champlain or something likes to drink. And he's coming to see if he can help us."

"Holy shit! You're meeting with the Oracle Of The Champlain? No way!"

"Yeah. Why, who is he?"

"Only the most powerful oracle in all of North America. Nobody gets to see him. Like literally, nobody. Especially not any of us mortals. And he's coming to see you? This can't be happening. What kind of magic did you work on that witch?"

"Just my normal charm. So this guy is a big deal? I wonder if he travels with security. Just the same, maybe we should put out a notice to all our peeno hunters in case anybody recognizes him. They need to be hands off, one hundred percent."

"Yeah, I hear that. We'll get right on it. And hang on a second, let me ask around the office about that wine."

Manny waited, driving along the winding road, hoping he wouldn't lose the signal. Finally, Jerry came back. "Do you mean *Petite Frimousse?* That's a high-end French wine."

"Yeah, that's what I said, Patty Free Moose. It needs to be twenty fifteen vintage too. And it must be provided without fail."

"Man, we gotta get you some culture."

"I'm pretty sure it's too late."

"Is that all? I mean, we can arrange to have the grapes pressed by the feet of a girl named *Manon* if you'd like."

"You're so funny. Just have it sent to the conference center. It needs to be there before Thursday night."

"Sure, no problem. You know it's only Tuesday and from a different continent. Just one bottle?"

"Hell, I don't know. How much can one oracle drink in a night? Then again, we must be prepared for an event as special as this. Better get a case of it. I'd rather be looking at it than looking for it."

"Your budget for this project is going to break our bank."

"You know better than that. I think that's it for now. Thanks, Jerry. I gotta let you go. Got a ton of shit to do."

"All right, man. Good luck and don't pick up any hitchhikers."

"No worries. I'm in no condition to be raped for a while anyway."

They shared another good laugh and hung up. Manny drove on. Things were hectic but seemed to be going well. He decided to call Max. He felt bad about not being there for him. The whole idea of their plan was Max's, and Manny wanted to be there all the way. But he told himself Max had been around and had a good way of looking at things. Once Manny explained why he was held out of touch, he would understand.

CHAPTER 15

Four days before the great Hero Of '70 Bash, with the weather a perfect 72 degrees and sunny, it was time to fire up Candy's Carriage and make a final test run of the boiler and all her fittings. Max didn't think of himself as a hero, and 1970 was a long time ago. But the celebration was good for the community. And it gave him a reason to fire up the old steam engine he had cared for over so many years.

He opened the large double doors at both ends of the shed, then pulled his old gray Ford tractor up from behind. Hooking a cable to the steel frame, he towed Candy's Carriage backward through the double doors where he connected it to an old caboose.

With the engine's smoke stack safely outside, Max checked the water in the boiler, ensuring it was at the right level. Then he went back inside the shed and fired up his air compressor. While wondering where Little Whiskey had gotten off to – probably chasing a squirrel somewhere – he unwound and dragged the rubber hose out to the firebox at the back end of Candy's Carriage.

Built during the 1940s, the old girl used diesel fuel to make steam. Max was glad of that. Having to tend a fire made of wood or coal like the older models used would have been too much work. As long as he was careful, he could operate everything by himself. And thanks to the folks in town anticipating the big celebration, the fuel tank was full. Opening the door to the firebox, Max lit a fuel-soaked rag and threw it into the bottom. He closed the door and opened the main valve, then the working valve on the fuel line. Inserting the compressed air nozzle into its coupling, Max forced the diesel fuel through a nozzle inside the firebox, atomizing it into a fine mist that burned with a flame that shot through the entire length of the boiler tubes.

Thick, black smoke initially came out of the stack. But it cleared up and was almost invisible as the fire grew hotter and burned more efficiently. Once the locomotive was in motion it would use its own pressure exhausting from the cylinders to force the fuel. For the time being, the air compressor would do.

After ensuring the pressure was correct and the fire was blasting through the boiler tubes, he allowed the fire to burn and heat the water inside. He didn't want to warm things up too fast, but the flame could only be turned down so low. Ensuring the old girl didn't get too hot too quickly would require a series of on-and-off-again firings. He pulled out his old, gold pocket watch and made a note to let the first cycle burn for ten minutes.

He rechecked the water level and let the fire burn while he looked the caboose over. Having sat mostly untouched for a year and expecting a few so-called dignitaries as passengers in a few days, Max didn't want there to be any surprises like mechanical issues or wasp nests.

As he inspected the caboose, his phone vibrated in his pocket. Finally, it was Manny. Max probably sounded overly excited when he answered, "Manny! Just how the Hell are you, boy? I've been worried about you. We have a lot to do before Saturday."

"Oh, I know. All I can say is I was unavoidably detained by the witch in the Catskills. But I'm free now, the spell is in place, and we're all systems go. I'm on my way up to Ferro now. How's everything with you?"

"I'm doing as well as can be expected. But that bastard Jasper paid me a surprise visit back on Thursday. I wasn't prepared for that and it's been weighing on me. No sense in crying about it though. I'm more determined than ever to go through with the plan."

Max hesitated, not wanting to bring up the subject of whether or not Jasper had read his thoughts about their plan. The moment of silence from Manny suggested he was thinking the same thing. Since there was no secondary plan – nor would there ever be one – it seemed best not to mention it.

Finally, Manny asked, "Another one? Damn. I just got done investigating a case up in New Hampshire. Jasper's work all the way."

"Yeah, I saw that on the news and figured it was him. It was a college kid for me this time."

Little Whiskey started yipping up front by the firebox. Max looked at his watch and shook his head, wondering just how smart the little dog was. He walked over and turned off the fuel for a few minutes. He continued his inspection of the two-car train while telling Manny all about his encounter with the young man from college, and how Jasper had left him on the side of a mountain in the middle of nowhere with no cell phone in the middle of the night.

They continued talking while Max ran the boiler through a few more sessions, carefully checking all the steam fittings as the pressure built up inside. He listened, laughed, and kidded with

Manny as he relayed his story of being held captive by Saavi.

"Taking one for the team, eh?" Max laughed as he said it.

Manny laughed too. "Oh, the things I do for my fellow man."

Before long the old locomotive was showing 200 PSI on the pressure valve. It was more than he was likely to use on Saturday, but it was good to run the test beyond the operating point just to be sure.

He turned off the fuel and shut the main valve while he and Manny said their goodbyes – expecting to see each other in a few hours anyway. With all systems ready for action, Max started pulling levers and opening valves to provide steam to the pistons – gently at first. With water inside the cylinders built up from condensation during the heat-up phase, injecting steam too fast could blow them apart. Once the steam slowly forced the water out through the petcocks, Max increased the flow. The steam began alternating through the pistons and working its magic. The two-car train slowly moved forward.

Little Whiskey jumped up into the cab, excited to be going for a ride. He was disappointed when the ride only lasted about a hundred feet. As soon as the engine passed through the shed and the smoke stack was outside again, Max shut it down. Everything was in great shape, and he felt good about the upcoming celebration. There was only one thing left to do, and that was to send a message to the folks in Ferro that everything was all systems go.

He looked at Little Whiskey. "Plug your ears, little one."

He reached up and pulled on the chain above his head. At 200 PSI, the old brass whistle screamed. Little Whiskey jumped out and ran like the devil himself was after him. Max sent three long blasts to the folks in town, then left Candy's Carriage to cool down while he went to look for his dog.

CHAPTER 16

Henry lay on his cot in the jail cell and stared at the ceiling. He wasn't sure if he was in protective custody, on suicide watch, or something else. Nor did he know much about the regular jail protocols. He was just glad he didn't have to share a cell.

Sleep was a thing of the past – a memory of better times. He had no idea what time it was. It was well past the evening meal and the eleven o'clock shift change. He wasn't even sure what day it was. He spent his time staring at the ceiling while playing out the events of his recent past, over and over.

He was in deep. The doctor had visited earlier. That didn't amount to a whole lot. But at least it temporarily broke up his mundane existence. The guards had started calling him Head Case Henry, and he wondered if the doctor had anything to do with that. Then again, as he looked into himself, they weren't wrong. So he really couldn't blame them.

Henry had plenty of time to reflect on himself, his life, and what had led him to his current predicament. It didn't make sense. That Jasper guy told him it was because he was such a bad person. Henry admitted to himself he was no angel by any means. But there were plenty of worse people in the world.

He almost wished Jasper would come back for a visit so he could ask him. His life was shot, but maybe some clarification would help. Then again, Henry thought maybe he was just crackers. Voices in his head? A body-snatching vampire forcing him to kill? Yeah, that was it, Henry was crackers.

Then he felt it, and heard—

GOOD EVENING, HENRY.

He closed his eyes, unable to respond. His jumbled thoughts tumbled over each other like a drum full of raffle tickets.

I SEE YOU'VE GONE AND GOT YOURSELF LOCKED UP. HOW DISAPPOINTING. I WAS HOPING WE COULD SPEND A LITTLE MORE TIME TOGETHER. IT'S GOING TO BE DIFFICULT FOR YOU TO HELP ME FIND A VICTIM IN HERE. AND HOW AM I SUPPOSED TO BRING YOU A WOMAN? I THOUGHT WE ENJOYED THAT LITTLE PARKING LOT ROMP LAST WEEK. I KNOW I DID. REALLY, HENRY, YOU DIDN'T THINK THIS THROUGH VERY WELL, DID YOU?

The voice in his head – the one that had caused all of Henry's troubles – was not only back to haunt him, but was actually complaining that Henry hadn't considered its desires when he turned himself in. But hey, why not? If you're going to go crazy, you should at least be able to call your imaginary friend a narcissist.

LET ME REASSURE YOU, HENRY, YOU'RE NOT CRACKERS. I AM QUITE REAL. I KNOW I'M NOBODY'S CUP OF TEA, BUT I CAN'T HELP BEING WHAT I AM. AND IF I MUST EXIST AS I DO, I MIGHT AS WELL MAKE MYSELF AS HAPPY AS I CAN. EVEN IF IT GOES AGAINST HOW HUMAN SOCIETY THINKS I SHOULD BEHAVE. THEY HAVE NO USE FOR ME, SO I HAVE NO MORAL OBLIGATIONS TOWARD THEM EITHER.

Henry still didn't respond. He couldn't think of a word to say.

I GUESS YOU DON'T FEEL LIKE TALKING. I WAS JUST KILLING SOME TIME. I'M GETTING READY TO FEED IN A FEW DAYS AND I THOUGHT IN THE MEANTIME MAYBE WE COULD HAVE SOME FUN. WE STILL CAN, IF YOU'D LIKE. I COULD BUST YOU OUT OF HERE AND WE CAN GO ON A SPREE. GO DOWN SWINGING IN A BLAZE OF GLORY. BUT MAYBE YOU'RE COMFORTABLE HERE. THREE HOTS AND A COT WITH NO PESKY RESPONSIBILITIES, DEADLINES, OR APPOINTMENTS. NO MORE SWEATING ON A HOT ROOF FOR AVERAGE PAY. I CAN SEE WHERE IT MIGHT HAVE ITS ADVANTAGES.

Finally, Henry spoke. Whispered actually. No sense in letting the rest of the jail hear Head Case Henry conversing with the voice in his head. Still, talking out loud to Jasper was the last lifeline to any kind of sanity he had left – though he knew in reality it was too late. "What do you want? Haven't you ruined my life enough already?"

I JUST THOUGHT MAYBE YOU WOULD LIKE TO HAVE SOME FUN TONIGHT. INSTEAD, I FOUND YOU HERE, ALL COZIED UP. I HOPE YOU ENJOY THIS TYPE OF LIVING, IT SEEMS IT WILL BE YOURS UNTIL THE END OF YOUR DAYS.

Henry couldn't stand it any longer. He sat up, grabbed his head in his hands, and began screaming "AAAAAAAAHHHH!! AAAAAHHHH!! AAAAAHHHH!!"

He kept screaming, even through what sounded like Jasper's laughter. After a few seconds, a guard came into view. A small, pimple-faced young man named Cassidy. In another time, Henry would have stolen his lunch money. But Cassidy had the upper hand, and shouted, "Hey, Head Case Henry! Knock it off!"

Henry stopped shouting. But before he could react, he felt Jasper move in. It was the same feeling he remembered right before he blacked out the night of their murder. He felt his fangs grow long. Then he felt himself blast an evil hiss toward Cassidy.

The young man's eyes widened so fast it reminded Henry of a Saturday morning cartoon. He thought Cassidy's eyes might pop right out of his skull. Cassidy didn't say another word. His face went from boss-man to scared little kitten as he spun on his heels and went out of sight.

As his fangs withdrew to their normal size, Henry said, "Gee, thanks. Like I don't have enough people giving me grief around here."

RELAX. WHAT DO YOU THINK HE'S GOING TO DO, GO TELL HIS BOSS WHAT HE JUST SAW? THEY'D LOCK HIM UP RIGHT HERE NEXT TO YOU. IT'S MUCH MORE LIKELY HE'S GONE TO HIS LOCKER TO SEE IF HE HAS ANY SPARE UNDERWEAR. DID YOU SEE THE LOOK ON HIS FACE? YOU CAN'T BUY THAT KIND OF ENTERTAINMENT.

Henry had to admit, watching Cassidy crap himself was satisfying. He laughed and spoke without whispering. "Scared the pimples right off his pussy face." He thought he heard Jasper laughing too. But his own laughter – fueled by a buildup of mixed emotions over several days – became hysterical, so he wasn't sure. He heard Jasper offer some sort of goodbye and felt him leave. But all he could do was laugh.

The rest of the jailbirds began yelling – mostly insults, calling him Head Case Henry and asking if the voices in his crazy head ever went to sleep. Henry ignored them and laughed until his stomach hurt.

When he finally settled down and the catcalls stopped, he began looking at his situation seriously again. He had been dealt a bad hand. And in the world of choices between bet, bluff, or fold, he admitted there was no way his hand was worthy of a bet or a bluff. That only left fold.

CHAPTER 17

It was finally Thursday. Toni and Tommy had spent the past few days having fun. A day and night at the casino. A drive up to Alexandria Bay for some fishing. There were plenty of yard sales and pub burgers for lunch. But it was time to get where they were going. An air of uneasiness hung over them, though they did their best not to let it show. As they made their way out of Watertown along Route 3 in the small, rented motor home, Toni plinked out some of their favorite songs on the old guitar George had left to her.

"It's not the same," Tommy commented as she finished the latest song.

"What? My voice? I'm not getting any younger, you know."

"No," he laughed. "Your voice is as angelic as ever. I mean this road. Back when we were just out of high school, some guys and I came up here on Memorial Day weekend. It was just after the Winter Olympics in Lake Placid, and this road was all spruced up. The pavement was brand new, and the roadside was all land-scaped. Now it just looks like every other road in New York State."

"Well, it was over forty years ago." It was her turn to laugh. "You ain't getting any younger either."

"Good point."

"Besides, look at the scenery. As we keep heading east the mountains are getting bigger. There are lakes everywhere. And the pavement isn't bad at all compared to most of the roads. Don't be such a Debbie Downer."

"Okay, okay. Stop yelling at me and play another song." Toni gave him a defiant look. So he added, "Please?"

She laughed and started a new song. It stayed like that for another hour until they found themselves on Route 86 heading out of the village of Saranac Lake. When the road to the federal correctional facility came into view, Toni said, "Turn here."

"We're going to jail?"

"No, the directions say the dirt road we're looking for is an extension of the road to the prison. Just turn here, and after the curve turn again towards the prison and go straight past the buildings."

Tommy did as she said. The road turned to dirt and they became lost in a tunnel of tall pine trees for over a mile. Eventually, the pine tree tunnel ended and gave way to a galley of about thirty old, two-story houses. Most had newer vinyl siding over the original clapboards and modern metal roofs. But they still stood in contrast to the present-day look of the Mountain View Conference and Resort center that suddenly appeared to their right, just as the string of houses ended.

"Here we are," Toni said. "This place looks pretty upscale. Your friend Manny has good taste."

Tommy parked in the half-full lot, and they grabbed their luggage. "I wouldn't call him my friend just yet. Besides, you have more in common with him than I do."

That was somewhat of an awkward thing to say. But both seemed to know it was true and the reason for their being there.

Toni shrugged it off as they headed inside. The front desk sat in a modern but ornate foyer with large plants, mirrors, and a friendly-looking, tall, brown-haired woman whose name tag said KAREN. There were only two single-story wings extending in opposite directions. Mountain View appeared to be a high-end place, but not meant for large groups.

"Welcome to Mountain View," the girl said with a smile. "I'm Karen, and you folks please feel free to let me know if there's anything you need during your stay. Do you have a reservation?"

"Chandler," Tommy said.

"Oh, the Chandlers. Mr. Richter has been expecting you. Your room is in the Scarface wing." She gestured toward the hallway to her right. "Number 7 on the left, at the end of the hall."

"Scarface?" Toni asked.

Karen smiled and laughed. "Yes, it's named after Scarface Mountain. You'll understand why once you look out of your window." She handed them their key cards. "I'll have David bring your bags."

"That's okay." Tommy put a hand up. "We're traveling light and can manage well enough."

Karen smiled. "Well all right then. You're the boss, and whatever you say goes here at Mountain View. Remember, there's always someone here, so don't be afraid to let us know if you need anything."

They picked up their bags and headed down the Scarface wing hallway. It was a short walk. The whole wing consisted of four rooms on each side. Just as they reached their room, a large door at the end of the hallway opened up and Manny appeared, smiling.

"Hey! Welcome. I'm so glad to see you. I hope you had a

pleasant drive up here."

They all shook hands. Tommy nodded while Toni said, "We did. It's been a nice few days away from the normal grind."

Before Manny could say anything else, that eerie, lingering uneasiness she and Tommy had reared up, and she added, "But I suppose we have lots to do, and you probably want to get down to business soon."

Manny straightened up, clearly not expecting that response. "Well, yes of course. But please, get yourselves settled in and freshened up if you like. Tell you what, I have to run a quick errand." He checked his watch. "I'll be back at five o'clock. When you two are ready just come into this conference room and we'll get to it."

They said goodbye and then found their room as upscale as everything else. There was a fireplace facing a hot tub, a huge bathroom with a walk-in shower, and plants everywhere.

They looked at each other and laughed. "Well, I guess it could be worse," Tommy quipped.

Toni looked around and smiled.

CHAPTER 18

Tommy opened the door to the conference room and held it for Toni. They entered to see a room almost as big as the rest of the wing. It was like two rooms in one. To the right was a kitchenette and a mini-bar with an oak table and six chairs. The apparent breakfast or dining area. There was a small space in front of them, then a long, dark wooden table made for meetings, with hardwood chairs at each end and two along each side.

Beyond that was what could only be described as an indoor-outdoor living room. A pair of leather sofas sat facing each other over a wooden coffee table, with two large, comfortable-looking leather chairs at the other two sides. On the wall to the right was a huge stone fireplace with four Adirondack chairs semi-circled around a smaller wooden table.

At the far end, there was more open space with the same hardwood floor as the rest of the room, which could serve as a dance floor or a display area. Finally, the far wall had a regular door next to a garage-style door that stood open. Outside they could see a large brick patio with several tables and chairs surrounding a fountain. Beyond that, curiously, and likely on a different property, was an old, oddly shaped building that appeared to be a tavern. Classic rock music filtered its way across.

The pair stood near the living room section, taking it all in. Finally, Toni said, "Wow. Manny sure knows how to put on a party."

"I do my best," Manny said, having sneaked in quietly behind them. "I hope you're both doing well. If there's anything you need just let me or Karen know." He made his way past the long table over to where they stood. Spreading his arms wide, he added, "I hope you find this conference room adequate. And since we all know why we're here, henceforth, it shall be known as the war room."

The two nodded that everything was fine. Before anyone could say anything more, they heard a soft whine as an electric side-by-side covered in camouflage pulled up on the patio. They turned to see an elderly black man step out and walk into the room. Elderly wasn't quite right. Tommy thought the guy must be a hundred years old if he was a day. But he carried himself well, even while cradling what looked like a large rat in his left arm.

The old man walked up within a few feet. He wore a short-sleeved, button-down shirt underneath a pair of denim bib over-alls, with a gold chain that likely connected to a pocket watch. An old, blue-and-white striped hat sat on his head – the kind you would see in an old picture of a railroad engineer. As Manny was about to make an introduction, the man took a grandiose bow. Rising back up with a big grin framed by a thousand wrinkles, he stuck out his hand and said in a deep voice that belied his small stature, "Maximilian Tiberius Beauregard, at your service."

If there was any ice to break, it was gone. As Tommy reached out to shake hands Manny said, "Max, meet Tommy Chandler and his lovely wife Toni."

"I'm pleased," Max said as he shook and turned to Toni.

152

Toni gave his hand a quick squeeze and said hello. She gestured at the large rat in his arm, which turned out to be a small, brown dog. "May I?"

Max nodded warmly and Toni put her fingers out for a sniff, bent down, and gave a little kiss between the ears.

"Little Whiskey, meet Toni Chandler."

Toni couldn't help but smile. "His name is Little Whiskey?"

"Yes ma'am, it sure is. Speaking of which—" Max said while turning to Manny, "—I've been here an awful long time, and ain't nobody offered me a drink yet."

"Oh me and my manners," Manny said as they all laughed. He went to the mini-bar and asked, "What's everybody having?"

Tommy gestured at Max. "I'll have what he's having."

Manny nodded. "Me too. Three Canadian whiskeys on the rocks. Toni? What's your pleasure?"

She looked at the fairly small bar. "I don't suppose you have any Riesling over there, do you?"

"If we don't we'll get some." He opened a cabinet next to the bar and suddenly it wasn't so small anymore.

Max made his way to the conference table and grabbed a chair. Toni and Tommy followed suit. A moment later Manny returned with their drinks and sat in the chair at the end of the table toward the open door. Then they became silent. It was time to get down to business. Manny reinforced that idea when he grabbed the remote and closed the garage door behind him. Tommy noticed when the door was closed, it blended in so well you almost couldn't tell it was there. Fine craftsmanship on somebody's part. He wasn't surprised, the whole place oozed fine craftsmanship.

Without the jukebox music filtering in it seemed eerily quiet. Manny got right to it. "Okay, we all know why we're here.

Though you two still don't know the plan. I apologize for keeping you in the dark. And I promise you will know it soon enough. But first, we need to know each other a little better. Max, here, has been used by Jasper on numerous occasions, going back five years. Used in the same manner your neighbor Bud Rogers was used. Jasper invades his body and uses it to suck blood from a victim. Max can tell us more about how it all goes down than anybody. So feel free to ask him anything you want to know about Jasper."

Despite having resigned himself to Toni's determination, Tommy still harbored reservations. He already had several questions. He started with, "Going back five years? How many people have you—?" He struggled, not sure how to word it.

"Six," Max stated flatly. "Soon to be seven."

Tommy shook his head. Looking at Manny he said, "That seems like a lot. I thought you said Jasper's . . . subjects . . . all go crazy or wind up committing suicide. Like Bud Rogers did."

"They do. Max is, to my knowledge, the lone exception."

Tommy turned back to Max. "Okay, pardon my bluntness, but what makes you so special? And how can you allow it to happen? Can't you resist?"

Max was anything but bothered by Tommy's candor. "No. Resistance is impossible. Jasper has a way of inflicting pain inside the back of your skull that's so severe it will put you down to your knees. He can make you pass out from pain. Sooner or later, you will succumb and do what he orders. Trust me. I've tried more times than I wish to remember. And it's the worst pain ever. Worse than being whacked in the balls. And we've all had that happen at least once." With a nod to Toni, "Present company excepted, of course."

Tommy couldn't argue that. "Okay, but what keeps you from

going insane or whatever? In our case, Bud Rogers lost his shit after two weeks. You're still going strong after five years? How? Doesn't it bother you?"

"Sure it bothers me. But let me try to explain. I don't think I'm anything special, but I've been around." Max reached down and absently began to stroke Little Whiskey's ears. "When I was eighteen years old our government sent me to Korea. What did I know about the world then? Nothing. I was filled with patriotic rallying cries of whatever the catchphrase was back then. Democracy, better dead than red – all that shit. Didn't question it too much. None of us did. Anyway, they gave me a flame thrower. Two tanks on my back connected to a hose and a nozzle that spewed pure carnage on whatever was in front of it. Did you ever serve?"

Tommy shook his head no.

"Well let me tell you, when you stick that nozzle into a pillbox full of soldiers and pull the trigger, all Hell breaks loose. You hear screaming as soldiers come flying out of every hole, only to be shot by your comrades. The noise and the screaming only lasts for a few seconds. But it stays with you forever, especially the smell. Not just the smell of the burning gasoline gel. You smell their clothes, their flesh, and everything that was inside the bunker that burns. Plastic and paper and wood and gunpowder. It smells and it gets into your clothes. And it smells for however many days it is until you can get it washed out. Then it smells in your mind – and in your dreams and nightmares."

Max stopped and took a big gulp of whiskey from his glass. Everyone stayed silent as he went on. "Then I came home and tried to turn it off. I went from the Hell of war to trying to hold down a job – every one of them boring compared to where I was.

155

But the Hell continues. You can't turn it off and you can't forget. I tried drinking it away for a few years. About killed myself doing so. And I thank God almighty that my wife Candy stuck with me through it all. I couldn't have blamed her if she cut and ran. I was a mess, and I'd be long dead if not for her."

Another sip. "But somewhere along the line, I realized it was never going away. I was either going to have to go on living and try to lead some kind of life, or I was going to end it all. Don't think for a minute I didn't consider it. And I had friends who did just that. But my wife pulled me through. Ever since then, I've come to understand that, yes, we've all done things we may or may not have done differently – and we have to live with that."

Another sip and the ice was rattling. Manny got up and made new drinks all around.

Max went on. "Now I don't mean I couldn't have controlled things beforehand. Sure, I could have tried to be an objector, or gone AWOL and spent my time in Leavenworth. But just like most of the guys, I didn't. And those decisions can't be undone. But it's the living with it after that can't ever be forgotten. Once I understood that – that it was never going to go away – then I made up my mind to live my life going forward, regardless of things I can't undo. But that's enough for any of us to bear. Living with your past demons is hard enough. Working yourself up over things you can't control and piling that on top will overload you and eventually destroy you."

A new drink, another sip. "Of course, I never expected to be involved with anything like this Jasper bastard. But the philosophy remains the same. And believe me, it's out of my control. He can't be stopped just by trying to resist. And that, for whatever it's worth, is my best explanation of how I manage to cope without going over the top. Trust me, it weighs heavily. I guess I'm just able to wall it off enough to live from day to day. If I have no control, I don't let it eat me up. But now I have an idea to try and stop the evil, rotten prick. That is something I can control. I feel obliged to act on it. And that's why we're here."

There was a long silence as everybody let that sink in. Toni reached across the table and put her hand on Max's. "Thank you."

Max seemed untouched. "Don't thank me yet. We've got the battle of all battles ahead of us."

After some more silence, Tommy gave Manny a look that indicated that yes, it was finally time for him to share the mysterious plan.

Manny cleared his throat. "Yes. Well, I guess that brings us to the heart of the matter. So what do you two know about how to kill a vampire?"

Tommy shrugged. Toni said, "Just what everybody knows I guess. Either a wooden stake through the heart or drag them into the sunlight. Are there any other ways?"

Manny shook his head. "No. And in Jasper's case, we don't even know if sunlight affects him. To my knowledge, no one's ever seen or been embodied by Jasper in the daytime. We don't know where he goes or what he does during those hours."

He reached down and produced a black duffel bag. As he set it on the table and unzipped it, he said, "That only leaves one other option."

"Right," Toni said. "But how do you get a stake into the heart of a spirit?"

Reaching into the duffel bag, Manny said, "The only way I know is to do it while the spirit is inside a human." He then pulled out a crossbow. One of the modern ones with the bows swept back to the sides so the whole thing was less than eighteen inches wide. He set it on the table where it could be seen that the quiver, attached to the bottom side, held three short, wooden bolts, about the same diameter as a pretzel rod.

Tommy looked at the contraption and shook his head. "Oh no. No. Nope. Uh uh. You're not going to suggest we use this thing to shoot a wooden stake into a living human while hoping it will kill a spirit."

Max jumped in with his gravelly voice. "We're going to suggest exactly that."

Tommy searched the old man's wrinkled face to see if he was going to smile, as though it were some kind of joke. None was forthcoming.

"And just who in the Hell is going to volunteer for that duty?"

Max never took his eyes off Tommy's. "Me."

Tommy jumped out of his chair and started pacing back and forth along the side of the table. "No. No way. There's no way I'm going to be a part of this. There's too many unknown variables. How do we even know it will work? How can we know for sure the spirit . . . Jasper . . . is inside? How can we know where and when he will be inside?" Looking at Max he said, "You don't expect him to invade your body at a certain time at a certain place and present himself to us so we can launch a spear into your chest, do you?"

Still calm, Max replied, "Actually, yes. Well maybe not that last part about presenting himself. But all the other stuff is bound to happen. And we know when and where."

Tommy was dumbfounded. "But . . . but . . . this is crazy." He looked at Toni, who didn't seem to offer anything either way.

Finally, he looked at Manny. "And just what the fuck? I mean, let's just say for a moment I could somehow agree to this madness. Why me? Why does everybody look at me when they talk about this crazy shit? Why don't you shoot him?"

Manny looked apologetic. "I can't. My night vision is horrible. I can't even trust myself to drive at night. And this is a once-in-a-lifetime opportunity, with a very narrow window. And we can't chance losing that because I can't see."

Then Max spoke again. "Please. Please, young man. Please sit down and let us explain everything. Just give us a chance to help it make sense to you."

Tommy didn't know what to say. He threw his arms up and looked at the ceiling. "You're all crazy."

A silence followed until Max, with a calm voice, simply said, "Please."

Bewildered, Tommy looked to Toni. She gave him an I don't know either shrug. Then she tilted her head and gestured toward Tommy's chair.

He finally sat down. "Madness. I can't believe I'm going to entertain this madness. But okay. Lay it on me." He hung his head in his hands, rubbing his temples. Toni reached a hand over and placed it on his thigh. It helped, but not much.

Max began talking. "First of all, let me explain something. I've been around a long time. My wife has been gone for twenty years, and our only son was taken from us tragically when he was only nineteen. We had a couple of beagles named Heidi and Fee-Fee that used to chase rabbits years ago, but they're long gone too. Except for Little Whiskey, I'm all alone in the world, and have been for quite a while."

It was time for another whiskey sip. "I just celebrated my

159

ninety-second birthday. But I have a disease, and I won't be seeing my ninety-third. That alone should help assuage your misgivings. At least I hope so."

Tommy didn't respond. He sat there with his head still in his hands.

"For now I'll keep it short and simple. On Saturday night I will be making a ceremonial run with an old steam locomotive. The whole run is roughly a half-mile, from my house to the back side of that tavern you saw across the way, beyond the fountain. Jasper will be there. He has some quirks, and apparently, the locomotive reminds him of when he was a child in the early fifties and some of the trains were still powered by steam. He likes to embody me as I drive the train. But that's not the important part. Later, after I fulfill my obligations with pictures, speeches, and whatever else they have planned, Jasper will visit me at home. And we will go out to find another victim. He's done it every year since 2020."

"As I understand it, Jasper normally leaves his subjects alone to get rid of the bodies. But in my case, since I'm ancient, he helps me dispose of them. The first time, in 2020, we dumped the body off the Route 3 bridge into the Saranac River. But that body was later found at a lock between Lower Saranac Lake and Oseetah Lake. So when Jasper returned the next year, I convinced him to try something different. I think he's happy to have found a subject like myself, who was still around a year later. I think Jasper considers me the closest thing he has to a friend. I hardly am, but that pain he can inflict keeps me acting like one."

"Anyway, for the past four years, we have taken the bodies on a trail through the woods out past my house. It's not an actual trail. It's not marked or anything. It's just a way through I know about having lived here forever and hunted the area. There is a creek that runs heavily this time of year, and it has a certain spot where the land juts out into the middle. My side-by-side can drive right to that spot. Then with Jasper's help, we throw the body out into the current, where it washes away through a series of rapids and eventually into Oseetah Lake. I take a couple of other precautions since the first one of those bodies was also found – though it was decomposed, leaving very few clues. The others, in the years since then, have never turned up. So we feel there's a very good chance Jasper will do the same thing this year."

"Now as luck would have it, directly opposite the place where the land juts into the creek, on the far bank, there is an old geological survey building the government used to monitor and document the water levels years ago. It's very small – only about six-by-four, but it's still in good condition and has a window. If you get there ahead of time you will be no more than twenty yards away. The crossbow is deadly accurate at that range, and at some point, you should be able to get a shot while that monster is still inside me."

Tommy finally looked up, still clearly dismayed. "I don't know. It all sounds incredible. And as a police officer – or any normal human being for that matter – I just can't justify shooting you."

Max changed his tone. Stronger and harsher. "Listen young man. That evil bastard has killed over two thousand people. Probably more since we can't know about all of them. He travels the world at a whim. He kills people that get eaten by crocodiles. Or hyenas and other wild animals, never to be seen again. It's impossible to know what his murder total is. His paranormal brethren have no solution or ability to reel him in either. This is a one-time shot, and it probably won't work anyway. But how can we not try?

If we don't at least try when we have the opportunity, then we're condoning the next two thousand dead. And the thousands after that as this monster will go on killing in a never-ending series of infinite possessions and murder – all the while causing misery to his subjects, his victims, and their family and loved ones."

Max was rolling, but whiskey time was whiskey time. Another sip and the ice was clinking again. Manny got to work while Max poured it on. "To you, it happened a long time ago, and you've probably been able to forget about it – or at least keep it buried. But make no mistake, the same son of a bitch that wrecked your little town is alive and well. Just over a week ago he struck up in New Hampshire. Another dead body. Then last week Jasper paid me a visit. We made a special run. Some poor, pimple-faced nineteen-year-old from the college up north. Oh, we buried him in a good spot. Even my old, scrawny ass is capable of incredible physical feats when Jasper is inside me."

Pointing to the eastern wall Max added, "We hauled him up that mountainside and dropped him into a ventilation shaft from a mine that's been closed for over a hundred years and almost nobody even knows ever existed. Now that young man's family will forever wonder what happened to him. And they'll never find out."

Manny came back. Another sip. "Then the dirty rotten bastard left my ancient, frail, scrawny ass up there on a rocky outcrop. Halfway up a mountainside, in the middle of nowhere in the middle of the night, with almost no moonlight, and no cell phone. He's a dirty rotten evil bastard who needs to go down. You can't say no to this and continue to live your life in peace."

Tommy had to admit, Max made a good case. Toni gave his thigh a reassuring squeeze. Of course, he knew which way she was leaning. But he wasn't ready to admit defeat just yet.

"But what you're asking me, it just doesn't sit right."

Max wasn't about to be dissuaded. "Look, young man, this isn't anything that fits into your normal way of thinking."

Tommy almost burst out laughing at how true that was. But Max kept going.

"I'm ninety-two years old. I've been blessed. For every day of every one of those ninety-two years, I've always been able to feed myself, pick my own nose, wipe my own ass, and hold my own pecker when I piss. Before long I won't be able to do any of those things, and I'm not looking forward to someone else doing them for me. This is the opportunity of the entire history of mankind, so stop pretending. You will put yourself in position, and you will pull the trigger. Or you will live out the rest of your days with the biggest regret you have ever known, or will ever know. So cut the shit, you know you're in."

Tommy couldn't believe it. He couldn't believe he was going to agree to the crazy idea. But one look at Toni and once again he knew he couldn't deny her. Everything Max had said about it being a super-limited opportunity rang true. Still, he couldn't bring himself to say yes. He let out a deep sigh instead, then leaned over and hugged his wife. And that amounted to the same thing.

Just then there was a knock at the hallway door. "Come in," Manny said, loudly.

Karen stuck her head inside. "Mr. Richter the caterer is here. Are you ready for dinner?"

"Perfect timing. Send them in please."

"Very well. Also, your other guest has arrived. Shall I show her in too?"

Manny brightened up. "Absolutely! Perfect timing."

Toni and Tommy looked up to see Tanya Lambert coming through the door. But of course, it couldn't be Tanya Lambert. Manny said she died four years ago. Besides, Tanya would have been around seventy if she were still alive. The girl entering the room looked to be . . . and then it hit him, in her late thirties.

They all got up to greet the newcomer, who came waltzing in with a flowing mane of red hair, blue jeans, and a white, button-down shirt that strained against a pair of large breasts. Tommy thought Tanya Lambert must have been cloned.

She gave Manny a big hug and said, "How ya doin' big guy?"

If there was any doubt who she was – even though there wasn't – it disappeared when Tommy heard the Texas twang. The girl ran over to Max, who also brightened up. He got a hug and a kiss on the cheek. A quick howdy, and then Little Whiskey became the object of her desire.

After a moment, realizing she was probably being rude, the woman turned to the remaining couple. Manny spoke up. "Toni and Tommy Chandler, I'd like you to meet Bianca —"

"Lambert," Toni finished for him. A quick understanding befell them all. Bianca greeted Toni, then she took Tommy's hand to shake.

The caterers began filing in. Bianca said, "Perfect timing is right. Something smells good."

They all nodded in agreement. Manny went to get Bianca a drink, and one for the rest of them. Tommy thought about what he was seeing. The timeline was perfect. Manny had said Tanya gave birth to a baby with a caul, sometime after she left for Texas. Tommy knew that meant the red-headed bombshell was conceived while a Jasper-embodied Tanya was having sex with Bud Rogers. He wondered if Bianca was touched in any way by that so-called inter-dimensional mumbo jumbo, as Manny had so eloquently put it.

He figured he'd find out soon enough so he might as well see what was for dinner. He thought about the day he opened the letter from Manny. Then he shook his head and wondered if his life could get any weirder.

CHAPTER 19

Manny insisted dinner be about getting to know each other better rather than getting into the bones of the upcoming plan. Toni told her story in more detail than she ever thought she would share. But everyone seemed to understand. None of it was a surprise to any of them. The only thing that seemed new to them was when Toni shared that while she had no idea if it was related to Jasper, she eventually discovered she was unable to bear children. Even that news only regarded a couple of hmms.

Max had already told his story. Manny's story involving Jasper had been shared with Toni and Tommy at their previous meeting. It seemed Manny and Max were already familiar with Bianca. That left only for Bianca to share her story with Toni and Tommy.

As they enjoyed their perfectly roasted chickens with mashed potatoes and candied carrots, Tommy started that ball rolling, asking rather bluntly, "So what's your story? Are you the spawn of Jasper? Do you possess inter-dimensional mumbo jumbo? And how do you fit into the plan?"

If Bianca was bothered it didn't show. Before she started she rose and went to where Toni was seated. She bent down and gave her a big hug.

Looking her in the eyes, she said, "Toward the end of my mother's life she talked with me about her experience with Jasper. She mentioned more than once how she wouldn't have been able to accept it as real if not for you sharing that you had a similar experience. I can't imagine what that was like. But I feel a bit of a soul connection with you, and I can understand your willingness to get the bastard – especially since he also killed your friend George. I don't have any personal connection to Jasper, but if for no other reason than I know his actions tormented my mother for years, I want to get him too."

Toni shed a small tear as Bianca walked back to her seat. Tommy felt his reluctance to the whole thing slip down yet another notch.

Then Bianca began. "As you have surmised, I am the product of my mother having had sex with the man you knew named Bud Rogers. During that time, she was fully embodied by the evil spirit Jasper Czymiak. As for inter-dimensional mumbo jumbo, I can't say I have any superpowers. I can't walk through walls or time-travel or anything of that nature. But that doesn't mean I'm completely un . . . touched either. I've never been sick a day in my life. Never had a cold or the flu. Never had the mumps or chicken pox. Never even had a cavity or a filling, or even so much as a fever."

She drained off her glass of Riesling. Manny got up to serve a fresh round of drinks for everyone while Bianca continued.

"Obviously, my mother was able to bear a child. However, I've discovered through the years that I don't seem able to get pregnant." Nodding at Toni she added, "I also have no idea if that's mumbo jumbo related. The only other thing I can add, and maybe have to offer, is that we've discovered I'm able to sense whenever Jasper is near, even if he's not embodied in anyone. I don't know if that will help, but I'm here to do what I can."

That was all interesting enough, but Tommy had more questions. "Okay. But how did a Texas girl come to be involved with Max – whom you seem to know – way the Hell up here in Ferro, New York? I can tell you've been here before, but why?"

Manny jumped in as he sat back down. "Maybe I can explain that part. It all goes back a few years. And while we don't believe in luck or coincidences at Monkey Beans, we don't turn our back on anything even if it seems to be just that. So let's give a little history. Back in the summer of 2020, the entire state of New York, like most places, was shut down because of COVID. People became restless. Camping became a popular pastime for visitors to the area – more so than usual. But with the restaurants, bars, and theaters shut down, local residents were looking for things to do."

"As you may have gathered, there is a big festival set to take place on Saturday. It's nothing official, but it's a local event that has taken on a life of its own, and grown bigger every year. It's become known as the Hero Of '70 Bash. It all started when a bunch of Ferro kids – and by kids I mean young adult spring chickens, unlike most of us here – convinced Max to fire up his steam engine and reenact what conveniently became the fiftieth anniversary of his heroic run of 1970."

Manny gestured to Max. "I think you can tell it better than me. Why don't you start from the beginning?"

The caterer knocked, stuck her blond head in, and asked if anyone wanted dessert. Everyone seemed satisfied so Manny asked if they could clear the table and call it a night. While they cleaned, Max went to the fireplace and gathered up Little Whiskey, who had dutifully sat out the dinner party.

After a few licks and kisses, Whiskey took his usual place cra-

169

dled in Max's left arm as he sat back down. Then Max spoke in his low voice. "First of all, I ain't no hero. But here's the story from its beginning. Way back, about a hundred and fifty years ago or more, about another half-mile past this little town of Ferro, there was a small iron ore mine in a large hill we all affectionately call Peckerneck Mountain. That's why this little hamlet of Ferro exists – houses for mine workers. In addition to the dirt road, there was a small, short-line railroad that the mine operated. It only ran from Peckerneck to the main line over in Ray Brook. That old main line is now a state-owned hiking trail. You probably saw the crossing as you turned off the main road heading back here."

Toni and Tommy both nodded. It was marked with signs and highly visible right before they passed the federal prison on their way in.

After a sip of whiskey, Max continued. "Back in the day, the mining company used to ship out pig iron from its location out to the main line. After I returned from Korea I got a job with the mine. Before long I was in charge of running the old steam engine and a handful of cars back and forth. Since the tracks were laid before automobiles, the company built a sort of depot where the track passed by Ferro so passengers could jump on for free any time the train went through. That building is now the noisy little tiki bar you see whenever that door is open." He gestured toward the garage door at the far end of the room.

"The mine was a small operation, but in the 1940s they upgraded their old steam locomotive from a coal-fired one to a more modern diesel-fired one. And being such a small outfit that only ran less than two miles, they continued using the old steam horse into the late 1960s, when the mining company finally went out of business."

170

Another sip. "I'm probably boring you so I'll move along. When the mine folded, my wife, Candy, and I purchased the building at the end of the line – at the base of Peckerneck Mountain. We converted it into a cozy house, surrounded by peace and quiet. I also convinced them to sell me the old locomotive and caboose rather than sending them to the scrap yard with the ore cars. This was in 1968. I made it my hobby to keep the old engine in working order. Since the mine took a few more years to finally tear up the tracks, we would occasionally run the old train up to where it used to connect in Ray Brook. Near where the prison is now, even though by then it no longer connected to the main line – which was also on its last legs."

"Anyway, in January of 1970, we suffered a nor'easter for the ages. With the wind blowing the snow sideways, all the low spots drifted in with several feet. That made the old dirt road from Ray Brook to Ferro – and also to my house – impassable. The storm was so widespread our little hamlet was anything but a priority for the state and county crews."

"Now everybody in Ferro had a wood stove and plenty of wood. So nobody was going to freeze to death even though the power was out. And most had plenty of food stored away. But after a week, in addition to cabin fever setting in, some residents ran low on needed medication, along with people's beer and liquor supplies running low. You know, emergencies."

Everybody chuckled. "I was no exception in those days. So I got to thinking, the road had several low spots and that's why the snow drifted in so deep. But the railroad tracks stayed on the level, with small trestles and culverts eliminating dips, and much less inundated with snow. So I decided to fire up ol' Candy's Carriage – named after my wife – and see if I could bust through. It took a

171

while to get as far as the little passenger stop building in Ferro, as I had to keep backing up and then plowing into one drift after another. Once I got that far, the Ferro residents realized my plan and began to help."

A sip of whiskey. "Now, twenty men with shovels can't clear a one-mile stretch very fast. But they can do a number on a drift in a hurry. Especially when all you have to do is knock it down enough for a small steam locomotive to bust through. Since the power was out, it was quite a chore to refill the water tank on the old girl, which we had to do twice that night by melting snow on the side of the boiler. It became a group effort."

"Then about seven o'clock she started running low on diesel fuel. Everybody scattered to their homes to find any fuel they could spare. They siphoned out of tractors and some took it right out of their home heating oil tanks. During that break, while waiting to fuel up again, a group of women came out with sandwiches and lots of other food. It was tempting by then, as it was cold and dark, to just quit for the night. But old Mrs. DuFour and a few other residents needed their medicine. And we were all low on beer, so we got off our asses and went back to work."

While the story was already known to all but Toni and Tommy, everyone stayed quiet as Max continued to lay it out.

"So we kept shoveling, backing up and ramming. And sure enough, all those low areas that had the road filled in were a lot less socked in with snow at the track level. Eventually, as some person noted, we punched through the last drift and rode up to the end of the tracks at 9:32 PM. It was just shy of the main line and a short walk to the road near the prison. The federal prison wasn't even there yet. But the state prison across the road was some kind of health treatment center back then, and was staffed full time."

"Civilization had been reached. By then the people of Ray Brook had heard the commotion and realized what we were up to. They graciously greeted us with vehicles and gave rides to and from Saranac Lake – the road there having been opened a few days earlier."

"It was another week before crews finally opened the road to Ferro. I made two trips a day with the old train – morning and night so people could get in and out. Most of them were able to secure rides with coworkers at Ray Brook to get to their jobs. Anyway, it was just me and a bunch of residents coming together and doing what we could for each other. There was no talk about heroes or any such drivel. It was just a story told through the years. A bit of local folklore and nothing more. That is until a bunch of bored kids got drunk one day during the COVID shutdown, and realized 2020 was 50 years from 1970. They decided the event needed a reenactment and a celebration. Apparently, the booze flowing that day made the fact that it was summer and not winter irrelevant."

"By the time they asked me if I would be interested in an anniversary run, they had already planned to elect a figurehead mayor who could appoint up to six cronies to take the commemorative ride in the caboose. I had extra time myself, so I agreed."

"In 1972 the mining company finally received official abandonment papers and tore up their tracks. I convinced them to sell me the roughly half-mile stretch from my house to the little town here so I could keep my hobby alive. Since it got them out from under having to tear up the tracks, they practically gave it to me. So that was the length of the re-enactment. A whole half-mile, from Peckerneck mountain to the new end of the line in Ferro – right over there on the far side of what is now that noisy tiki bar."

"There was no tiki bar in 2020. It was just an old three-sided building with a steel roof that the residents kept up, along with the land around it. Sort of an unofficial park. And that was it. They bought a bunch of kegs of beer and we timed the ride – which took less than fifteen minutes – so the arrival would coincide with the historic 9:32 PM breakthrough."

Max took a long pause, with several whiskey sips, before proceeding." It was during that first run that the rotten bastard Jasper made himself known to me. Now I've gone on long enough. Let's just say he was once a young man in human form, and he doesn't fit in with other paranormal beings, nor is he like a demon or other spirit that has always existed as one. Having once been human, and with no friends in the spirit world, Jasper gets his enjoyment through human experiences. But he can only do so by temporarily embodying them. That inter-dimensional mumbo jumbo thing prevents him from any full-time human occupation."

"It seems when Jasper was a child there were still some steam-operated locomotives running, and he's maintained an affinity for them. I don't have to tell you, I was frazzled having a voice in my head pestering me to blow the steam whistle every thirty seconds, and telling me how he loved trains as a kid. As it turned out, that was the least of my problems."

"Later that night Jasper came back and spelled out his story, then proceeded to use me to go up the hiking trail on Scarface Mountain in my side-by-side. We found a camper for a victim, brought her corpse out, and loaded her into my truck. I've already told you how I tried to resist, but it's useless, so I won't rehash that. And yes I was a basket case the whole time Jasper decided we should drive out to the bridge on Route 3 – where it goes over the Saranac River – and dump the body there. "

"I've come to learn that Jasper usually leaves his subjects alone with their victims to dispose of as they wish. But I think even then he must have figured the train ride would be an annual event. If he could help me then maybe I wouldn't go bonkers or wind up in prison, and he'd be able to come back the next year. I don't know. I just know he was willing to help me get rid of the body. Though ultimately it didn't work out that well and the body was discovered a few days later."

"Anyway, the commemorative run became an annual event, growing bigger every year. And now, with the addition of the tiki bar and this high-falootin' resort, it seems it will keep growing. Except, of course, without me." Max paused and drained his whiskey. "And every year Jasper shows up for a train ride, and then we go get a victim. Dirty business I know. Now I think I'll let Manny take over again."

CHAPTER 20

Bianca got up and served the next round so Manny could continue. Before he could, Tommy jumped in, "Well I guess we're getting somewhere. But I still don't see how, where, or why Bianca came from Texas and wound up here."

Manny gave an understanding nod as he spoke. "I know. This is where we get into the coincidence, or luck, or whatever it is. Here's what happened. When that first body was found in the lock, the police were baffled. Loss of blood, curious marks on the neck. No idea where the actual killing took place, or by whom or why. Much like I'm sure you remember when police found my friend Mateo years ago." A quick look at Tommy, who nodded to confirm. "But to me and Monkey Beans, it had all the earmarks of a Jasper killing."

"So I came up to Ray Brook and poked around. There wasn't much to go on. I made notes of all the facts, convinced it was the work of Jasper. Then I went on about my business, figuring I'd never be back here."

"Then, almost exactly a year later our Monkey Beans watchers and cross-referencing database noted that a hiker near Ray Brook had gone missing. According to friends who had seen her last, it was the same date as the Hero of '70 bash. Hikers go missing around the world all the time, but the coincidence seemed too precise. So I returned to the area to poke around some more. Again, I didn't find out much. No body was recovered so evidence was scarce. Still, I decided to keep an eye on things around here, and persuaded Monkey Beans to give anything related to the fledgling annual event some extra vigilance just in case."

"Nothing happened around here until there was another disappearance at the same time in 2022. Again, there wasn't anything to go on, and no body was found. But the following year, in 2023, I received a Monkey Beans report that the girl in Texas—" He nodded at Bianca, "—the one born with a caul – and born to Tanya Lambert, whom I had by then been able to talk to and confirmed her involvement with Jasper – was making plans to be in Lake Placid and Ferro at the same time of the fourth Hero of '70 bash. I didn't know why that would be. Coincidence? Maybe. But I was damned sure going to be here when it happened."

With a nod to Bianca, "Your turn, I think."

Bianca started with her Texas twang, "I work for an online magazine that specializes in little-known pieces of Americana. My boss told me to pack my bags for New York, as there was a growing event happening where a historic train ride was reenacted by a Korean War veteran who had just turned 90 years old. I gotta tell y'all, when they said New York, like most people where I live, I expected plenty of tall buildings with millions of people living on top of each other. Imagine my surprise when I arrived at my hotel in Lake Placid. Then I found myself in Ferro surrounded by lakes and mountains. And what's the population, like seventy?"

She opened her palms for effect. "Anyway, my job was to see what this party was all about and write an article for the magazine. The night before the re-enactment I came to Ferro. That Tiki bar had just opened a month before. I saw this brand new conference center, but it was too expensive for my company's budget. Anyway, I set about interviewing people. Many of them were young and very drunk. Horny bastards too." She laughed as they all did. "But it's nice to be wanted."

"Anyway, I found that they were coming in from all over. The college up north, and from not only Lake Placid and Saranac Lake, but from even farther away. Places like Tupper Lake and Keene Valley. I even met a couple from Plattsburgh who drove down just for the event. But it was getting late. And since my room was in Lake Placid, I couldn't stay here and get loaded. Even though that seemed to be everyone else's agenda."

"I sat down at a picnic table away from the action to make some notes on my laptop before I left." She pointed at Manny. "This big lug sat down next to me. I assumed he was yet another horny bastard coming to lay a line on me. But at least he wasn't some snot-nosed kid, and he looked pretty good for being old enough to be my father."

She reached out and punched Manny's shoulder. "No offense."

"None taken." Smiling.

"Before I could begin to protest, he told me all about how he knew my mother and about her secret and how he was investigating the same thing that had haunted my mother for half her life. The next thing I know we're back here in this brand-new building and I'm spilling my guts about everything I knew. At that point, it wasn't anything except what my mother had told me. But I was impressed by Manny's knowledge of the subject. Then he floored me when he said he was in town, not just for the celebration, but because he was investigating that evil Jasper bastard."

"I was interested, not just because of my mother's connection, but because I live for being an investigative reporter. His stories about Jasper weren't the kind I could write up and expect anybody to believe. But they sure as Hell interested me. Unfortunately, I really did need to get back to my room. I had traveled all day and wasn't feeling my best. I agreed to come back early the next day to meet with Manny so we could talk some more. We agreed to watch the event unfold together. Which didn't bother me, as I figured it might help keep the horny twenty-one-year-olds at bay."

"The next day I arrived around seven. The whole event was ridiculous but fun-filled. Young people spent two days celebrating something that would only last a few minutes. It reminded me of the Groundhog Day celebration in Pennsylvania they sent me to a few years back."

"As darkness fell the votes were counted. A new mayor was inaugurated and went on to make a big production of naming his six dignitaries. With much fanfare, the seven of them were shuffled off in the back of a pickup to Max's house. Minutes later the little train was chuffing toward us. It came into view with the mostly drunken dignitaries riding on top of the caboose – or hanging out the windows while they took pictures and selfies."

"Then something strange happened. As the train moved closer, I was overwhelmed by the presence of evil. I felt it right in my bones. Manny must have noticed and asked me if I was okay. I was, but damn it was an eerie feeling that disappeared shortly after Max parked the train. The party went on with more selfies and pictures. Most of them posed with Max in front of the engine – Candy's Carriage – or in front of the huge Hero Of '70 banner."

"The whole thing was crazy in a young adult kind of way.

And it was fun. But we were on a mission. Especially Manny. He was convinced I was probably feeling the presence of Jasper – which made sense since the reason Manny was here in the first place was because he was suspecting a Jasper reappearance."

"Later that night, I felt the sensation again, just as I was leaving. It didn't last long, but Manny made a point to note the time. Not much more happened that night except, as you may have guessed, there was another disappearance. This time it was a homeless person from the little community of them that spends their summers over in an abandoned sawmill. As such, it wasn't reported right away, and we didn't know about it until after I'd gone back to Texas. But Manny's investigation led him to believe that if my feeling of evil was indeed when Jasper was near, then we could narrow down his embodiment to one of the people on that train – and possibly to someone who may have passed near me at the later time."

She paused and sipped her drink. "I think it's time to let Manny tell the rest."

The story was getting longer instead of shorter. But Tommy realized he was enthralled. He stayed quiet and let Manny pick it up again.

"We still didn't have a lot to go on. But my hunch was that Jasper had embodied one of the people on the train, as the feeling Bianca got arrived with the train and left when it stopped. After I left that year I continued investigating those seven passengers and Max. I found that of the seven, only two of the passengers were anywhere near Ferro during the bash the year before. And of those two, neither was anywhere near here the year before that. That left me with Max, as unlikely as that seemed, as the only one of the eight on the train who was present during the time frame when each of the disappearances occurred. At his age, I couldn't see him moving dead bodies regularly. Though I did have my own memory of how powerful the embodied Bud Rogers became while attacking my friend Mateo all those years ago."

"Anyway, I think my stories had Bianca hooked on the whole Jasper saga. I asked her to return last year to help me investigate further and she jumped at the chance, even though it wouldn't be on company time. We went under the assumption that Max was the main character. Sure enough, as the train neared the station again, Bianca was overwhelmed with the feeling of evil, and it disappeared shortly after the train stopped. During the photo sessions and all the hoopla, I planted a tracking device in Max's pocket. I had my car and a nice, quiet, electric side-by-side ready so we could follow him wherever he went."

"Once the hoopla died down so Max could slip away, we noticed he had his own side-by-side already waiting so he could leave the little train overnight and go home. We stealthily followed him in the side-by-side down the dirt road back to his house. It took some time, and we weren't sure we were close enough, but eventually Bianca got the evil feeling again, and we were convinced Max was our man. It was hard to follow him the rest of the night without being detected, but we learned enough, and another homeless person disappeared. There was no more doubt."

"The next day we confronted Max. He was, of course, very defensive and denied everything. But once he realized we were not the enemy, he became awash with the relief of finally being able to share what he'd been through with somebody who would believe his story."

Max had been quiet the whole time. He finally jumped in. "Unbelievably relieved. I can't tell you how good it felt to be able to unload on these two. And to learn that Manny had so much knowledge of something I thought was mine alone to deal with. We've shared so much in the past year. And I just hope somehow our plan will work and rid the world of that rotten son of a bitch."

Tommy had been listening intently. It was finally his turn. "I guess you've all been through a lot. Our experience with Jasper was years ago and mostly buried – at least by me. But I have to say, the more I hear, the more I'm climbing fully aboard. Sometime soon, though, I do wish somebody would share the details of this crazy plan."

Manny got up, "Yes, it's time we laid it all out. Let's take a quick break and we'll get to it."

CHAPTER 21

The group re-situated themselves at the meeting table, next to the lounging area. They seated themselves in what was becoming a pattern, with Manny at the head on the far end toward the dance floor and overhead door. Max was to his right, with Bianca on his left. Further away on Manny's left, sat Tommy, and Toni sat at the other table end facing Manny, with an empty chair to her left between her and Max.

Tommy was visibly elated to finally get to the meat and bones of what they had planned. So far all he knew was that Max was supposed to be at a certain place and time with Jasper inside him, and Tommy was supposed to shoot him with a wooden bolt from a streamlined, modern-day crossbow. While he had been steadily accepting that crazy idea as an actual logical plan, he needed more to go on.

His eagerness was not lost on Manny, who finally began. "Okay, based on what Jasper and Max have done for the past four years in a row, and since each of those times it has worked out well with the bodies never appearing like the first one thrown off the bridge was, we expect the same series of events to unfold this year. And we want to be ready."

"If all goes according to plan, here's what should happen.

Sometime after Max finishes with his photo shoots and grand-standing, he will exit the party and go back to his home at Pecker-neck Mountain. Once there, Jasper will greet him and they will take Max's old pickup out onto Route 86 and head out past Lake Placid. Eventually, they will turn onto an old driveway that leads to an abandoned logging mill."

"During the summer months that old mill becomes a haven for about two dozen homeless people. Nobody knows where they go in the winter, but they've become a sensation among some well-meaning tourists. It's gotten to the point where some of these tourists, mostly city folks from New York, will go live with these homeless people in what amounts to a feel-good exercise. Of course, for them, it's really just tent camping. You'll see them in town with their hairy armpits and bad hairdos using credit cards to buy bottled water and ribeye steaks. But it makes them feel good when they go home and tell their friends how they went to live as the homeless do. For some, it's a week or two. Others have made it an annual trek that lasts all summer."

"Regardless, the word is out. And since these people love to share their ribeyes and other things, it's pretty much guaranteed there will be a good contingent of homeless persons there again this year. The remote location makes it easy for Max and Jasper to grab one without being seen. They park a ways away, walk in un-der the darkness, grab a victim, and do their thing. Then Jasper helps Max carry the body back to his truck where they drive back to Max's house and finish disposing of the body at their leisure – with no prying eyes."

Tommy rolled his eyes but didn't say anything. Manny con-tinued. "That's where you come in. We've got to get you – and Toni if she'll join you – to the little old government building on the opposite bank from the point where they will go to toss the body into the current."

Tommy put a hand up. "Why can't I just wait along the trail in the woods and shoot him when he drives by?"

Max jumped in then with his low voice. "Because the trail goes through a forest of tall pine trees with so many boughs and branches almost no light gets through. Especially with barely a quarter-moon right now. And if it's cloudy besides, forget about it. You wouldn't be able to see your hand in front of your face. You will have a night-vision scope, but the trail isn't exactly marked out – we only do this once a year so there's not a trail at all – there's no exact path we'll take. The only lights will be from the side-by-side. Even though you'll have a good scope, we'd be guessing and hoping for you to be in the right position – which we don't want to do. This is a limited opportunity and we have to leave as little to chance as possible. And we need you stationary, with a bench rest so you can't miss. You're only going to get one shot in a limited time frame."

Tommy looked doubtfully as Max sipped some whiskey and added, "We can't have you guessing the route – shooting at a moving target in almost total darkness with the only lights coming straight at you, likely blinding you from seeing the target anyway. If things go as they should, we will drive to the point, which is also a natural clearing just big enough to be a turnaround. So when we stop, ideally we'll be halfway turned and the headlights won't be pointing at you, but will still provide enough ambient light to help you see."

"It will happen quickly, so you will need to be ready. And when we stop, Jasper will fully overtake me, we will grab the body and heave it into the current. At that point we should be facing you, only about twenty yards away. For a split second you should have a perfect shot at my heart. At only twenty yards and with a night-vision scope – and some practice – you should be able to hit a dime."

Tommy still had questions. "Why can't you plan the route ahead of time? That way I can just be there when you get there. Or can't we just go out to the point ahead of time and sit? Why do we have to be across the water?"

Max countered. "It's just not feasible. There's no place on the same side where we can be as certain you will stay hidden and get off a clean shot. The little shack provides a perfect cover and a bench rest. And it's practically guaranteed that for the short moment after Jasper helps me toss the body but before he leaves me, we will be facing you. We have to give this our best shot and this is the best way to increase our chance of success."

"But what about me just picking a different spot ahead of time," Tommy countered. "And you making sure to drive past that spot?"

"Well, that's a problem we've had to iron out. Jasper can read my thoughts. So we've gone to great lengths to ensure that while all this is happening, I won't know anything about our plan."

Tommy shook his head. "What? Just how the Hell are you going to pull that off? Hypnosis? How can you keep yourself from thinking about the plan? That's impossible."

Max looked at Manny, who cleared his throat and took over. "We actually discussed hypnosis, but were never able to find a way to make it strong enough to be sure it would work. And we have to be sure, so we had to go a different route. Believe it or not, just before I came here I spent five days in the Catskills convincing a powerful witch to cast a spell. On Saturday, Max will forget everything he knows about our plan. He won't recognize you or Toni as anyone he knows either. So it will be important not to act like you know him if you should contact him earlier in the day."

"A witch," Tommy stated more than asked.

"Yes, a witch," Manny said sternly. "We've been through this before. There are many other peenos besides Jasper. And this witch is one of the most powerful witches alive. It took plenty of urging from the big wigs at Monkey Beans just to get me to see her. The peenos are no better at reigning in Jasper than we are, but would be just as happy to see him gone. Since we have a plan – albeit one with a slim chance of working – it's in their best interest to call a temporary truce and help us. So I visited the Good Witch Of The Catskills, and came away with a powerful spell that will be applied to Max on Saturday."

Tommy was overloaded, getting hit with a lot at once. Yet all he could think of to ask was, "It took you five days?"

Manny looked sheepish and smiled to himself. "Yeah," was all he said.

But the crew wasn't going to let him off that easily. Toni and Bianca broke their silence simultaneously and started prying.

Suddenly all ears, Bianca said, "Oh come on. There's more to this story."

Toni added, "Yeah. What gives? Five days is a long time just to come away with a spell from someone with the same interest in casting it as you have for wanting it."

Manny sat in silence for a minute, but eventually spoke. "Okay, I guess we're all in this together and it's no time for secrets. The spell is quite specific, has to be cast a fair distance, and has to last almost a whole day. It was very expensive."

He paused but everyone waited for more. "And the powerful

witch doesn't need money. She's well-fixed in that department. So payment was demanded in a more traditional, witch-to-mortal fashion." Manny paused there while the others pondered what that meant.

Then Max laughed and blurted out, "She made him a sex slave!"

Realization set in and the others – even Tommy – all began to laugh. It was a good time for it. The mood needed lightening up and it was perfect. Bianca gave Manny a devilish grin and said, "I knew you were holding out on me you big stud muffin. Five straight days. You da man!"

Manny just laughed. "Yeah well at my age it's a good thing I had just refilled my prescription of little pills." He tapped his left front pocket. "Never leave home without 'em. I ain't no spring chicken you know."

* * * * *

They took a break then. But they weren't finished so it was back to the table. They all sat back at their places. Manny said, "Okay, where were we?"

Tommy said, "I was asking questions about this plan. But before we go any further, I need to ask, why don't we use a rifle with wooden bullets?"

Manny nodded and said, "We did a lot of research on that. Wooden bullets, and rubber ones too, are used sometimes in riot control situations. But those aren't actual bullets. They come out of a shotgun and aren't designed to penetrate and kill. They're just supposed to hurt like Hell. But when trying to force a bullet down a rifled barrel with enough spin to be accurate and enough force to penetrate a rib cage, the wood doesn't hold up under the extreme amount of pressure required to send it out with that kind of speed and energy. By the time the bullet exits the barrel with all that force, its structural integrity breaks down and it splinters into a thousand tiny toothpicks that scatter once it hits the open air. We tried backing off on the gunpowder, but then the accuracy suffered and we couldn't guarantee enough penetration. I know I sound like a broken record, but we only have one shot at this. You will be in plenty of range for the crossbow, and it won't fail."

Tommy seemed satisfied with that answer and shifted back to the plan. "Okay, Max won't know what's going on. The consensus is I need to be in the shack across the stream—."

"We." Toni interrupted. "We will be there."

Tommy shook his head. "No, I don't think so. There's not much you can do and you would be unnecessary." He knew that was the wrong choice of words, but it was too late.

"I'm not missing this for the world." She smacked Tommy's arm. "No way are you leaving me behind while you go play hero. I want to see the son of a bitch that killed George dead with my own two eyes, and you're not stopping me."

Tommy was sure he wouldn't win that argument. But he looked at Manny in case he could offer some help. Manny had other ideas, tilted his head, and said, "I agree. I think it's best if she goes along. For one thing, I may need to communicate with you and we don't want anything distracting you. I don't want you try-ing to answer a text or something when you should be aiming and shooting. Remember, the window of opportunity will be small. If I have something you need to know I can text Toni and not bother you if the timing is wrong."

After a moment he added, "Besides, the current in the stream picks up pretty good right before the bend, and you will likely need both of you to paddle the boat to shore to keep from getting swept downstream."

"The boat," Tommy stated more than asked again. The surprises kept coming. "What boat? I was expecting to swim across the stream with the crossbow in my teeth like a special forces ace. You're telling me I have to use a boat? Not my style." He nudged Toni, who slapped his arm again. "I'm a hero, dontcha know?"

Manny chuckled at Tommy's reaction. But the explanation followed. "Well, it's like this. We can't just drive you through the forest to the point and have you make your way across the stream. That would leave tracks in the soft ground of the forest floor – mostly pine needles. And since the point you're headed to is quite remote, the tracks left behind could cause Jasper to become suspicious. We don't know that he would. But as with everything we're doing, we're trying to eliminate anything that could possibly work against us. That means we have to put you in a boat at an upstream location and let you make your way downstream to ground zero."

Tommy decided to roll with the flow. "Of course we do. Why wouldn't we?"

Manny remained serious. "The problem is, upstream is in the middle of nowhere. If you look out your window and see Scarface Mountain, the stream we need you in is basically on the opposite side of there from here – but to the south, away from everything."

Tommy's turn to have fun. "Oooh! So let me guess. Helicopter? I always wanted to ride in a helicopter."

Many chuckled again. "Sorry, nothing quite so grandiose. We have a way in, though it is somewhat convoluted."

"Of course it is. But hey, lay it on me. I'm loving this mission more and more."

"The area we need to get you to is closer to a little place called Averyville. Naturally, we have friends over there who will help us out. We'll take you there and drop you off. Our friends will see you and a small boat through the forest from there, to a spot where you can get into the water. Then you have to go downstream until you get to the shack. Paddle over there, pull the boat up, drag it behind the shack so Jasper and Max don't see it, then wait for Jasper and Max to show up."

"And what will you be doing this whole time?"

"I will be monitoring Max. I will have a tracker and a transmitter on him, so I can see where he is and hear what he says. The fact that he usually talks out loud to Jasper should help. Hopefully, I can keep tabs on how everything is going and relay their progress to you. I will also have Bianca ready with my car in case we have to drive anyplace, as my night vision sucks."

"I want to urge everyone to stay vigilant. We hope everything goes according to plan. But if it doesn't, we still only have this one opportunity. We should all be ready to move and improvise as needed. Keeping ourselves safe of course. But the truth is, we don't know what will happen, and we might have to play things by ear to give ourselves a different opportunity should things veer off course."

Tommy wasn't done with questions. "So how far downstream do we have to float? How far away is this Amityville place?"

"Averyville," Manny corrected. "Straight over the mountain? It's probably a mile and a half. Though it's more like ten miles by the time we drive out to Ray Brook, east to Lake Placid then south and west to Averyville. Once we get there and our friends take you another mile through the forest, you will only have to float about three-quarters of a mile. Just think of it as a dozen football fields or so. Not far really, considering it's all downstream and you will have paddles to speed your progress."

"So we're making a big circle. Are there any more aspects to this exciting plan?"

"None I can think of at the moment. Besides, it's almost time for the oracle to arrive, so we can finish any details tomorrow."

Oracle? What oracle? Tommy wondered. But he was finally getting info on the plan and wasn't about to let it sidetrack. He kept going. "Okay. But let me run through this so I've got it all straight in my head. Correct me where I'm wrong. On Saturday, the witch will cast a spell on Max so he doesn't remember any of this and therefore won't accidentally telepathically tip our hand to Jasper. Later, a bunch of drunk kids will elect a mayor who, with some friends, will go to Max's house at Peckerneck Mountain. They will climb aboard an old steam-powered train consisting of one locomotive and one caboose. With much pomp and circumstance, they will make about a fifteen-minute ride back to here, more or less."

Tommy paused and pointed in the direction of the tiki bar while Manny nodded. "Later that evening Max will go home and then he and Jasper will likely go out past Lake Placid to find a somewhat homeless person for Jasper's dinner. And it's our expectation they will then take the dead body back to Peckerneck Mountain, load it into a side-by-side and then go through the woods to a point on a stream where the current picks up. There they will chuck the body into said stream."

At that point Tommy stopped himself. He looked at Max and asked, "What makes you think you guys will go to that spot again?

I mean, didn't you say the last time you dumped that college kid down an old mine shaft? Why not use that again?"

Max sipped his whiskey and said. "Good question. Jasper can bounce around inside my head all night, but whenever he needs to fully embody a person, it takes a lot of energy. When he helped me lug the kid up on that hillside it took so much energy it wasn't worth the trouble of killing him in the first place. Jasper said so, and used that as his excuse to leave me stranded up there in the darkness – the rotten prick. Anyway, we'll go back to what works. Jasper just needs to help me get the body to my truck. Then we drive home. A quick transfer from the truck to the side-by-side with his help again, and we drive to the point where he helps me toss the body into the current. Much less energy is required on his part. And the past four years, since I started poking holes in the abdomen, the bodies have stayed hidden."

Bianca jumped in then, as they all looked at Max with surprise at that statement. "Poked holes in the abdomen?"

Max continued without emotion. "Yes. It helps keep the body from floating once decomposition forms internal gasses."

Toni, having heard enough. "Okay, can we just move along here?"

Tommy seemed satisfied with Max's answer. Looking back at Manny he started again. "Okay so meanwhile, Toni and I will catch a ride from you and Bianca all the way around to Amity—Averyville, where we will then catch a ride through the forest with some friends of the Monkey Beans. We will take a boat downstream to where we expect Max and Jasper to show up across the stream from a long-abandoned government shack. You and Bianca will stay mobile while keeping tabs on Max and giving us progress reports. Max will show up and while Jasper has him fully embodied, I will plug him with a wooden bolt from the crossbow, ending both of their existences. Is that it?"

Manny nodded. "Easy peasy."

The whole group chuckled, knowing it would be anything but. Manny added, "We all know this has a slim chance of working. But we've agreed to try. So let's remember to give it our all. Stay vigilant. Be ready for anything. Failure will suck for the entire future of all mankind. Any questions?"

Tommy spoke up. "I probably have a hundred or more. But right now I can only think of one."

"Shoot."

"This powerful Good Witch Of The Catskills that held you captive, is she old and ugly?"

Manny grinned and laughed silently, shaking his head. "No."

Tommy laughed too. "Oh, the things you do for your fellow man."

They all laughed. It was a good way to end the meeting. As Manny got up and headed for the door, he looked at the clock in the kitchenette, and said, "We have about ten minutes before we meet with the oracle. Let's all get freshened up and get back here. We don't want to keep him waiting."

Tommy still didn't know what that meant. He looked at Toni who was similarly perplexed. They looked at Bianca and Max who also shook their heads. He thought about stopping and questioning Manny, but he was already to the door. Besides, Tommy was getting used to being in the dark while things unfolded one piece at a time – and it was only ten more minutes. He shrugged his shoulders and went to make a fresh drink.

CHAPTER 22

The group reunited, each of them naturally curious. Bianca started it off. "So Manny, what the Hell is this oracle you've been talking about?"

Manny looked around and suddenly realized he had never told anybody about the expected visit. "Oh, I'm sorry. I failed to mention that before I left the witch in the Catskills, she informed me that in light of our mutual interest, she had arranged for a visit from someone called the Oracle Of The Champlain. He's supposed to be here at nine o'clock and requires a rather expensive French wine. That's pretty much all I know. I haven't heard anything since then, so we can only wait and be ready."

Toni asked, "Oracle? Like a fortune teller?"

Manny shrugged. "I guess so. I've never heard of the guy, but when I mentioned him to the folks at Monkey Beans they were all highly impressed that I managed to secure an audience with him. I'm told this Oracle Of The Champlain is a big deal. And an audience with mortals like us is practically unheard of. So I guess we should be impressed."

Tommy couldn't help but add his cynical two cents. "Oh yay. As if there isn't enough crazy shit going on this weekend. Now we get to throw in some quack with a crystal ball. Saturday night can't come soon enough."

Manny smiled as he seemed to understand Tommy's frustration. "I wouldn't be so sure. Monkey Beans is well informed on things like this, as they've been studying them for centuries. If they say he's a big deal, he's a big deal. Please just humor us for a bit longer."

With a kick from Toni under the table Tommy knew he was beat again – and probably a little out of line. But somebody had to be the cynical nitpicker in the group just to keep everybody level-headed.

Right at nine o'clock there was a quick knock at the door. Karen stuck her head in and said, "There's a mysterious man here who calls himself the oracle to see you."

Unfazed, Manny told her to send him in. A bit surprised, Karen did so. They looked on as a clean-cut, brown-haired model of a man came through the door wearing a leather biker jacket, blue jeans, and black engineer boots. He also carried what appeared to be a large bird cage with a black, cloth cover.

As he strolled in he smiled and said, "Hello, I am the Oracle Of The Champlain, here to offer my services at the behest of Saavi, the powerful Good Witch Of The Catskills."

Noting their mostly blank expressions, he added, "But you can just call me Jack."

Everyone remained silent as Jack made his way toward the table. He kept smiling and with a laugh, said, "Let me guess, you were expecting some old guy with a gray beard to his knees in a purple tunic, right?"

Bianca chimed in with her Texas twang. "Well no, we didn't know what to expect. But a middle-aged, male-model biker carrying a—" she gestured with her hands, "—bird cage? We weren't expecting that either."

The rest of the gang nodded and grunted in agreement.

"No, I don't suppose you were." Looking around he asked, "Which of you is Mr. Richter?"

Manny rose from his chair and greeted Jack with a handshake. "That would be me. But please, call me Manny."

Jack shook hands as he looked up to meet Manny's gaze. "Good enough. Hopefully, we can all use first names. I suppose there's no reason not to get right down to business. Do you have the *Petite Frimousse?*"

Manny nodded and headed for the minibar. "Coming right up."

Jack proceeded to the head of the table where Manny usually sat, and set the bird cage in front of him. He hung his jacket on the back of the chair and plopped down like he owned the place. Before he could speak Manny called over, "I know it's red wine, but would you like it chilled at all? And I'm afraid my presentation skills probably aren't what you're used to."

Seeming less and less like an exalted wizard, Jack's reply still surprised the room when he said, "Nah, just dump the shit in a glass." Then after a brief pause. "And give us all a glass. Plus a little more in a separate rocks glass if you will, please."

While Manny filled the glasses, Jack removed the cover of what did indeed turn out to be a bird cage. Inside, on a T-shaped roost, were two birds about the size of crows, facing in opposite directions. One was dark brown, almost black. While the other had lighter brown feathers.

"I'm going to ask you all, please refrain from touching these birds, or attempting to communicate with them. They are *venēficus* birds, highly cultivated, and older, by far, than any of you would imagine. But their purpose is explicit, and distractions help no one."

Manny came over with a serving tray and began doling out the wine. "Six-and-a-half glasses of warm Patty Free Moose for your pleasure." He set the extra, small glass in front of Jack.

Jack laughed at Manny's pronunciation. Manny, apparently not bothered by Jack stealing his seat, set the tray on the table and took the only empty chair – at the side of the table to the right of a mostly silent Max.

With a more serious look, Jack said, "As I said, my name is Jack." Looking to his left at Bianca, she offered her name while the rest followed suit. When they got to Max he stood up from his chair and offered his hand. Jack also stood and they shook hands.

Max asked. "Will my dog bother any of this?"

Jack looked at Little Whiskey. "I don't think so. He seems rather well-behaved. What's his name?"

"Little Whiskey."

Jack smiled, as though he and Max had just created a silent bond. He said, "Hello Little Whiskey," and reached out his hand for a sniff and a quick pet. Then it was back to business. "All right. Now that we all know each other, it's time to meet my friends." Nodding at the roost before him, he said, "This is SusieBird and JulieBird. Say hello, SusieBird."

The bird facing away from Jack, with the darker feathers, said in a scratchy bird voice, "Hello, fuckers!"

Caught off guard, the whole group broke out in laughter. All except for Tommy. Tommy shook his head. When the laughter died down he asked, "Is this supposed to be some kind of a joke?" Toni reached her hand over to his. But it didn't stop him. "Really? You expect us to take you seriously?"

Jack nodded at Tommy. "Please, let me apologize. I should have warned you all. Usually, the greeting gets the desired laughter. But I should have heeded the seriousness of what we're all doing here, and not have sprung it on you like I did. You see, these birds came to me from my mentor and predecessor, the Oracle Of The Concord. She lived on top of a mountain in Vermont and was, by all accounts, the most miserable witch that ever graced the earth. Quite the contrast to the wonderful enchantress named Victoria who still lives on the other side of the mountain."

"Lady Concord – as the miserable one was called, though she was anything but – trained these birds. She cultivated their ability to connect with unseen dimensions and bring forth a specialized knowledge of properly prompted prophecy. Unfortunately, they also learned their English language from the miserable wretch. And now we're stuck with two foul-mouthed, but very productive and insightful *venēficus* birds."

Looking back at Tommy, Jack went on. "Again, I apologize. But please, don't let my carefree demeanor and the birds' crassness deter you. We are all here for the same purpose. And I assure you, whatever these birds tell us here tonight will be important in our mutual quest to eliminate Jasper Czymiak."

With a squeeze from Toni's hand, Tommy lightened up. He didn't speak but nodded to Jack that all was well and he should continue.

With that, Jack spun the roost so the lighter brown bird faced the group. "Now say Hello, JulieBird."

In a similar, scratchy bird voice, she cackled, "Bitches! Bitches everywhere. Hello bitches!"

It was too much even for Tommy to resist, and they all shared another round of laughter. Finally, Jack took his glass and raised it. "To a successful prognostication. May our joint effort result in victory against our foe."

They all took a sip, expecting great things considering how Manny had said it was expensive. Nobody seemed overly impressed as Jack grabbed the extra, smaller glass of wine and offered it to SusieBird.

She dipped her head and stuck her beak in. Coming up she said, "Mmm . . . smooooth."

Jack again spun the roost and offered a sip to JulieBird. "Bitchin'!" She scratched.

As she dipped her head for another sip, Jack pulled the glass away.

"Not until after we're finished. Moderation, JulieBird. Moderation."

As he set the glass aside JulieBird scratchy-whispered, "Bullshit."

With more laughter, the toast, and bird treats out of the way, Jack looked around and said, "Okay, time to get down to the bones. Which of you here, if any, have ever been embodied by the spirit, Jasper?"

Max and Toni both raised their hands. To the others, Jack asked, "And have any of you been personally touched in any other way?"

Bianca spoke up. "Sort of. I was conceived while my mother was embodied by Jasper. And I have the ability to sense whenever he's near."

Jack looked at her with genuine admiration. As though he considered maybe she was more of his kind than of the mortals. But that would have to wait for another time.

"Really," was all he said. Then it was back to business. "Okay,

I need Toni to please sit here to my left. And Bianca, if you could take Tommy's chair while he moves to the end, please? We need the four of us to join hands, with the two who have been embodied touching me. I'll scoot over a little so Toni can slide in and Bianca will still be close enough to reach Max across the table."

As they rearranged themselves, Max moved Little Whiskey onto his lap to free up both hands while Jack asked Manny to dim the lights. With four sets of hands connected in a circle around the birds, Jack spoke. "I will ask you all again, please don't speak or touch the birds during this session. The quieter and stiller we all remain the better. It'll take about ten minutes, so if anybody has to use the can, now is the time."

Nobody did, so it was on with the show. "Okay, here's what's going to happen. I'm going to begin repeating a chant. It will be repetitive, and you will find it very boring. Please just be patient. And when the birds begin to move, don't be startled and make any sudden movements." Looking around he asked, "Are we ready?"

The group all nodded yes. So Jack said, "Okay, let's begin." He reached forward and pressed a button on the base of the birdcage. Soft sounds of waves gently washing ashore began to filter up, though no speaker was visible. "Now, we should all relax. Just listen to the sound of the waves. Breathe deeply and slowly."

After a minute or so Jack began to chant softly. The language was foreign, but Tommy thought it sounded like Latin. After about ten words he heard the name Jasper Czymiak, followed by another ten words or so. Then Jack spoke the chant again.

And again.

And again.

Tommy grew frustrated until, after about five minutes, a feeling washed over him. A euphoric, calm feeling. He glanced around and could tell the others felt it too. Still, Jack kept on with the chant. Ten foreign words – Jasper Czymiak – and another ten words. Over and over. Never faster or slower, or louder or softer. The euphoric feeling was pleasant, so Tommy remained patient.

After another minute, the T-shaped roost the birds sat upon began to rotate, and their heads began to bob up and down in rhythm with Jack's chant. There was no new sound or visible motor. But there they were, following each other in circles on their private merry-go-round. Heads bobbing. Around and around. Over and over.

Finally, after a few more minutes that seemed longer, during one of the chants, when Jasper's name was uttered, SuzieBird softly said, "Fuuuuuckerrrr." It happened again the next time around. And the one after that. Tommy decided it was a good thing they were all hypnotized – or whatever it was – because the whole thing was the perfect setup for a case of, don't look at your friend during a serious function because you know it will cause you both to start laughing. The euphoric feeling held that in check. But Tommy kept his gaze from wandering to any of the others just to be safe. He also admitted to himself, yet again, something powerful was happening and his cynicism was probably unfounded. One more rung on the ladder to his being fully committed.

After the third round with SuzieBird's Jasper description, Jack finally stopped the chanting. The birds' rotating roost, as well as their head bobbing, likewise stopped. The only sounds were the gentle ocean waves from the hidden speaker and the soft hum of the ceiling fan over the coffee table by the sofas in front of the fireplace.

They stayed in silence for a full minute. Each of them dutifully remained still and quiet. Finally, Jack spoke softly. "SuzieBird, you have channeled the dimensions. You know our quest toward Jasper Czymiak. We ask you to share your secrets now. What will help us rid the world of Jasper Czymiak?"

SuzieBird bobbed her head up and down for about thirty seconds. Finally, in her scratchy bird voice, she said, "Arrogant fucker. Kill the Jasper. His arrogance will kill him. Kill the arrogant Jasper."

The silence continued until it seemed Jack was satisfied SuzieBird had nothing more to offer. He then posed the same question to JulieBird.

Her scratchy response was, "Redhead bitch. Kill the Jasper, redhead bitch must involve. Redhead bitch to help kill the Jasper."

Jack waited a bit longer, and then it was over. He broke the circle and everyone snapped back to their regular consciousness. They took a few moments to look around at each other, affirming they had all seen, heard, and felt the same things. Toni looked down the table at Tommy and said, "Wow." Tommy nodded in agreement.

Bianca shook her head and said, "Whew."

Max reached down to bring Little Whiskey back into his arm cradle. Even Little Whiskey let out a surprising yip.

Jack reached for the small glass of wine, first giving another sip to SusieBird, who remained silent. JulieBird seemed not to have that ability. "Bitchin'," was her response after the first sip. After a second sip but denied a third, she once again said, "Bullshit."

That produced a round of laughter. They all sipped their expensive wine while Jack turned off the ocean sounds and placed the cover back over the bird cage. As the birds disappeared from view, SusieBird let out one last scratchy comment. "Lights out, Bitch!"

JulieBird answered, "Bullshit."

Jack then addressed the group. "Well, it's quite clear. And don't take these words lightly. To be successful in eliminating Jasper, you will need to stay vigilant and be ready. At some point, his arrogance will make him vulnerable. That will be your opportunity. Also, I don't know your plan, but unless you have another redhead in your group, it needs to include Bianca." He paused briefly while they all, including Bianca, looked around at each other, questioning. "And these birds don't make mistakes. If mistakes are made it's always on our end, where people either didn't listen or weren't ready when opportunity knocked."

He stood up and reached for his jacket. Manny asked, "Would you like some more wine? We didn't know how many bottles to get, and have spent a small fortune on it."

Jack smiled and said, "No thanks. I'm on my motorcycle and need to stay focused."

Bianca summed the group's surprise when she asked, "You're riding a bike? What do you do with the birds? Strap them to the handlebars?"

"No, they ride in the sidecar."

Manny said, "Oh man, I gotta check this out. What kind of bike? You got a Harley?"

"No. It's a seventy-two Moto Guzzi with a custom-built sidecar. I inherited them both from Lady Concord, along with the birds."

Manny said, "I'll walk out with you and take a look."

Jack put up a hand in protest. "Not so fast. I'm here on a

truce. But you and I are still at odds, despite our current mutual quest."

"Aww come on. A truce is a truce."

Jack smiled then. "Well okay. Just don't tell anybody I was nice to you."

As they walked toward the door Manny asked, "You want to take a couple bottles of Patty Free Moose with you? We've got plenty left."

Jack shook his head. "Nah, thanks. I can't stand the stuff."

Manny spread his arms as if asking, what gives?

Jack nodded at the bird cage. "It's the only thing the girls will work for. Other wines won't do. Yet another thing Lady Concord left me with."

They both laughed and headed for the door. Before going out Manny turned to the rest and said, "I think that's it for tonight. I'm sure we're all ready for bed anyway.."

Bianca agreed. "I know I am. I started this day in Kentucky and a pillow sounds real good right now." She looked at the group and asked, "Anybody want the rest of my wine? I think it smells like dirty socks."

Max jumped in. "Tastes like dirty socks too." He offered some to Little Whiskey, who shook his head no.

Toni sipped her wine. "I don't think it's all that bad. It's aromatic. Starts off bold and has a nutty finish with a hint of elderflowers."

The others rolled their eyes while she laughed. Then Tommy got up and pushed all the unfinished glasses in front of Toni, who began combining them into her glass. He looked at Max and said, "How about I go find that good Canadian whiskey and fix us a real drink?"

"Now you're talking." Max pulled the gold railroad watch out of his pocket and opened the flap, briefly looking inside. He smiled and reached down to scratch Little Whiskey's ears while he waited. Before Bianca could leave he said in a soft voice, "I won't recognize any of you after tomorrow – and hopefully I'll never see you again after that." He paused as they all knew what he meant. He finally added, "I wonder if one of you would look after my dog. He's well behaved, though I admit I have always spoiled him with people food."

Bianca ran over and gave Max a big hug. "I have a big back yard with an oak tree and about five thousand squirrels. I'll be happy to give him a home."

Max couldn't speak, but his expression spoke volumes. Tommy brought the drinks back. Bianca said goodbye again and left for the night.

Once they settled back in, Max spoke to Tommy in a quiet but stern voice. "Young man, I want you to listen to me. I know what we're planning goes against everything you believe in. And I know you seem to be convinced it's the right thing to do – and it is. But I also know in the next two days you will have doubts creeping back in. It's only natural. On Saturday, your normal in-stinct will be to know that if you stop me from leaving my house on Saturday night, you will save a life. And that is technically true."

"But you have to understand – and I learned this stuff in the war – there are extraordinary times when you have to allow things like that to happen for the greater good. Rest assured, even if your oath and training and moral compass kick in and you save a life by stopping me, it is a one hundred percent certainty you will be trading that life for another one. And in this case, failure on our part means thousands of lives in the future – until the end of time."

"It won't be easy to accept. But you must prepare yourself now to be ready to accept it. The only way to stop the evil bastard is to let the plan work. It's dark. It's unnatural. And it goes against everything that you are. But it has to be. There is no other way. One more person will die, and technically you can stop it. But in the grand scheme, you won't be stopping anything. Let it go."

Tommy closed his eyes. Toni rose and embraced him. But there was nothing more to be said.

CHAPTER 25

Friday was a cloudy, dreary day, with off-and-on light rain showers. A good day to stay inside. Manny took Toni, Tommy, and Bianca into town for breakfast, then left Toni and Tommy back in the war room while he went off somewhere with Bianca, saying they'd be back in a while.

Tommy used the time to practice with the crossbow. Sitting at the kitchenette table he set the target on the floor at the far end of the room – past the meeting table and the lounge area by the fireplace, and across the dance floor. All told it was just about twenty yards to the far end. It made a nice, makeshift shooting range close to what Manny had said the distance would be.

Toni looked on silently as Tommy loaded the crossbow for the first shot. To draw back the string, Tommy had to put the crossbow on the floor and insert the toe of his shoe into a steel loop. Then he used a heavy cord with a T handle on each end and two hooks with pulleys attached. The cord went around the butt stock, then the ends with the handles and pulleys dropped down each side of the main beam. Once Tommy hooked the pulleys to the drawstring, using his foot in the loop to hold the bow down, he pulled up on both T handles.

Even with the mechanical advantage of two pulleys, it still

took some effort to draw the string back until it latched into the catch. As it did it made an audible click as the safety catch on the trigger automatically engaged. Once the drawstring was firmly held in the loaded position, Tommy unhooked the cord and pulleys and set them on the table.

While he placed a bolt onto the main beam and nocked it onto the string, Toni said, "Sheesh. I don't think my little ass could even pull that string back. It's a good thing you're big and strong."

Tommy gave her a loving look before aiming at the target. "Yeah, I'm pretty impressed how they can make these things so compact but powerful. And with the stock, scope, and trigger, it's almost like shooting a rifle. The old compound bow I used to hunt with wouldn't hold a candle to this thing."

With that, he took a deep breath and let it halfway out. He put the cross hairs on the bullseye and squeezed the trigger. Like a flash of lightning, the bolt shot across the room and smacked the target with enough force to knock it over.

Toni jumped and let out a yelp. "Holy shit! That thing is crazy!"

Tommy walked to the target. The far wall had a wooden table near the door, with a vase of flowers on it. Setting the vase on the floor, he slid the table over to the back end of the range. He put the target on the table and shoved them both tight to the wall, hoping to keep it upright through future shots.

As he walked back, Toni said, "That thing is awesome. It's nothing like a regular bow-and-arrow. How many feet per second do you think it shoots?"

Tommy shrugged. Toni decided to look it up on her phone. Tommy went about shooting some more. With the target secured, he could shoot all three bolts before retrieving them. When he did he was surprised at how tight the group was. Accuracy was incredible compared to his old compound bow. He took the center of the group, measured to the center of the bullseye, and made a scope adjustment. He repeated the process a few more times until he was consistently hitting the quarter-sized bullseye.

After a while Toni noticed since Tommy had stopped adjusting the scope, he was only taking one shot at a time before retrieving the bolt and reloading. She asked him why.

"One shot is all I'll get, so I need to practice that way. If my first shot is a little off, it doesn't do any good to sit here and reload and make a better second or third shot. My frame of mind must be that one shot is all there is. So I shoot once and remind myself not to screw it up, because this is a once-in-an-all-time opportunity and failure is not an option. Plus this particular bolt," he held it up for effect, "seems to be the most accurate of the three. So it makes sense to practice with just this one."

Toni decided that made sense. She teased him a little with some brave warrior comments. But doing so didn't have the desired effect. Instead, it seemed to remind Tommy, and herself, of what they were going to do. Suddenly, even though they both knew it needed to be done, the thought of talking about shooting Max to kill Jasper seemed taboo. Toni decided to get her guitar and play some songs while Tommy kept shooting.

It went like that for over an hour. Toni played and sang while Tommy would shoot once, walk the length of the room to retrieve the bolt, return, and repeat. Eventually, Manny and Bianca came back. They had been shopping. Toni thought that was a bit odd. But decided there wasn't much else to do until the next day. Tommy was practicing and everything else was in place.

Manny carried a cardboard tray with four paper cups of trendy, flavored coffee, and a bag of muffins. He set them on the table as he and Bianca sat down. Tommy aimed and fired a bolt into the bullseye again. It was Bianca's turn to be surprised by the speed, power, and impact the bolt had when hitting the target.

"Holy shit!" she said as she jumped. "Damn, that oughtta do the trick." Just as before, the comment eerily reminded them of what they were preparing to do, and the room fell silent again.

As Tommy returned to the table for another round, Manny cleared his throat in an attention-getting manner. "We have to talk about a change in our plan." He waited for Tommy to sit and grab a cup of trendy coffee. Then he continued, looking at Toni. "I believe we have to switch places with you and Bianca."

Before he could go on Toni sat up straight and shot back, "What do you mean switch places? I'll be with Tommy and Bianca will be your night-time chauffeur. What's wrong with that?"

Manny tried to give her an understanding look, but she wasn't interested. Still, he went on. "You were here with the oracle, and I know you felt what we all felt. That dude has some serious mojo, and everybody with knowledge of him swears by his ability to see. And while I don't know exactly what role Bianca will play, if the oracle says she needs to be there for us to succeed, then we need her to be there – with Tommy, as it happens."

Toni stared at Manny for a full minute. She finally turned to Tommy for help as he was getting up to come around and sit by her side. He put his arm around her and said, "I feel the same way. I want you there more than anything. But Manny's argument is right. It sucks. But we all felt the power that oracle emitted."

Toni wouldn't have it. "I don't like it. I have every right to be there to see that bastard killed. And to be with you." She felt like saying more but was afraid she would cry, and be damned if she would do that right then and there. More silence followed. It seemed everybody – including Toni – knew it was the right plan. She just needed time to accept it.

Still, she wasn't done. Looking back at Manny she argued, "You said you recruited us because we have no family, and this could get ugly. We thought long and hard about that before we agreed to come here and join you." Then looking to Bianca, "But you have family. You have three brothers if I'm not mistaken. Are you prepared to put them, and yourself, through whatever might happen? Including your possible death?"

Manny jumped in and tried to lighten things, but Bianca cut him off, saying, "It's a fair question." She looked across the table into Toni's eyes. Then she reached across for her hand. Toni tried to pull away but Bianca grabbed and held on, firmly but with sincerity in her eyes.

"I know I can never know what you went through. But I watched my mother live with it all of her life. And I had to grow up without a father because of Jasper – the dirty, evil bastard Jasper. I've also known Manny for a couple of years now, and he's told me stories of hundreds, even thousands of people murdered by the evil son of a bitch. So now I'm in the same boat as the rest of us. I can't let myself not take this one-time shot at putting an end to it. If I back down I'll never be able to live with myself. And I admit I have no idea what I might bring to the table in all of this. But I'm with the rest of us when I say I believe in the power carried by Jack the Oracle. He had something going on like we've never experienced before."

Toni softened a little. Very little. But Bianca wasn't finished. "As for my brothers, yes, I have three. But the truth is, they are all older than me by at least a decade. They were all grown and moved out long before I blossomed as a teenager. And now we're spread out all over the country. We share holiday cards and the like. But the truth is, we've never been close. We certainly don't hate each other. But if I were to come up missing it wouldn't affect any of them or their lives."

The room went quiet again. Finally, Tommy squeezed his wife and said, "I know it's hard. Early on you asked me to trust Manny and Max and their plan. And I had plenty of misgivings. But the more we all talked and listened, and the things we've heard, well, I'm on board now. I know it has to be done. We all do. But these guys are right. What we're doing, and the fact it's a one-time thing, well, we have to give it every possible chance and give ourselves every advantage we can. And like everybody else, I can't imagine what difference it makes having Bianca with me instead of you. And I wish I could ignore the words of the oracle. But even I have to admit, he had a way about him during that . . . seance or whatever it's called . . . and we do need to listen to what he said if we want to have the best chance of success."

He gave her a few moments. Then with another squeeze, he whispered, "We need your trust now my beautiful, wonderful, loving wife, best friend, and life partner."

Toni had been slowly accepting that they were all right. And Tommy's over-the-top shtick at the end almost made her laugh. But she still didn't like it. She gave them all a look of resignation before finally saying, "Yeah, but I still think it sucks!"

"Fair enough," said Manny. "I'd like to mention now, I just got a call from Monkey Beans. It seems Jasper's latest subject – a young man named Henry up in New Hampshire whose body Jasper employed to feed on a camper last week – couldn't take the stress and has packed it in. I know I probably say this too much, but it's not just Jasper's victims that get affected by him. There's a whole lot of collateral damage too. We really need to give this our all and put a stop to the monster if we can."

Nobody said anything, but it was a good reminder. Still, there was no sense in dwelling on what they already knew. Eventually Manny asked Tommy, "How's the practice going?"

"Hell, with the pistol grip, rifle stock, scope, and a bench rest I could shoot a bug off a bull's ass with this thing."

Manny nodded. "Good. Keep it up."

The uneasy silence crept into the room again. They all seemed to know what had to be done. The closer it got to game time, the more ominous the planned shooting of Max seemed.

Manny finally broke the silence. "I have a suggestion. I think we all need a little wind-down time tonight. So for dinner, I think we should go over to the tiki bar and take advantage of their health food menu. Have a few drinks and try to relax before the big day tomorrow."

"Health food?" Toni asked dubiously.

"Yes. They have a wonderful menu full of things like tacos and bacon cheeseburgers. Or some poutine with a side of mac and cheese. And I'm prescribing a little indulgence for us all this evening."

They all laughed. It was still early so Tommy loaded up another practice round. Bianca said she would make doubly sure her new dark clothes and hiking shoes fit.

Toni shrugged and said, "I guess a little mac and cheese won't hurt." She grabbed her guitar and started another song.

✦ ✦ ✦ ✦ ✦

At seven o'clock Manny rounded up the gang and met in the war room. They had skipped lunch and were ready for drinks and tiki bar health food.

"I believe it's time for some R and R," he stated. "It's going to be crowded over there with everybody gearing up for tomorrow. The event revolves around Max, and he'll make an appearance over there tonight. But if we somehow manage to pull this crazy scheme off, he'll become a missing person. We should steer clear of Max from here on out. The less any of us are seen with him the better for all of us."

Tommy gave a knowing nod and said, "For sure. We need to act like just what we are – guests at the conference center who are checking out the party. Though I'd be a little concerned about Karen at the front desk. She's seen us visiting here with Max. That could cause problems if she or one of us winds up getting grilled."

"Don't worry about her," Manny said flatly. "She's one of us."

Tommy shook his head. "Monkey Beans really is everywhere, aren't they?"

Manny just smiled. With that settled, they walked over, past the fountain, and into the craziness that was the Hero Of '70 Bash pre-celebration. The entrance to the tiki bar was a regular door in a regular wall, which seemed out of place with the other three walls hinged at the top and propped open – creating an indoor-outdoor pavilion with a handful of regular tables and chairs on the inside, and a large number of picnic tables on the outside.

Above the entrance was a painted sign featuring a busty blonde girl wearing a button-down shirt tied into a halter top, a pair of cowboy boots, and a pair of extra-short, cutoff denim shorts. She was facing away, walking along the edge of a cornfield under a full moon. Beneath all that were large, orange letters that read, *DIRTY BUTT'S TIKI BAR*.

Manny always got a kick out of the sign. It reminded him of something from long ago that he could never quite put his finger on. In front of him, Toni pointed to it and smacked Tommy and they both laughed. Unnecessarily entering through the door, just because it seemed like the natural thing to do, Bianca immediately made her way over to a portable Margarita bar. Toni and Tommy went to the regular bar which, while quite busy, was staffed well and had an opening.

A middle-aged man with a black mullet that had an off-centered white stripe running the entire length greeted them. "Hi, welcome to Dirty Butt's. This is my place and if you need anything you come see me. I'm Badger – and yeah, I know, they should have named me Skunk." He gave them a big smile and they all laughed.

Manny and Tommy each had a bottle of beer while Toni ordered a Riesling. They took some menus as Badger asked if they were there for the celebration or just staying at the conference center.

Manny answered for all of them. "Just at the center. Looks like you've got a Hell of a party going on here though. We might have to check it out tomorrow."

"Oh yeah," Badger said, in a high voice that belied his tough-sounding nickname. "It's the event of the year for sure. We even have a special permit from the state to stay open 'til four AM tomorrow night." He nodded at the tables that made up the outdoor seating. "If you find yourself a table one of the girls will be by to take your food order."

219

The three of them sat down at a table on the outer edge. The place was packed but after just a few minutes a tall, purple-haired girl named Morgan showed up to take their order. The three made small talk while they waited, and the food came out surprisingly fast. They talked about how long Tommy had been a cop. And about Toni's diner which George had left her. Of course that brought them back to the subject they were all trying to avoid discussing. But it was all good, they knew why they were there, and it couldn't be ignored.

As they chatted and ate, they watched Bianca work the crowd. Even in her late thirties, she was a knockout bombshell with her long, fiery red hair. And a natural flirt. They watched and laughed as she moved about, engaging and laughing with all the – as she had put it the day before – young, horny bastards. They would stop her and hit on her, and she would blow them off and have them laughing at the same time.

Toni commented, "She would make a Hell of a bartender. Just like her mother."

Manny smiled and Tommy added, "Yeah, Tanya was the best. That girl is a chip off the old block if there ever was one."

Bianca swung by the table a few times to say hey. But she seemed uninterested in eating. The other three, however, took Manny's prescription advice seriously. Toni had a plate full of Buffalo chicken macaroni and cheese. Tommy had the bacon cheeseburger with jalapenos. Manny had an open-faced steak on garlic bread with mashed potatoes drenched in brown gravy.

They washed it all down with more drinks as they people-watched. Max showed up and played his celebrity role well. As they watched, Toni noticed that Max seemed to check his old, gold railroad watch often – something she had seen him do whenever he was around. He'd pull the watch out of his pocket, the old chain glistening. Then he would open the cover and check the time, close it up, and put it back in his pocket. All one-handed of course, as his left hand was always occupied by his companion, Little Whiskey.

"That seems like a peculiar habit," Toni said. "I wonder why Max always checks his old watch. I know he has a cell phone. And there's at least two big wall clocks in the bar here."

Manny gave a soft, loving laugh. "He's not checking the time."

"What then?" Toni asked while Tommy looked on, also questioning.

Manny smiled. "He has a picture of his wife in there. She was the last family he ever had, and has been gone for several years now."

Toni frowned. "Awww man, I should have known that. Now I think I'm going to cry."

"Don't cry. Max has been around a long time and has a great understanding of the ways of the world. But he also knows his time is short."

Again, the silence in the middle of all that noise was haunting. It didn't need to be said, but they all knew the best thing in the world for Max – the thing that would make him the happiest – was for them to succeed in their mission.

Manny excused himself and headed for the men's room. As he made his way back, he passed the bar where Badger called to him. "Everything okay tonight, sir?"

"Just fine," he called back. Making his way through the rows of tables, he suddenly found himself face-to-face with Bianca.

She let out a hoot and pinched Manny's cheek like a grandmother would. "Aren't you just the cutest thing?" It seemed the margarita bar was working. Bianca's stress level was at zero.

Manny didn't say anything. He just smiled and laughed.

She leaned in closer and whispered, "You know how I told you about how I've never been sick a day in my life?" It wasn't a question. "Well, I've also been blessed with a very healthy appetite."

Bianca spun and walked away. But as she did, she made a point to not-so-accidentally brush the back of her hand across Manny's crotch. It didn't take a rocket scientist to know she wasn't talking about food. Though he was surprised. He was, after all, no spring chicken, and old enough to be her father. She could take her pick from the horde of young men there. But he resigned himself to his fate. Their mission was tremendously important, and the oracle had said they needed Bianca to succeed. Manny decided to do whatever was needed to keep her around and satisfied. He instinctively reached down and tapped the little pill box in his front pocket, and thought to himself, *Ahh, the things I do for my fellow man.*

Arriving back at the table he noticed Toni and Tommy were doing their best to act like they hadn't seen what just happened. But they weren't very good at disguising it. Finally, while giggling, Toni said, "I think she likes you."

Manny did his best to keep a neutral expression and changed the subject. He picked up his beer and motioned to Toni's glass. "Finish that up it's my turn."

After that it went unmentioned. They spent their time chatting and people-watching. Doing their best to pass the time and not dwell on their upcoming macabre mission.

CHAPTER 24

The room was dark. Manny lay on the king-sized bed, bare naked, just as Bianca had requested before she slipped into the bathroom. Having been told to get undressed and be ready, he felt a bit awkward but was determined to see the mission through. He reached down to confirm, with the backing of a little pill from his box, his toy soldier was standing at full attention. Hard as a rock and ready for action.

Bianca came out of the bathroom and walked across the room, wearing nothing but a purple T-shirt that was about three sizes too large. By the time it made the detour over her twin peaks, however, the bottom was just low enough to let the imagination run wild. And it did.

As she neared the bed and turned to face him, the shaft of light from the bathroom illuminated the front of her shirt just enough so Manny could make out the words BIG MATT'S LAST MINUTE TOUR. He wondered briefly who Big Matt was. Judging by the size of the shirt, he hoped it wasn't some jealous boyfriend who would come busting through the door.

That didn't seem likely, so he decided it was probably just a former conquest, and wondered what ever happened to Big Matt. The question was quickly forgotten. And any questions Manny had about what kind of foreplay Bianca might require were swiftly answered. She hopped onto the bed and straddled him. Taking command of the toy soldier, she lowered herself down – placing the eager troop directly into the front lines where the action was.

Letting out a quick gasp, Bianca charged immediately into full-speed rock and roll. There was no warm-up period. From zero to one hundred in point five seconds. The toy soldier was caught off guard but quickly responded to the duty for which he was trained. Manny was caught off guard too. His previous encounter (the one that lasted five days – *Ahh, the things I do for my fellow man*) with Saavi was full of tender, slowly building foreplay on almost every occasion. The redhead above him was a polar opposite.

Manny and his toy soldier quickly caught up. But it was her show and he decided as long as Bianca felt like taking the lead, he wasn't going to argue. He was, after all, just doing his duty to the mission and keeping her on board by supplying her with whatever she requested. Somebody had to do it.

So he let her go on rocking and rolling. Her mountains were kept reigned in by the BIG MATT shirt, but they wrestled around underneath like two wildcats in a pillowcase. He let his hands roam up her thighs and everywhere. He considered taming the wildcats, but before long she began to moan and growl. Sensing that she didn't need any more stimulation from him right then, he decided to save the mountains for later. Hands back to her thighs and butt cheeks, gripping them firmly and keeping with her rhythm.

The lustful moaning intensified. Yet Manny noted, even in her hot and heavy attack, Bianca managed to keep her lips pursed, muffling her pleasure sounds. Even as her frenzy escalated, she maintained consideration for the fact the walls might not be well insulated.

It had only been a few minutes, and the toy soldier was standing strong. But Manny didn't see how she could last much longer without something giving. Sure enough, the redhead above him shuddered and shrieked as her body tensed, slowing the pace but driving herself onto the toy soldier while her fingernails dug into his shoulders.

He wondered what her round two expectations would be. She answered by leaning forward and giving Manny a deep kiss. Then she settled into a slow, soft grind. Manny had to remind the little guy that it was her show for the time being and to calm down. Let her do her thing if that's what she wanted. He let himself enjoy the velvety, gliding action. Slowly massaging him with every soft, smooth cycle.

After a few minutes, to Manny's delight, the redhead's pace gently increased. The toy soldier complained that it still wasn't enough, but it stayed that way. Every few minutes she increased her speed and intensity, little by little, while Manny reminded himself and his faithful soldier to be patient. On they went.

After several rounds of steady increases, his red-haired rider was back to about half the intensity she exhibited the first time through. The low, guttural moans returned. Less intense than before, but still telling. She was building herself up again, one stage at a time. Still going, she dug her nails into his shoulders again. The intensity increased and the under-shirt wrestling match was back on.

Manny decided he'd had enough of BIG MATT and his LAST MINUTE TOUR. He grabbed the shirt and raised it over her head. She raised her arms, lost the shirt, and returned her nails to his shoulders, all without missing a beat. The wildcats, free from their burden, bounced and flailed savagely. Her pink, rock-hard nipples threatened to destroy anything in their path.

In the interest of public safety, Manny reached up and took them in his hands. He gripped the violent nipples in the crook of his thumb and palm, while he let his fingers massage her breasts from the outside in. The result was another increase in intensity, tightening fingernails on his shoulders, and more moaning.

A lot more. During the second round, however, Manny noticed the redhead no longer seemed to care about the possibility of thin walls. Her fury approached the same level she displayed the first time, but she didn't seem to care who knew about it.

Meanwhile, the heavy frontal assault took its toll on the toy soldier. Manny's comrade began to lose control. He ordered a cease-fire, but the toy soldier was headed for the big bang, and it seemed there would be no turning back. Manny refused to admit defeat, however. He closed his eyes and tried to think about unpleasant things. He thought about the time he was in prison. He thought about his childhood in Newark, with thugs on every corner forcing him to become one of them or get his ass beat every day.

Finally, he thought about a truckload of dead puppies – and that did the trick. Not the dead puppies themselves, but the absurdity of what he was doing. He was thinking of dead puppies to maintain control, under the pretense of satiating a beautiful woman to keep her on board for a crazy project that had a slim, if any, chance of success. All because a middle-aged biker dude with two foul-mouthed, wine-swilling birds in a sidecar told him she was important. He almost burst out laughing at himself. But it worked. The toy soldier was back under control and determined

226

to see the job through. Failure was not an option for the overall mission, nor their current one.

With the situation handled, Manny returned his attention to the dueling wildcats while the redhead intensified her assault. He wouldn't have thought it possible, but round two grew even more intense. Fingernails dug madly. Guttural moans turned into a series of shrieks – neighbors be damned. Bianca let loose. Her flood gates opened as she shuttered and shrieked and moaned and squeezed and ground herself into him.

Then it all stopped. The girl was unpredictable for sure. When she finished she threw her arms above Manny's head on the bed, fell forward with her breasts squashing into his chest and her face next to his – and just stopped.

Manny took a moment to figure her out. He didn't want to play the wrong hand, but women were so different from one another. He decided patience was best for the time being, even as his mind raced. Was it time for him to flip the script and take the lead? Should he have his way with her? Toss her around like a rag doll and show her who's boss? Then he thought maybe she was done and that was it. The toy soldier screamed that damned well better not be it.

He let himself run his hands over her butt cheeks, then traced his fingers up her spine until they were lost in the mess of red hair that seemed to be everywhere. Then he just held her – their hot breath huffing in each other's ear. Nothing else moved.

Well, almost nothing. Manny wondered if Bianca could feel the toy soldier's German helmet throbbing inside her every time his heart pumped. It didn't seem possible she couldn't. Still, she just laid there, motionless except for her breathing. It went on until he could no longer stand it. Eventually, he gave in to the toy soldier's demand for action and allowed himself a tiny thrust from below.

At first there was no reaction. But after a few seconds, he felt her cheek against his begin to smile. He gave another thrust, a little bigger. And she pushed back. Then she moved her lips over his and gave him another deep, passionate kiss. Before long his questions were answered again. She started with the ever-so-slow grind. Once again she took the lead, with Manny declining to argue the point. Not that he minded.

It was a repeat of round two, and Manny saw no reason to interrupt. It was her show after all. He didn't know if things would change at any point, or how long it would last. The only thing he knew for sure was when his time finally came, Manny figured he would likely blast his rocket all the way to the moon.

Or Venus.

Or whatever otherworldly place it was the redhead belonged. So once again, he let her lead. A clench, a little faster. A shudder, a little faster. A quiver, a little faster.

And so, together, they danced their dance into the night.

* * * * *

The room was warm. Toni and Tommy lay atop their king-sized bed, laughing at the sounds coming through the wall. The conference center was nicely built. But somebody had skimped on inside wall insulation.

Toni rolled over and buried her giggles into her pillow. Tommy, wearing just a pair of boxers, propped himself up on one elbow and looked down at his beautiful wife of thirty-six years.

Besides being his best friend, confidant, nurse, lover, and everything else, Toni had kept herself in great shape, and it showed even as she approached sixty. She wore one of Tommy's white, V-neck cop tee shirts. When she rolled over it rode up a bit, exposing most of her behind. Every time she giggled, a cute little dimple formed in each of her butt cheeks. A trait that, even after all the years, never failed to turn Tommy on.

He grabbed her by the shoulder and turned her back towards him. Then he ran a hand up her shirt and cupped her breast. As he nuzzled his lips into her neck he whispered, "Hey little girl, you want to fool around?"

Toni couldn't help but laugh. But through the giggling she managed, "We might as well. No telling how long they'll be keeping us up."

With that said they lost their shirt and shorts. Before Tommy nuzzled into her neck again, he smiled and said, "Let's see if we can outdo them, shall we?"

Toni giggled some more. "Ohhhh no. You're not getting one peep out of me!"

"Not even a peep?"

"Not a one."

"Hmmm," he said as he flooded her neck with his hot breath while his hand slid up and worked her nipple. He worked his way down and began to nibble. He let his hand slide down and gently stroked her inner thigh. He'd learned much about his partner through the years. One thing was that she was a total sucker for the inner thigh stroke. It even prompted a slight, "Hmmm." Which was nice, he thought. But certainly not a peep. But there was still plenty of noise from next door to go around.

Tommy took his time. Toni could be as hot as an oven, but

she liked to warm up slowly. He patiently kept up the nibbles and strokes. Occasionally letting his fingers tease her a little. He kept working her, gently. Eventually, his nibbles worked their way down her belly, and he placed himself between her thighs where the long-time policeman assumed temporary duty as an oral surgeon.

Once Toni's fire was lit, it didn't take her long to start cooking. She had his head in her hands, while Tommy's hands cupped her butt cheeks, where he could feel the dimples pulsing in and out. He kept up the magic, feeling and reading her. Eventually, when her belly began to do its own little dance, he knew it was time. He ran his hands up her thighs to her knees and spread them wide. Then he pinned her legs to the mattress, knowing how much Toni enjoyed the contrasted feeling of being held down while she tried to buck against him.

And buck she did. Trying to raise herself, then twisting her upper body first one way, then the other, while Tommy held her down. He watched with pleasure as she tightened and tensed and squirmed. Still, he was a bit disappointed when all she let out was a muffled "Mmmmph."

He decided that still didn't count as a peep. But with the next-door noises taking a break, he figured it was their turn. So he kept after it. Giving Toni a few moments to collect herself, he returned to the inner thigh stroke. Gently, up to the knee and back down again. Slowly and softly, he built her back up with pleasant strokes until he finally felt a tender tug on his head.

It was time. But Tommy pretended not to notice. He ran his hands up, then back down her thighs. Then he let his fingers tease her sex from the bottom up, only to pull away just as they reached the magic at the top. The following thigh stroke was accompanied by a not-so-subtle tug on each ear – letting him know he hadn't gotten the message the first time. But he still wasn't done. He finished the down stroke by inserting both thumbs as far as he could, then quickly removing them as she tried to move against him. The next thigh stroke was met with a playful, yet right smart smack on the top of his head.

Knowing not to push things any further, Tommy raised himself above her. And when he finally entered her, despite her earlier resolve, Toni gave a peep. It was nothing compared to the earlier sounds from through the wall. Just a spontaneous affirmation that his timing had been perfect.

But theirs was not a frenzied orgy. Theirs was a well-rehearsed choreography of love and sensual sharing. Every motion and every slide of flesh on flesh was the product of their years together. Tommy settled into a slow, gentle pace. And with the sound barrier having been broken, Toni settled into a steady, "Mmm . . . mmm . . . mmm," that matched his rhythm.

And so, together, they danced their dance into the night.

CHAPTER 25

Saturday was game day. But the game wasn't until night-time. The crew spent the day nervously trying to stay busy. Nobody spoke much. Toni sat at the kitchenette table and played some songs. But her heart wasn't in it. Tommy practiced with the crossbow, but it was dialed in well. He was occupying his time to keep from dwelling on what they were planning to do. Not that it worked very well.

Eventually, the day wore on, and at seven o'clock Manny had another dinner catered. Beautiful slabs of beef sat untouched in front of each of them while Manny went over the details of the upcoming plan.

"Okay, so we're all systems go." Looking at Tommy he said, "At nine forty-five we'll take you and Bianca over to our friends in Averyville. It will take us about twenty minutes to get there. Then they'll take you through the woods and get you and the little boat started downstream."

At that point, Manny produced a small paper bag containing two small, disposable flashlights and two pairs of thin gloves.

"It's a warm night but you'll want to wear these the whole time. When you're done you can go downstream until you see a little clearing on your right with a couple of picnic tables. That

233

area is just down the hill from the back side of the tiki bar. You can just let the boat go downstream from there. But there's no sense in leaving fingerprints anywhere. Max will, after all, officially become a missing person. And that will require investigating."

Tommy nodded. "Okay, so you say our shooting position is about three-quarters of a mile downstream from where we get dropped off. That shouldn't take too long. But let's say we get to your friends in Averyville at a little after ten. By the time we get through the woods to the stream, get into the boat, get downstream to where we're going, then get the boat out of the water and behind the building, we'll be pushing eleven o'clock. What's the expected timeline for Max and Jasper to do their thing?"

"Well, Max is getting up there in years, so he usually manages to get his photo ops and meet and greet stuff done in an hour or less. He tells everybody he's old and it's past his bedtime and stuff. That puts him home by around 10:30. Jasper usually leaves Max for a while during the meet and greet. But he will be anxious to get started and will return as soon as Max goes home. There shouldn't be much delay in their leaving. According to Max he usually parks his side-by-side and checks in on Little Whiskey. Then they get in the truck and leave."

Tommy just nodded so Manny went on. "The abandoned mill is off a side road on the other side of Lake Placid. It should take them about twenty minutes to get there and park the truck. Then, according to Max, it doesn't take long for them to do their thing. Although Jasper has him fully embodied so for most of that part there's no memory. They just walk in and find an isolated victim. There's no struggle, as once the victim looks into the vampire's eyes they become helpless and inviting. Jasper uses Max to carry the body however far it is back to the pickup, and they drive back to Peckerneck Mountain."

Manny paused for a sip of wine. "The whole thing should take about an hour. Figure them back at Peckerneck around eleven-thirty. From there it's not far through the dark woods with the side-by-side to your location. If we get you to our friends before ten-fifteen you should have plenty of time to be in place and ready. Just be sure to have the crossbow loaded and ready. Your shooting window will likely only be a few seconds long at the most."

They all stared at their food. The silence that occurred every time there was a break in the conversation was a telling sign of their mission's foreboding nature.

Manny finally broke the silence again. "I will be with Toni, in my car but with her ready to drive if the need should arise. Max says he usually leaves his cell phone at home on these missions as it would make it harder for authorities to pin him at any particular time or location should he ever become a suspect. But I have a GPS tracker on his truck. And I've inserted a listening bug into the bill of his engineer's cap. He usually talks out loud when speaking to Jasper. Of course, I'll only be able to hear what Max is saying. And he won't remember our plan due to the witch's spell, so he won't be dropping any info on purpose. Hopefully, it will be enough, and this plan will go just how we're drawing it up. But while I can't imagine any scenario that will play out differently, we need to be ready for anything. It's our only chance to get rid of this monster."

More silence followed until Manny asked Tommy, "I guess I should have asked this earlier. We bought Bianca some dark clothing to wear while shopping yesterday. Do you have any dark clothes?"

Tommy nodded. "I've got a dark green hoodie in our room. It's a warm night but it's a lightweight one, so I'll be fine."

It seemed everything was as in place as it could be. Nothing to do but pick at their food in ominous silence and wait.

✽ ✽ ✽ ✽ ✽

Max gave Candy's Carriage and the caboose one last inspection. The fire was lit and the boiler was up to pressure. Any minute a shuttle carrying a newly elected mayor and six of his or her closest friends would show up for the fifteen-minute re-enactment of the historic run made back in 1970 – minus the snow, of course.

Little Whiskey followed him as he circled the back end of the caboose. Max picked him up and said, "Sorry, little one. You don't get to go on this trip. I know you don't get along with Jasper, and I don't blame you. But he's coming and there ain't nothing I can do to stop him. So into the house you go."

As Max walked toward the house Little Whiskey began to whine. He loved the train rides. He didn't like the steam whistle, but he loved the rides. He clearly didn't understand why he was to be left behind.

Max felt bad too. He was almost in tears as he apologized again before shutting the door, leaving his dog to howl in his high-pitched bark. Dealing with Jasper had turned a supposedly fun event into a distasteful chore that Max had no way of avoiding. He almost felt glad his disease meant the upcoming run would be his last one.

He heard the hooting and hollering before the headlights

came through the trees. A pickup truck carrying seven young males came into view. They jumped out before it stopped, ran over to the train, and started snapping selfies while acting like a bunch of kids. Which, as far as Max was concerned, they were. Each wore a different-colored Hero Of '70 shirt tee shirt.

But it was all good. Max was happy for them and the fact they had found something to celebrate in their local history. He put on his best face and greeted them all. Handshakes and selfies all around while the shuttle driver turned around and returned to the party. Then, with a grand gesture of checking his old, gold railroad watch, Max announced, "All aboard the Peckerneck Mountain, Ferro and Ray Brook limited! Next stop, Ferro!"

He shook his head and laughed as the seven young men scrambled, pushed, shoved, and made their way into the caboose. He climbed into the cab of the little locomotive and checked the boiler pressure. Just before he put the old girl into motion, he heard the, unfortunately, familiar voice.

HELLO MAX. LET'S GO FOR A RIDE, SHALL WE?

"Jasper," Max said out loud. Being separated from the passengers and the noise of the locomotive eliminated any chance of him being overheard. "Where ya been? I was starting to wonder if you were sitting this one out."

NOT A CHANCE. COME ON, BLOW THE WHISTLE!

Jasper was acting like a kid too. It was out of character, but Max noticed it every time they made the run. He supposed it had to do with Jasper having once been human and only being able to enjoy human things. Also, having ceased being human at a very young age over fifty years ago, memories of Jasper's past while he was alive would be limited compared to an old fart like himself. So Max tried to understand and took it all in stride.

237

And it was time to blow the whistle anyway, to let the folks in Ferro know they were on the way. He reached up, pulled the chain, and let out a pair of blasts. The old brass whistle came to life. WHHAAAHOOOO! WHAAHOOOO! The pitch was higher than the air horns of modern-day trains. But there was an underlying depth to the sound that no doubt could be heard for miles around.

The passengers in the caboose hooted and hollered, and started chanting something. But there was too much noise and other things going on for Max to be able to make it out. Meanwhile, Jasper laughed and carried on – so unlike his normal personality.

YEAH! YEAH! WOOT! WOOT! DO IT AGAIN! DO IT AGAIN!

Max shook his head. "I can't blow the whistle all the way there. This old boiler can only take so much pressure, and I'm running it on the low side as it is. We're only going about two miles per hour, but I can't be running all the steam through the whistle. We'd never make it to Ferro on time."

OH, WHATEVER. PARTY POOPER.

The scenery slowly changed in the darkening night, from the open area near Max's house to a tunnel of old-growth pine trees.

CAN'T YOU MAKE THIS THING GO ANY FASTER? COME ON, WE'RE GOING TO BE LATE FOR THE PARTY. CASEY JONES IS ROLLING OVER IN HIS GRAVE.

"I've been running this train for over sixty years, and we're right on time." Max took his watch out and gave it a quick look for effect.

LAME. COME ON, BLOW THE WHISTLE AGAIN. Jasper, sounding out of character. Lost in his remembrance of human youth.

Max shook his head. "Hold your horses."

The banter went like that for the next fifteen minutes. Jasper bugged him for the whistle, and Max occasionally acquiesced. All while the passengers hooted, hollered, and posed for pictures of each other hanging out the windows.

Eventually, the tree tunnel opened up and the depot-turned-cabaret came into view. It looked to Max like a record crowd again. The event was growing as word spread from year to year. That pleased Max and he smiled, wondering if the tradition would continue without him. As the train approached the station, he let out three long blasts. He could almost picture Jasper jumping up and down with joy inside his head.

The passengers – celebrities on this night – jumped off even as Max brought the train to a stop. He immediately turned off the fuel to the firebox, then placed a few padlocks on certain levers to keep any crazy kids from trying to take a joy ride in the middle of the night.

COME ON, MAX. GIVE US ONE MORE BLAST.

With no more reason to conserve steam pressure, Max gave the standard crossing signal blasts. Two long blasts followed by a short one, then another long one. Jasper cackled like a kid on a roller coaster while the mass outside scrambled to get a video of the steam rolling out of the whistle. Max shook his head at the thought of how different things would be before long. Soon enough the little kid inside his head would revert to his evil self.

The ride was over. Max turned to exit the cab, pausing first so everyone could take a photo of the Hero of '70. He smiled and waved while Jasper spoke inside his head.

OKAY, HERO. THANKS FOR THE TRIP DOWN MEMORY LANE. I'LL BE BACK LATER. DON'T BE HERE TOO LONG SOAKING UP ALL THIS ADORNMENT.

Max felt Jasper's exit before he could respond. He stepped down and began the task of shaking hands and posing for pictures with hundreds of people – many of them strangers. Going about the business of carrying on the new tradition. Secretly, he hoped to get it over with so he could get through the night's ugly business and have it behind him.

CHAPTER 26

The foursome rode in Manny's car, with Toni driving, as Manny hated driving at night. Tommy, sitting in the back with Bianca, got on his cell phone to check the map. He needed to wrap his head around where they were going. They were on a two-lane road that seemed to bypass Lake Placid. Entering the words Ferro and Averyville into the directions field, he saw they were traveling about ten miles but just completing most of a big circle – ending up south of Scarface Mountain but on the opposite side from where they started.

Nobody said much. Toni turned down another road that led them to Averyville, which didn't seem to Tommy to be much of a town. More of a dead-end collection of cabins and houses and trails that would be perfect for anybody wanting to get away from it all. It was hard to get a feel for anything in the darkness. He decided it didn't matter as they wouldn't be there long. Toni followed Manny's instructions until they drove down a long driveway. When they reached a beautiful log cabin Manny instructed Toni to keep going past it, down a much less used driveway that disappeared into the darkness of tall pine trees.

Eventually, they came to an area where there was room to turn around. There they saw a small boat on a trailer connected to

241

an ATV. Tommy wasn't up on his boats. He knew it wasn't a canoe. He thought maybe it was called a guide boat, but then decided that was probably wrong too. Of course, it didn't matter. A plain-looking man with a brush cut who appeared to be about Tommy's age and wearing camouflage leaned against the seat of the four-wheeler.

They exited the car and Manny greeted the man. Then he turned and made a brief, group introduction to the rest, identifying the man only as Daniel. Daniel didn't say anything. He just waited by the four-wheeler while the group said their goodbyes.

Toni gave Tommy the hardest hug he'd ever received from her. She shook her head and said, "I still think it's bullshit that I don't get to go with you."

Before Tommy could try assuaging her, she added, "But yeah, I get it. The oracle and all that shit. But I don't have to like it."

There wasn't time for much else. Manny moved everyone along. With another hug and a long kiss, Toni finally pulled herself away from Tommy, saying, "I hope you get the bastard. But no matter what, you make sure you come back to me."

It was a hard goodbye. But it was too late to turn back, and everybody knew it was less than a once-in-a-lifetime chance to rid the world of the evil that was Jasper Czymiak. But a chance they had to take. So they forced themselves apart. The man named Daniel seemed to understand as, after they all said their goodbyes, Tommy watched until the taillights were out of sight. As soon as they were gone, Daniel was all business.

In the darkness left behind, he motioned to the boat on the trailer. It was small, with two bench seats. The way it was built, there didn't seem to be a front or a back. There were two loose paddles and nothing else. It took a minute for Tommy and Bianca to realize those two seats were where they were supposed to ride.

Daniel helped Bianca up into the boat seat toward the rear and Tommy climbed into the other, placing the duffel bag and crossbow in the space between. Then without much fanfare, Daniel started the four-wheeler and drove down the narrow path, into the darkness.

Tommy noticed Daniel didn't use the headlights. They seemed to be in the middle of nowhere, but the fact that Daniel was being so cautious made him wonder just how much he knew about what they were doing.

Bianca finally spoke. "This is not how I usually spend my Saturday nights. You sure are a fun date, Tommy Chandler."

Her candid tone and the extreme nature of what they were doing rained down on them and they laughed at themselves – nervously. Riding in a boat on a trailer through the woods in the middle of nowhere to go kill a spirit vampire by shooting a wooden dart into a warm, living, and kind human being, certainly wasn't a typical Saturday night date.

Their laughter drew a puzzled look from Daniel. But he didn't say anything, and the ride was over quickly. They found themselves at a clearing where Daniel made a turn and backed the trailer down into the water. Bianca and the "front" of the boat began to float. She let out a startled yelp, then covered her mouth as though she realized she shouldn't be making any noise.

Daniel set the brake and made his way back to them. As he untied the knot – the last link to anything that resembled normalcy in their world, Tommy thought – he said to them, "I'm hoping you both know how to swim 'cause there ain't any life jackets. But it's only about three feet deep at the most. The current is slow here but will pick up right before you get where you're going. When you find the current increasing as you go around a large bend to the right, make your way to the far side as your destination will be right on that bend."

As Daniel pushed the boat the rest of the way into the water, Tommy, the cop, couldn't help but ask, "Aren't you curious what we're doing? Or do you already know?"

Daniel stopped pushing for a moment. "Curious? Hell yeah. But I'm a member of Monkey Beans and I know what we do. And for right now, no. Maybe someday you or Manny or somebody will tell me all about it. But right now I don't want to know anything more about what you guys are up to. I was asked to do Monkey Beans a special favor and here I am. I wish you all the best. But right now I want to finish this and get back to my fireplace and a good book."

Tommy gave an understanding shrug. "Well, thanks for the ride."

As Daniel gave the final push and they floated away, he added, "I'll say a prayer for you though. Godspeed."

Then they were on their own. Two souls dressed in dark hoodies, floating into the darkness. Tommy grabbed a paddle and handed it to Bianca, who was facing him instead of downstream. She took the paddle and shifted herself around. Then they both helped themselves move with the current.

It was dark. The stream cut a swath through an old-growth forest of tall pine trees. There were stars aplenty but only a quarter moon. And because of its angle, they were in it's shadow too.

There didn't seem to be much to talk about, so they paddled downstream in silence. After about a quarter-mile they suddenly heard voices. Bianca looked back to Tommy, who gave her a puzzled look. As they rounded another winding bend, they saw flickers of light on the trees on the bank. The voices grew louder and they realized they were approaching a small group of young people and a campfire. Tommy wondered where they came from and decided they probably weren't quite as far into the middle of nowhere as he thought.

He also knew the last thing they needed was to be seen by anyone who could identify them. The cop in Tommy kept seeing scenarios of Max becoming a missing person. An abandoned boat eventually turns up downstream from Max's house, followed by a group of kids telling the police, "Oh yeah, we saw that boat go floating by us that night. There was a gray-haired man and a red-head about half his age."

Maybe he was overreacting, but many crimes had been solved by small bits of information being pieced together. Before they floated into view, he acted quickly. He moved up onto the forward seat, sitting next to Bianca but facing the opposite way, like on an old-fashioned loveseat.

He quickly took Bianca's ponytail and stuffed it down the back of her sweatshirt. Then pulled up both hoods to hide their hair color. As they floated into view of the campers, he turned his head to hide his face, then wrapped his arms around Bianca and laid his lips onto hers – hoping to give the impression of a young couple in love, just out for a midnight float.

It seemed to work, as one of the voices by the fire suddenly said, "Hey, check this out."

There was laughter from about four people. Bianca showed she was all in on the act by opening her lips and slipping her tongue into Tommy's mouth. He was caught off guard, but managed not to break his cover even though the moments it took to float by seemed to take forever.

It was working though. As they slowly moved past the group, one of the young men called out, "Yeah, give it to her, Buddy! You know she wants it."

That was followed by a girl's voice and what sounded like a slap. "Shut up, Joey!"

Tommy gave a wave to indicate he'd heard the kid but wasn't interested in breaking away from his embrace. As they floated out of sight, the one called Joey, still speaking loudly enough for them to hear, asked, "Hey, do you know how drinking light beer is the same as making love in a canoe?"

"No, how?" Another man from the party asked, also a little extra loud so the couple could hear the joke.

Joey answered, "They're both fuckin' near water!"

More laughter followed, then the girl's voice again. "You asshole."

Tommy and Bianca both laughed as Tommy snuck a peek to make sure they were out of sight. They were, and he quickly returned to his own seat, not saying a word. Still, he admitted, Bianca was a huggable, kissable package – and smelled nice too.

She looked back over her shoulder. "And so, the one-of-a-kind Saturday night date takes a turn."

He felt like she was laughing at him, and she probably was.

"Oh shut up and get paddling. I only did what I had to do."

"You sure did," she said softly, still laughing.

Tommy tried not to dwell on it. But a little of whatever she was wearing had rubbed off on him and lingered with every breath. He would have some explaining to do to his wife, no doubt. But he figured if he could nail the – as Toni liked to put it, son of a bitch who killed George – she would likely forgive him no matter what he did. Not that he was going to do anything, he reminded himself. Besides, they had bigger fish to fry.

A few minutes later, just as Daniel described, through the shadows they saw a large bend to the right, and the current started picking up. They both paddled in silence to get the boat to the far side. Sure enough, as they came to the middle of the bend, through the darkness they could make out a tiny shack that stood opposite a point that jutted out into the stream, just as it had all been described.

They pointed the little boat to shore, paddling faster to keep up with the current trying to drag them away. When the boat hit the shore Bianca jumped out and tried pulling it onto land, but with Tommy still in it, it was too much for her. Seeing her struggle, he jumped ship and went into water well over his knees. Together they pulled the boat out of the water.

As they dragged it behind the shack, Bianca drawled, "Y'all call this a creek around here? Where I come from this would be a river."

Tommy didn't respond. He just finished moving the boat out of sight. While it looked like it was made of wood, it was much lighter – made of some newfangled material. The folks at Monkey Beans paid attention to detail. That fact was reinforced as they entered the small shack. It was an old building, probably built around a hundred years before. But the roof was in good shape, and the inside had been kept dry. A quick check with the flashlights Manny provided showed it had been thoroughly swept for spiders, etc., just as Manny had said it would be.

The window facing the opposite bank was open. There was a bar stool and a small bench where he could rest the crossbow while shooting. Monkey beans had readied the place in anticipation of their arrival.

Tommy gestured at the lone bar stool. "Have a seat."

Bianca shook her head. "No. You are the heart and soul of this mission." She pointed to the duffel bag on the floor. "You need to get that thing loaded and in place on the bench in front of you, then sit your ass on that stool and be ready. You don't want to have to go back and say we screwed this mission up because you were being chivalrous, do you?"

She made a good point. Tommy took the crossbow from the bag and went through the process of getting the string pulled back and nocking a bolt. He set it on the bench facing out the window and adjusted the stool so he would be in position to shoot.

Then they were alone in the darkness. Bianca pulled her phone from her pocket.

"What are you doing?"

"Checking the time and texting Manny that we're in place and ready"

"What time is it?"

"Eleven ten," she said.

That seemed about right and Tommy nodded. Manny sent a text back. Bianca read it and responded. Then she said, "Max is through Lake Placid and almost to the abandoned sawmill where they should finish their business and make their way here. We have a while to kill. What would you like to do?"

She ended that with a suggestive laugh. Tommy caught the innuendo but hoped she was just teasing.

To make himself clear he said, "We're going to sit right here and be ready, just like you said a few minutes ago."

CHAPTER 27

Max slowed down as he and Jasper approached the driveway to the abandoned sawmill. But Jasper surprised him.

KEEP GOING. WE'RE NOT GOING TO THE SAWMILL TONIGHT.

Max hesitated, but he knew arguing with Jasper was a bad idea. So he drove on by.

"Okay. But what's up with that? And where are we going instead?"

JUST DRIVE. I'LL TELL YOU WHERE TO GO.

Max kept driving east on Route 86 for about another mile. The road was deserted, but then a driveway appeared on the left.

TURN IN HERE.

Max did as he was told and pulled the old truck into the driveway. It turned out to be a long driveway that disappeared into the woods. Max's curiosity got the best of him. "So what's up? Why the change?"

BECAUSE I'M ONTO YOUR PLAN. YOU AND YOUR RIGHTEOUS FRIENDS THINK YOU CAN LAY A TRAP FOR ME. THEREFORE, INSTEAD OF TAKING WHAT YOU ALL CONSIDER TO BE A LOWLY HOMELESS PERSON TONIGHT, WE'RE GOING TO GET OURSELVES A FAMOUS AUTHOR FROM VERMONT, WHO HAPPENS TO BE STAYING

IN A BED AND BREAKFAST ROOM HERE WHILE SHE WORKS ON HER NEXT BOOK. MAYBE A HIGHER PROFILE PERSON OF SOME WORTH WILL REMIND YOU ALL THAT, WHILE I'M NOT THE MONSTER YOU THINK I AM, I CERTAINLY CAN BE. AND YOU ARE ALL FOOLS TO BELIEVE YOU CAN STOP ME. WHEN THIS FAMOUS PERSON COMES UP MISSING, YOU CAN ALL BE REMINDED FOR THE REST OF YOUR LIVES THAT YOU WERE A PART OF IT. IT'S YOUR FAULT AS MUCH AS ANYONE'S. AND IT WON'T BE SO EASY FOR YOU ALL TO FORGET ABOUT HER AS JUST ANOTHER VICTIM OF MINE.

Because of Saavi's spell, Max had no idea what Jasper was talking about. "What the Hell are you going on about? What righteous friends? What trap? Have you been taking drugs or something?"

Jasper sighed. Max didn't remember ever hearing him do that, and it seemed odd.

I KNOW, I KNOW. YOU'RE RIGHT, OF COURSE. YOU DON'T KNOW WHAT I'M TALKING ABOUT. I'LL FILL YOU IN LATER. BUT FIRST, WE HAVE WORK TO DO.

* * * * *

When Max regained consciousness he was standing at the back of his old pickup truck. In the darkness was the outline of a pretty, dark-haired woman, probably in her thirties, that Jasper and he had just killed and loaded into the truck. Without being told, Max closed the tailgate and got behind the wheel.

DRIVE.

Sure. I'll have us home in no time. But what the heck was all

250

that nonsense you were going on about? He turned the truck around.

WELL, IT SEEMS YOU HAVE BEEN UP TO NO GOOD. UPON YOUR REQUEST, YOUR FRIEND MANFRED CONSPIRED WITH A MISERABLE WHORE OF A WITCH DOWN IN THE CATSKILLS, WHO HAS PUT A SPELL ON YOU SO YOU WOULDN'T REMEMBER ANYTHING. YOU SMARTLY DIDN'T WANT TO TIP YOUR HAND, ACCIDENTALLY INFORMING ME OF YOUR PLAN JUST BY THINKING OF IT. BUT REST ASSURED, WHEN WE GET TO THE SPOT ON THE STREAM WHERE WE USUALLY DISPOSE OF THE BODY, YOU AND MANFRED AND HIS OTHER FRIENDS HAVE CONSPIRED TO LAY A TRAP TO SHOOT ME – BY SHOOTING YOU – THROUGH THE HEART, WITH A WOODEN CROSSBOW BOLT. I KNOW IT ALL PROBABLY SEEMS INCREDIBLE SINCE YOU HAVE NO MEMORY OF IT. BUT I LEARNED OF YOUR TREACHERY LAST WEEK WHEN WE TOOK THAT COLLEGE BOY. THE SPELL WASN'T ON YOU YET, AND YOU COULDN'T HELP THINKING ABOUT IT.

Max was dumbfounded. He had no idea what Jasper was talking about. Yet he knew not to argue too much. He wondered if maybe the fiend was suffering from some kind of inter-dimensional dementia. Everything Jasper said sounded nonsensical – as though the evil spirit was metaphysically discombobulated. He shook his head as he drove out to the end of the long driveway.

ANYWAY, ALL YOU NEED TO KNOW FOR NOW IS THAT WE ARE NOT GOING BACK TO YOUR HOUSE. I HAVE A GOOD MIND TO JUST LEAVE THE BODY HERE, BUT I'VE DECIDED THAT SINCE WE BOTH KNOW YOU'RE NOT GOING TO BE AROUND THIS TIME NEXT YEAR, I'M GOING TO BE USING YOU A FEW MORE TIMES BEFORE THEN. AND A MISSING BODY, EVEN IF IT TURNS UP LATER, WILL AT LEAST DELAY ANY INVESTIGATIONS AND PUT YOU FURTHER IN

THE CLEAR IF ANYTHING GOES WRONG. HAVING YOU LOCKED UP DOESN'T DO ME ANY GOOD. I ALREADY HAD ONE OF THOSE THIS WEEK. I'M GIVING YOU THE BENEFIT OF HELPING TO DISPOSE OF THE BODY, EVEN THOUGH I'M UPSET AND DISAPPOINTED WITH YOU AND YOUR PLAN TO TRY TO ELIMINATE ME. SHAME ON YOU, MAX.

Max was still lost. Jasper was usually straightforward even while being cocky and condescending. It sounded to Max like he was just spouting gibberish. But without much choice, he asked, "So where to, then?"

I DON'T FEEL MUCH LIKE SPENDING MY NEWLY ACQUIRED ENERGY HELPING YOU. SO I THINK A NICE, QUICK DUMP OFF THE ROUTE 3 BRIDGE WILL SUFFICE. IT'S MORE THAN I SHOULD DO FOR YOU, CONSIDERING WHAT YOU'VE TRIED TO DO TO ME. BUT BELIEVE ME, YOU'LL BE PAYING FOR IT.

Still confused, all Max knew was the last time they dumped a body off that bridge it showed up later in a lock downstream in the river system. "That plan didn't work all that well the last time. Remember the body showed up a few days later?"

IT WILL BE FINE. EVEN IF THE BODY SHOWS UP LATER, ALL ANYONE WILL KNOW IS HER DOOR GOT KICKED IN AND SHE DISAPPEARED. THEY WON'T HAVE ANY IDEA HOW SHE GOT THERE. YOU DON'T HAVE YOUR CELL PHONE AND THIS OLD TRUCK DOESN'T HAVE GPS. SO UNLESS SOMEBODY SEES YOU, NOTHING SHOULD EVER POINT TO YOU. THAT'S ALL THAT'S IMPORTANT. WELL, THAT AND THE FACT YOUR FRIENDS LYING IN WAIT WILL JUST BE SITTING IN THE DARKNESS WAITING FOR US TO SHOW UP. THE JOKE'S ON THEM NOW. THE BEST OF THE IRONY IS, THOUGH, THE REASON THAT THIS WOMAN'S BED AND BREAKFAST HOSTS WEREN'T HOME TONIGHT IS BECAUSE THEY ARE ATTENDING

YOUR HERO'S BASH. THEY PROBABLY EVEN HAD THEIR PICTURE TAKEN WITH YOU.

Jasper actually laughed. Other than during their train rides Max couldn't remember ever hearing that. He shook his head and turned right onto Route 86, heading back toward Saranac Lake to pick up Route 3. "Whatever you say, Jasper. Even if I don't understand most of it."

JUST DRIVE. LET'S GET THIS OVER WITH. I'M SUPPOSED TO BE HAVING A NAP BY NOW.

CHAPTER 28

Tommy sat on the stool and looked out the window. Bianca moved to stand next to him, at his side. Though the shack was so small, anywhere she stood would still be next to him. After a few minutes of silence, she put her hand on his thigh.

"Don't do that, please."

"Why? Don't you like it?" Again, teasing.

"Of course I like it. That's why. I'm a happily married man, and this is hardly the time for any distractions."

Bianca removed her hand and gave an exaggerated sigh. After a few more agonizing minutes, sitting next to the woman who just radiated sexuality, he wondered if she was just teasing, or if she would seriously let things escalate if he decided to go there. She surprised him with her next comment.

"I'm scared too, you know."

That caught Tommy off guard, but as he thought about it, of course she was scared. He was too. What they were doing was hardly normal. And the monster they were after had no qualms about killing thousands of people. It was a dangerous mission they were on, and she had every right to be scared.

He let out a sigh of his own and looked up at her as she looked into his eyes. Yes, there was a fear there which they both shared. He reached his arm around her and pulled her close. But it was different. It was a platonic hug they both needed. Of course, with him sitting and her standing, Tommy naturally got a face full of boobs.

That fact wasn't lost on either of them and they laughed. It was a sign they were in it together and determined to be successful. And neither would let that be ruined by petty distractions. Waiting in the darkness became much easier.

But as the minutes passed, the inaction gave them time to think. Tommy began to dwell on what they were doing. It had all been rationalized to make sense, and seem like they were doing the right thing. But the longer they sat the more ominous it became. He suddenly realized he was breathing hard and shaking. He'd never had a panic attack and wondered if that's what it was.

He started shaking way too much to be able to fire off an accurate shot when the time came. Worrying about that made things worse, and it piled up on him. Bianca saw what was happening and moved behind him. She calmly grabbed his shoulder and neck muscles and gently massaged them.

Speaking softly, almost purring. "You're okay. You got this. We got this. It will all be over soon. And it's all okay. It's what Max wants and it's what the world needs. We know it. You're fine. Just close your eyes and breathe slowly with me."

She made a point to take slow, deep, gentle breaths. Tommy didn't respond right away. But eventually, as he listened to her soft voice, it began to work. And the massage was divine. Tommy loved his wife, but one thing about her massages, every time she tried it felt like she was using chicken bones. Some people just weren't made for certain things. And Toni wasn't made for muscle-relaxing massages.

Bianca, on the other hand, was a master, and Tommy didn't complain. Nor was he surprised. Everything about Bianca oozed success. He finally calmed down and got back to business. "They should be on the way by now. I wonder why Manny hasn't texted an update."

As if on cue, Tommy's phone vibrated. It was an incoming call from Manny, which was odd because he had said earlier that one big reason for sending Bianca was so he could communicate through her and not tie him up. He decided it must be important, so he put on the speakerphone and answered.

"Yeah, what's up?"

"Tommy, there's a change of plans. I don't know much because I can only hear Max's side of their conversation. But the bottom line is they're not coming to your location."

Tommy hesitated, not sure what that meant they should do. He looked at Bianca who shrugged.

Before he could think of a response, Manny started in again. "We're now looking at a longer shot than the long shot we had before. But my best guess is they're heading for the bridge on Route 3, west of Saranac Lake, where they dumped a body a few years ago. I'm not sure how or why, but if there's any chance in Hell of this plan ever working, it depends on you getting there first and somehow, some way, finding a place to hide and get off a shot when they stop. It's probably just a last desperate thread of hope. But as long as it's still a thread and you're still all in, you've got to get to the little picnic area that's down the hill behind Dirty Butt's. A trail leads up from there to the back of the parking lot. Haul your asses downstream to that spot, get to your car, and try to get out on Route 3 before Max does. It's our only chance."

Bianca didn't need to be told twice. She was already moving

to get the boat back in the water. But Tommy had questions.

"I don't have a car, we came in a motorhome. We'll have to take your car when we get back."

"No!" Manny screamed. "We have to go out on the road now and try to find a way to slow them down so you can get there first. You'll have to take Bianca's car. But if there's any chance left at all you've got to move. NOW!"

Tommy decided he was still all in and said, "Okay we're on our way." Before disconnecting he added, "Be careful out there, you've got my wife with you!" But he wasn't sure if Manny heard it.

He unhooked the crossbow bolt from the string and placed it back in the quiver. He left the string drawn back. Not the best protocol, but he figured they'd be in a hurry to get reloaded. He checked to make sure the safety was on, then stuffed the crossbow into the bag with the string still drawn. Bianca already had the boat headed into the water as he exited the shack. She jumped into her front seat as Tommy tossed the duffel bag in, then gave a final shove before jumping in. And they were off.

The current was stronger than before, and they paddled for all they were worth. It was only about another half-mile – or as Manny put it – eight or nine football fields. Going downstream with adrenaline pumping, they covered the distance quickly. They weren't sure what they were looking for, but soon enough they heard the sounds of the Hero bash going on up the hill, and in the dim light they could see a little picnic area on the bank.

They jumped ashore and Tommy shoved the small boat back into the current where it floated away. As late as it was, the picnic area was deserted. Everybody in town was up at the celebration. They were glad the path was fairly smooth, and running up the hill didn't result in any broken ankles. As they reached the top of the hill the woods opened up. They skirted the party by going around to the left towards the parking lot.

Tommy, breathing heavily as he was no spring chicken, said through his huffs, "We have to take your car, I'm in a motorhome."

Bianca turned and ran toward the conference center. "I gotta grab the keys. Red Mustang."

Tommy went through the small park to the parking lot which was shared with the conference center, and found the red Mustang. He set the duffel bag down and rested as he caught his breath. After only a minute he saw Bianca running across the lot, but toward the far end from his location. He saw the lights of her red Mustang light up as she hit the unlock button.

"Shit!" He realized he was leaning against the wrong car and took off. By the time he got there, Bianca was in the driver's seat with the engine running. Tommy jumped in the passenger seat with the duffel bag in his lap. They were moving before he closed the door.

Also panting, Bianca asked, "Where the Hell is Route 3?"

"It's the way Toni and I came into town. Go left on the main road," Tommy said between huffs and puffs. "We take 86 into Saranac Lake and pick it up there."

When they turned left onto 86 they were still in Ray Brook and the speed limit was only 40. Tommy cautioned Bianca not to go too fast because getting pulled over would suck. She pushed it anyway and they made it into the village in a few minutes.

Manny called again. Tommy answered, "Yeah."

"We just spotted Max outside of Lake Placid, heading your way. We'll try to get in front and slow him down, but we don't want to be too obvious or cause an accident. The last thing we need is for Jasper to just up and leave Max with a body in his truck. Where are you?"

"We just turned onto Route 3, and if we can catch the lights we'll be headed out of town soon."

"At least you're in front of them and have a little space. Give it all you got. I don't know how you can, but it all depends on you getting there before Max and finding a place to shoot."

"Understood. Hold him up as best you can. But be careful, you've got my wife with you."

"Will do. Godspeed to both of you."

They did catch a light and they began to head out of the village as Tommy disconnected. It was getting late and traffic was light. As soon as they saw the sign for 55 miles per hour Bianca put her foot to the floor. Tommy pleaded with her to slow down. She did, but only a little. And sure enough, about a mile outside of town the vehicle coming the opposite way hit its brakes and made a U turn.

"Oh, Piss!" Bianca looked at Tommy who closed his eyes in frustration. The cop lights came on and they pulled over. Bianca put the window down while the Franklin County deputy – a veteran with gray hair and a wrinkled face – slowly approached them.

"All the way from Texas just to speed through my town? License and registration papers, please. And proof of insurance too."

"I'm sorry officer," Bianca said as she searched for the documents.

"It's deputy, not officer. But good-lookin' girls get a pass."

Before he could say anything else, Tommy had his wallet and badge out, saying, "We're sorry, deputy. We just got carried away. I wonder if I could get a courtesy?"

The old timer lowered his head and looked in at Tommy, then at his badge. "Genesee County Investigator? Damn, you came all the way across the state to meet up with this pretty little thing from Texas. Well, can't say I blame you."

Tommy decided to roll with it. "Yeah, we just spent the day acting like a couple of tourists in Lake Placid. Now we're heading back to our room in Tupper Lake and got a little excited." He put his hand on Bianca's thigh and stroked it, hoping the deputy would fall for it."

The deputy let out a laugh. "And she's only half your age." He put his palms up and said, "But I don't want to know anything more. Be safe." Then to Bianca, he added, "Slow down. I've got a reputation to uphold in these parts."

Without another word, he turned and walked back to his cruiser. Bianca waited until he killed the emergency lights before pulling away. The deputy did another U-turn and as soon as his tail lights were out of sight, she floored the pedal again just as a pair of headlights appeared behind them, in the distance. This time Tommy didn't bother to try to slow her down. They were lucky. They were still in front of Max. But those lights could very well be him. He pulled out his phone and called Manny, who didn't bother with pleasantries.

"Please tell me you're on the bridge and in place."

"Not quite. We had an incident. But we're back on the road so we should be there soon."

"Your wife is a hell of a driver, and we did manage to slow Max down. But he's already outside of town and we're breaking off. We've done all we can do. Give it all the Hell you can."

As Manny said that, Tommy saw a green light in the distance. Manny was about to say goodbye but Tommy said, "Hey we might have caught a break. I remember this bridge now from our drive into town earlier. It's under construction and down to a single lane, with an automated traffic light at each end. And the construction lane has all sorts of equipment on it. If we can get there in time, we might still have a shot at this. Keep your fingers crossed."

Before Manny hung up, Tommy heard Toni yell, "I love you."

He echoed her comment but doubted it got through.

At the speed they were traveling, they reached the bridge in no time. But the light changed to red and Bianca hit the brakes.

"Go," Tommy said.

"But what if there's a cop hiding and watching?"

"If there is we're screwed anyway. And I sure as Hell don't want him to see us doing what we're about to do. So let's hope there isn't one. Go."

Bianca ran the light.

The bridge wasn't very long – only about a hundred feet. The section of the river it crossed was just a narrow spot where the water flowed from one small lake to another. Just as Tommy remembered, there were various pieces of construction equipment placed in the closed lane.

As they crossed over Tommy pointed and said, "There."

Just past the bridge was a ramp through some trees that led down to an area where fishermen could set up and small boats could launch. As Bianca turned, Tommy looked back and saw the headlights behind them drop just out of sight, into a small dip. Hopefully, luck was with them, and Max wouldn't see them pulling off.

The space was deserted. Bianca killed the lights and they got out. Tommy grabbed the crossbow out of the bag and nocked a bolt on the already cocked string. Then they ran up the ramp, hoping to get onto the bridge before Max. As they neared the top they saw Max's old Chevy approaching. But for him the light was green, and they weren't going to make it. His truck slowed down as it approached the single lane. They ducked behind the last of the trees to stay out of sight, even though there was almost no moonlight. Then they watched in surprise as Max kept driving across the bridge without stopping. He went by and sped up as though the bridge wasn't his destination after all.

They looked at each other in wonder, but quickly realized another vehicle was coming from the other direction. Max kept going because he didn't want to be seen stopping on the bridge. They stayed hidden while the approaching car waited for the light to turn green. As soon as it did and the car drove off, they made their way onto the bridge.

Though it wasn't quite halfway, there was a large generator, or air compressor, or something that was on wheels. They crossed over the temporary concrete barrier and carefully stepped down onto the construction lane. As they did they saw headlights coming. Max had turned around and was on his way back.

The construction side of the bridge was a gridiron of reinforcement steel bars. The pair had to be careful in the darkness. Stepping between the bars was possible, but a broken ankle was just a trip and fall away. They managed to get behind the compressor in time, and it turned out to be just the right height for Tommy to stand behind while resting the crossbow on the flat top. It even had a large exhaust pipe that he could get behind. It didn't completely hide him but would break up his profile in the darkness if Max decided to look his way. The quarter moon slipped behind a cloud and it became even darker.

It seemed the whole thing was coming together after all. Bianca got behind Tommy and put those reassuring hands on his shoulders. She seemed to know it was what he needed, and he was grateful. His heart still raced in anticipation, but her soft hands kept him calm enough.

They stayed motionless as Max's truck approached. The light was red, but with no traffic, Max must have decided the time was right. He ignored the light, drove out to the middle of the bridge, and stopped. Not wasting any time, Max exited the cab, walked to the back, and dropped the tailgate.

They were less than twenty yards away, and Tommy felt confident if he could get the right shot he couldn't miss.

Then Bianca whispered, "He's here."

That meant Jasper was there and the mission was a go. Although she needn't have bothered, the red glow in Max's eyes was a loud and clear display of Jasper's embodiment.

Tommy trained the scope on Max and suddenly realized he hadn't switched on the night vision. But the scope was high quality and gathered what little light there was. Being so close, he wasn't worried about missing – but didn't want to make any unnecessary movements. He remained still, with the unlit scope trained on JasperMax.

They watched in horror as he pulled out a large knife and matter-of-factly stabbed the corpse's abdomen several times. He had previously mentioned doing that to help keep the body from floating. Tommy felt Bianca's fingers clasp his shoulder muscles, obviously not prepared for that either. Then it got worse, as JasperMax used the knife to mutilate the corpse's neck – destroying any evidence of vampire activity. If discovered, all anybody would find was a mutilated body full of holes and no blood.

264

He grabbed the corpse and turned away to throw it off on the downstream side, away from them. Tommy let his training kick in. He took in a full breath and let it halfway out, allowing him to hold steady without any chest movements affecting his aim. He fixed the crosshairs on the back of Max's chest. Front or back didn't matter, as long as he hit the heart. But before he could get a shot off, Max's body twisted sideways as the Jasper embodiment allowed him to throw the body an unbelievable distance. Still, he held the scope steady, ignoring the loud splash, waiting for his chance.

Then JasperMax surprised him. He turned to face Tommy and Bianca. It happened quickly, but Tommy still had time to think about the oracle, and how it was just as he'd said. Jasper was arrogantly daring him, while the redhead was there, keeping him calm so he wouldn't miss.

While doing his best to ignore the red eyes drilling holes in him, Tommy fixed the crosshairs on JasperMax's heart and squeezed the trigger. The bolt shot out with all the speed over two hundred pounds per square inch of pressure could generate. It closed the distance in a millisecond. But he couldn't believe what happened next.

In one lightning-quick motion – with unbelievable speed that could only be chalked up to inter-dimensional mumbo jumbo – JasperMax raised his right hand and caught the bolt, stopping it just a fraction of an inch before it reached his chest. The two watched in horror as JasperMax displayed the bolt before them with both hands. Then, with a laughter that was much higher pitched than Max's normal voice, he casually snapped the bolt in two and flung it into the water.

The glow faded from Max's eyes. Bianca said, "He's gone."

They watched quietly as Max regained himself. He looked around beneath him to see if he'd dropped anything. Then he closed the tailgate, hurried back to the cab, and drove away.

Just like that it was over. Mission failed. Suddenly deflated after coming so close, they stood speechless for a few minutes.

Bianca took a deep breath and summed it up. "Well, shit."

Tommy couldn't argue with that. They ducked down behind the compressor while a car came through, then carefully made their way through the gridiron. After re-crossing the barrier they walked back to the car in silence.

Tommy put the crossbow back into the bag. He threw it behind the seat and got back to business. "I guess I should call Manny and give him the bad news."

"No, dumbass, you should call your wife. No doubt she's worried sick about you right now."

Sheepishly, "Yeah, that's what I meant."

He pulled his phone from his pocket and dialed up Toni, who answered instantly.

"Are you okay?"

"Yes, I'm okay." A quick look at Bianca. "We both are."

"Good." After a few seconds, she added, "Did you get him?"

There was no way to sugarcoat it, so Tommy just answered, "No. We were close but came up short. I'm sorry."

He waited while she relayed the information to Manny before returning. Toni hid her disappointment well. But after all the years together Tommy still heard it in her voice when she finally said, echoing what he'd overheard Manny say, "Well, we knew it was a long shot. And you guys are safe so that's the main thing. I was worried sick and I love you. I love you. I love you."

"I love you too, more than anything. I'll see you soon."

"I'm glad you're safe. And Bianca too. Are you on the way back? We're going to pick up Max and break the spell. Then Manny wants us all to meet in the war room to debrief and decompress. He says we still have about nine thousand dollars worth of wine to drink."

Tommy had a lingering, nagging feeling. It had to do with the fact that Jasper knew they were there, trying to kill him. He worried that Jasper might come after some or all of them in a vindictive way. He didn't mention it but decided they would be better off, somehow, if they stayed together for a while anyway.

"Okay. We'll be back in a few minutes. I need a quick change, I got soaked in the stream. Pour me a glass of Patty Free Moose. Might as well be miserable in our misery."

Despite the dismal mood, Toni giggled at that and they hung up after a final goodbye. It being quiet in the car, Bianca had heard everything.

"Lucky girl," she said again.

"I'm the lucky one. Try not to speed. We don't need any more excitement tonight."

Bianca gave the back of his neck a quick, heavenly rub and said, "Buzz killer."

They drove back in silence. They had failed and Jasper would go on killing throughout eternity. It was hard to find anything to talk about that didn't seem insignificant compared to that. They parked near the outside entrance of the war room. As they climbed out they could see and hear the party at Dirty Butt's in full force. Not everybody was gloom and doom.

Just before Bianca closed her door she surprised Tommy by saying, "I wouldn't have done it you know."

"Done what?"

"You know what. I can't help it, I'm a quintessential flirt. But I'm not a home wrecker, and you and Toni have something special. Something many people only dream of having after all your years together. Ain't no way in Hell I would ever try to spoil that."

Tommy wasn't expecting that particular conversation at that point in the evening. He just said, "Yeah, I know. It's just part of your charm."

She laughed. "Yeah, yeah. You wouldn't have done it either. Everything I said is true and you would never do that to your woman. She's a lucky girl."

"I'm the lucky one. But you're right. I couldn't do that to her."

Besides, as he remembered all the noise coming through the wall the previous night, he doubted he could keep up anyway. Still, as Bianca made her way around the front of the car, there was a natural, primal part inside that couldn't help envision him polishing the hood with her ass.

Obviously on the same wavelength, Bianca smiled and teased, "Sure is fun to think about though."

She blew him a kiss and walked toward the war room.

As he walked behind her, he was forced to agree.

CHAPTER 29

Toni drove Manny's car past the hamlet of Ferro and up the dirt road to Max's house at the base of Peckerneck Mountain. As they pulled into his parking area they saw Max closing up his shop, having left the short train at the depot near Dirty Butt's for the night.

Max looked confused, as though nobody had any business driving to his place at that time of night. When Manny jumped out, Max recognized him and looked a little more at ease, but still confused. Manny walked up, looked into Max's eyes, and said, "Pretty hippie gypsy. Pretty hippie gypsy. Pretty hippie gypsy."

It took a few moments, but Saavi's spell was broken. Max's expression changed to one of understanding. Confusion turned to sorrow as he realized his presence – being still alive – meant the attempted assassination had failed.

To say he looked disappointed would be an understatement. Toni got out, walked over and gave Max a big hug. He seemed to appreciate that, but still said, "Crapped out, huh?"

Manny answered. "Unfortunately. They said they got close but came up empty. We don't know the details yet. We're all going to the war room and drown our sorrows while we get the lowdown. Why don't you come with us?"

"Not without my Whiskey."

As he turned to go into the house, Toni wondered if he meant a bottle or his little dog. Not that it mattered. But she wasn't surprised when he came back wearing a denim jacket over his denim bibs, carrying Little Whiskey in his arm.

They drove the half-mile back to the conference center in silence. Toni parked Manny's car near the war room's end of the building and they entered without going through the foyer up front. Toni saw the duffel bag on the table where Manny usually sat, and the Mustang was outside, so she knew Tommy was back. Bianca was in the kitchenette opening a bottle of Patty Free Moose. As she looked up, Toni noticed Bianca also saw the disappointment in Max. He walked toward the table with his shoulders uncharacteristically slumped.

"Max? Whiskey?" Bianca asked, trying to sound cheerful, hoping it might rub off on him.

Max nodded and took his normal seat to the right of Manny's seat. He waited in silence, petting Little Whiskey between the ears.

Manny made his way over to Bianca and gave her a tight hug, then looked at Toni. "Some wine? We have plenty. And I don't want Monkey Beans to know I spent so much money without needing to. So let's drink it up."

Toni said, "Sure. I love the stuff. Unlike the rest of you." But she was walking toward the hallway door, wanting to go to her room and see Tommy as soon as possible. He came through the door before she reached it, comfortably dressed in sweatpants and slippers. They embraced in a long, tight hug and began kissing. A little excessive maybe, but nobody commented. She and Tommy walked toward the table and took their usual seats.

"Whiskey or wine?" Bianca called out to Tommy.

"Both. It's been a long day."

Bianca poured the wine and Manny poured the whiskey. They brought everything to the table and sat down – Bianca across from Max and next to Manny, as usual.

They took a drink and there was silence as nobody seemed to know what to say next. Manny finally cleared his throat and started. "Well, I'm glad we're all safe." Looking around the table and then at Tommy, "Can you share with us how it went? We're curious."

With a little help from Bianca, Tommy relayed the story as it happened. He explained how everything went smoothly until the plans changed and they had to scramble. When he got to the part where JasperMax caught the crossbow bolt in flight, he stuttered, as though he still couldn't believe it. Some reassurance from Bianca, confirming the lightning-fast reaction, seemed to help.

Then Max, still sad-looking and slumped in his chair, spoke up. "I can believe it. I know when that rotten bastard is fully inside of me I have no memory of what happens, but I've seen the results. There's no way my skinny old ass could have ever hauled that young man up the side of Scarface Mountain without some supernatural help. There are very few people, if any, who could do that. I have no doubt when that son of a bitch has me fully embodied I become super-human."

They took a moment and revisited their drinks. The winding down period had them doing that often. Tommy finally began again. "There's something we all need to know. Right as I was trying to get Max in my sights—" he paused, realizing what he had just said. But Max was unconcerned, as were the others. "Jasper turned and presented himself to us. I mean, he knew we were there. He stared right at us and dared me to pull the trigger."

271

At that statement, Tommy reached for Toni's hand under the table and squeezed it tightly. She realized he was more than a little concerned.

Manny nodded and said, apologetically, "You're right. We all knew this mission was a risk, but now we're facing the unsuccessful aftermath. I'll feel horrible if anything happens to any of us."

Tommy spoke again. "I don't know what difference it will make, but I would feel better if we all stayed here together, at least throughout the night. Though I doubt there's much we can do if Jasper decides to show up and have his way with us."

They all nodded. Discussing the subject made each of them realize they could be in danger. At least being together would give them a sense of fellowship that might ease their anxiety. Even Max, who had been around the world, seen much, and was used to being alone, nodded his head in agreement while Little Whiskey licked at his fingers.

Then there was a silence again. Bianca tried to lighten the mood. "I have to leave early for home, but yeah, I'll feel better hanging with you guys until the sun comes up. Should we start an all-night game of Monopoly or something?"

The gesture had the desired effect and they did lighten up. Max drained his glass and said, "I could use another if one of you kind souls would be so gracious."

It seemed they had all been hitting their drinks. They drained their glasses, then Bianca and Toni went to the mini-bar to pour fresh rounds.

Max spoke up again. "You might as well just bring the bottles over here. I know I don't plan on stopping after just two."

Toni looked back across the room at Max with sorrow. Though not big in stature, Max always carried himself upright, with a sense of dignity. But his dark tone when speaking, and the slumped head and shoulders, looked like a man who fought the good fight for many years but had admitted defeat. He hoped to go out with nobility, but instead was resigned to the fact that his health would soon begin to deteriorate, leaving him at the mercy of others in his final days – and there was nothing he could do to stop it. It seemed as though he was surrendering the rest of his life. It brought a tear to her eye, which she quickly wiped away before anyone could see it.

Tommy took a turn. "Maybe we should start a game of strip poker."

"I'm in!" Bianca said quickly and laughed.

"I think I'm too old for that," Toni said, giving Tommy a swift kick to the shin as she set his drink down. But it was a playful kick, and they laughed too.

Max suddenly sat up straighter and said in his deep voice, "Hell honey, you don't know what old is. And the last thing I think any of you want is to get my old, wrinkled ass into a strip poker game."

He laughed at himself, and they all joined him. It was a much-needed moment and everyone seemed glad to have the old Max back. But the moment was short-lived. Just as Bianca set down their drinks she straightened her back and stood up sharply.

"He's here!"

Nobody had to ask who was there. Silence prevailed as they glanced around nervously. After a few seconds, Bianca's eyes took on the red glow. Then she, with Jasper inside, jumped up on the table and began dancing suggestively – like a stripper without a pole. They sat motionless. No one dared to do anything to bring Jasper's attention to themselves. Meanwhile, the embodied Bianca

273

strutted down the table. A voice that wasn't hers and with no Texas twang chanted a seemingly homemade song while staring at Toni.

Funky ass bitch with eyes of blue
Just can't wait to have my way with you!

At the last words, she grabbed her crotch and thrust it directly at Toni, who stayed motionless.

They remained still until the red glow left Bianca's eyes and she found herself standing on the table. Looking confused, she hurriedly made her way back where Manny helped her down.

As she sat down she said, "He's still here, somewhere."

Again they stayed still, glancing around. The helplessness was overwhelming and nobody dared to move. Then it was Tommy's turn. As it became obvious he was Jasper's next host, Toni reached out and put her hand on his shoulder. The embodied Tommy ignored it, sat up straight and stuck his chest out proudly with an exaggerated stature. With a big, fake smile, he spoke in the same voice they'd heard earlier.

"Hi there. I'm a long-time, tax-sucking pig-cop. Do you know me? I don't solve any crimes. I just collect paychecks. Thanks, taxpayers, I love you all."

As before, everyone stayed still and silent. But the show continued. Pointing at Manny he said, "You see that man down there? He's been a fugitive from justice for decades. But I don't care, I'm just a tax-sucker who likes to pretend I'm a ghost hunter. Busting crooks is too much trouble. It's much more fun to ride around in my company cruiser and eat doughnuts. I love doughnuts."

The stillness and silence of the group likely wasn't Jasper's intended response, so he switched subjects.

Still possessed, Tommy turned to Toni and said, "Do you all know my wife? She's a good wife. Here I'll show you."

He grabbed Toni by the hair on the back of her head and pulled her face down into his crotch. Toni was caught off guard and tried to resist, but with Jasper in charge that was impossible. A scream tried to escape but was stifled. She could barely breathe with her face planted firmly into Tommy's privates.

"Oooh yeah, baby! Give me that good wifey treatment. Oooh, you do it so good. Just like you did it to Bud Rogers that night." Looking around the table he added, "You all remember Bud Rogers, don't you? Poor guy just couldn't handle a little adversity in his life."

Then it was over. Jasper left Tommy, who regained consciousness – surprised to find himself forcing Toni's face into his lap. He quickly raised her head and hugged her. Not knowing what had just happened but seeing her crying, he naturally held her.

Toni hugged him back. She knew it wasn't anything Tommy did. And she needed his comfort more than anything right then.

Meanwhile, they played the waiting game, wondering who – if anybody – was next. They all looked at Bianca with the same thought. She nodded her head. Yes, Jasper was still near. The silence seemed to last forever. Toni managed to compose herself and stopped crying. And still, the wait continued.

Suddenly Little Whiskey jumped out of Max's arm. He hit the floor and ran to the front of the coffee table between the two small couches – pacing back and forth, staring at Max and yipping.

Yip! Yip! Yip!

The red glow appeared in Max's eyes, but JasperMax just sat in the chair leering at them, one by one. Then he started laughing.

It was the same voice they'd heard through Bianca and Tommy, instead of Max's normally low, gravel voice.

"You all think you're so cool. The high and mighty trying to rid the world of evil." He kept laughing while he reached down and removed the crossbow from the duffel bag. He threw the bag onto the floor and held the bow up, looking at it from different angles in mock admiration.

Yip! Yip! Yip! Yip!

JasperMax stared at the little dog with contempt before returning his attention to the group. "I laugh at you all, thinking you could come after me with this little toy. Was this supposed to be some kind of joke? And your filthy, ugly whore-witch in the Catskills, with her little spell? How cute."

As he spoke, JasperMax placed the crossbow on the table. Toni noticed the cord with the handles and pulleys she'd seen Tommy use to cock the string was nowhere to be seen. But it wasn't an issue. JasperMax stood and placed the butt stock against his hip. With an index finger on each side of the main frame, he pulled the string back as though it were nothing but a rubber band. Once it clicked into place, he plucked one of the two remaining bolts from the quiver and slid it into its groove, nocking it on the string. After an exaggerated display of clicking off the safety catch, the crossbow was loaded and ready to fire.

Yip! Yip! Yip!

He grabbed the bow by its pistol grip in his left hand, with his finger on the trigger, and pointed it at Manny's face. They all watched in horror – their eyes as wide as wide as Manny's had become. He didn't move an inch. It was obvious Jasper was in control, and any type of defiance likely wouldn't end well.

Yip! Yip! Yip! Yip! Yip!

Toni grabbed Tommy's hand under the table again. Things were getting serious. She had watched Tommy practice shooting the crossbow and saw how hard the bolts hit the target. Even though she had never hunted, it was evident that despite not being tipped with a hunting broadhead, if that trigger was pulled, whatever, or whoever was in front of it would have a pretzel rod-sized hole punched into him.

Yip! Yip!

That person at that moment was Manny. He looked straight into JasperMax's eyes, doing his best to appear stoic. JasperMax started berating him. "You. You have been chasing me around the world now for, what, thirty-some years? Seriously, don't you have anything better to do? You and your gang at Monkey Farts? Then this is the best you can do? A rag-tag team of novices trying to sneak up on me in the dark with a toy from the Middle Ages? You should be ashamed of yourself. Trying to vanquish me from your perfect world with your silly plan. Hypocrite."

Yip! Yip! Yip!

Then he pivoted until the bow pointed at Bianca. She did an amazing job at showing no fear. And Jasper was less harsh.

"I feel a bit of kindred spirit with you. After all, I did help your mother bring you into creation. I would think that would buy me a little leniency from you. But no, you want me gone too. Such a disappointment, my child."

That last bit stung her. But she only showed a quick flinch, causing JasperMax to smile before moving on to Tommy.

Yip! Yip! Yip! Yip!

Aiming the crossbow at Tommy's chest, he started in. "And you, the pig-cop. It wasn't good enough for you to let things be. You had to come dragging up the past like some sort of crusader."

Leaving the deadly bolt aimed at Tommy, JasperMax moved his gaze to Toni. "Speaking of the past, I see you married the little guitar player from the diner. Yeah, I remember her." Shifting his red-eyed gaze between the two. "Did your pretty little wife ever tell you about the night we banged Bud Rogers?"

Yip! Yip! Yip! Yip!

Toni knew enough not to do anything rash, but if looks could kill she was shooting daggers, which made JasperMax smile even more as he continued. "Did she tell you about that spectacular blow job she gave him that night? Ol' Bud was in his glory, let me tell you." Then he mocked, "Let me see, was that before or after you two started dating?"

Yip! Yip! Yip! Yip! Yip! Yip!

JasperMax quit smiling, apparently having had his fill of yips. He swung the crossbow back towards Little Whiskey.

"SHUT UP!"

In what would normally have seemed to be a casual, off-hand shot, he pulled the trigger. But of course, the shot was right on. Poor Little Whiskey was no match. The bolt, without any razor-sharp broadhead blades, went through the little dog's chest, hit the floor, and ricocheted back up – nailing the poor little dog to one of the coffee table legs. His tiny feet dangled just off the floor.

With the pretzel rod-sized bolt through his chest, poor Little Whiskey could no longer yip yip yip. He couldn't do much of anything except wiggle around for a few seconds, like a grub on a fish hook.

Toni was already of a mind to lash out at JasperMax, and that last act put her over the top – common sense be damned. But as she tried to rise out of her chair, her level-headed husband held her down. She looked down the table and watched as Bianca, who had no such restraint, flew out of her chair and jumped across the table with fire in her eyes.

"YOU MOTHERFUCKER!!"

As she reached for JasperMax, likely intending to choke him or punch him, he put up his free right hand and caught her between her twin peaks. He gave her an upward shove which sent her high in the air toward the coffee table. Her head smacked the ceiling fan with a clunk, then she fell back to the floor with a thud – lying on her back between where Manny was seated and the pinwheeled Little Whiskey. Her arms lay above her head. Her red hair splayed out in all directions on the hardwood floor like a child's refrigerator drawing of the sun.

Bianca didn't get up right away. She just lay there and stared at the ceiling fan, moaning softly. Manny tried to get up to help her but a supernatural strong-arm from JasperMax planted him back into his seat.

So they all sat still. JasperMax once again held the crossbow up in front of him. "You pathetic mortals think you're some kind of match for me? I laugh in your faces. How dare you think you could wipe out my existence with this little toy?"

He grabbed the crossbow by the main beam with both hands and twisted. While the shaft didn't completely break, the changing shape caused one of the strings to come off its pulley where it snapped free with a loud crack. JasperMax flung the broken bow aside to demonstrate its worthlessness. It slid down the table where Toni put out a hand to keep it from falling into her lap. She looked at the remaining bolt in the quiver but knew it was useless. Even if Tommy had the cocking cord with the handles in his pocket – which she doubted, the broken beam and derailed string meant the crossbow was never going to fire another bolt.

JasperMax laughed again, then spoke. "You pathetic mortals. Look at you all now, cowering in fear. Are you afraid I'm going to do you all harm? Make no mistake, I could easily kill each one of you. But I'm not that kind of monster. I'm a vampire, and I only kill people to take their life force because I have to."

"Still, I can't just let you all off the hook now, can I? What kind of retaliation is fitting for a band of misfits that tried to vanquish me?" He looked at Bianca, who had stopped moaning and showed signs of returning to consciousness. A sinister smile accompanied an even bigger, ugly laugh.

"Of course. I haven't had a double meal in a long time. But that fiery redhead is going to be a sweet, juicy snack. A little overindulgence on my part and a long, peaceful nap. Then you can all live the rest of your lives feeling responsible for her death."

He waved his hand. "And you can't stop me. Your little bow-and-arrow is broken. Ha ha ha! I dare you mere mortals to try to stop me. This will be your hardest lesson ever learned, so learn it well. Then maybe you'll think twice about ever coming after me again."

Toni watched in horror while JasperMax's fangs grew. Manny tried to rise but JasperMax forcefully planted him back in his chair as he went by and kneeled next to Bianca. Bianca's eyes had regained some clarity. But while gazing into his eyes, they took on a lustful, inviting look.

As JasperMax leaned in for the kill, Manny jumped out of his chair and grabbed him from behind. Jasper, just as he had over thirty years before – this time through Max instead of Bud Rogers – reached back with one hand and gave Manny a shove that sent him flying at least twenty feet toward the open dance floor. He landed with a grunt and a thud as he slid on the hardwood.

As JasperMax again leaned in for the kill, Tommy desperately ran at him and met a similar fate. He was sent back over the meeting table and onto the walkway.

Toni considered doing the same thing. But it was her turn to be the rational one, and she realized it was pointless. Meanwhile, JasperMax leaned in, only to be interrupted again by Manny, who went flying the other way, toward the kitchenette.

Toni cursed herself. *Do something!!* But what? The two grown men were getting tossed around like rag dolls in what began to look like a poorly choreographed fight scene in a low-budget movie. Toni maybe tipped the scales at one-twenty. Still, something had to happen. While the two-man onslaught momentarily saved Bianca, it was hardly a sustainable defense – especially at their age.

Come on Toni! Do something! She scolded herself. She wondered briefly where Tommy's pistol was. But of course that would only succeed in killing Max and not Jasper. She watched in horror as her husband went in for another round of abuse. She almost cried out as he flew toward the coffee table – smashing into it and causing it to flip up on its side. Doing so made the poor, pinwheeled Little Whiskey fly up – his head and legs waved like a flag while the rest of his corpse stayed pegged to the leg. The bolt stuck straight into the air, holding fast and keeping the tiny dog pinned as his little feet and legs flopped down and hung motionless.

She gazed at the bolt. Of course! *This is it, Toni!* She thought quickly. It was just as The Oracle described. *This is it. Jasper is distracted by his arrogance. And the redhead is as involved as she can be.*

With no further delay, she knew what she had to do. She grabbed the last bolt from the quiver in front of her and shoved the broken crossbow off the table. Then, with the adrenaline-fueled alacrity of a spring chicken, she hopped onto the table and headed for JasperMax. Even with her short legs it only took four steps to reach the other end.

But time slowed to a crawl. At step number one she was reminded of her mother telling her not to run with a sharp object. By step two, as she watched a weary and beaten Manny go flying yet again, she flashed back to when she and Tommy first started flirting and hanging out after a chance meeting in Letchworth State Park – thirty-seven years before.

By step three she was thinking she probably looked like a half-assed pole vaulter, running with a steel-tipped pretzel rod in both fists out in front of her. By the fourth step she was back in real-time, making sure not to trip over Manny's wine glass. As she reached the end of the table Toni jumped as high as she could, realizing almost too late that the ceiling fan was there. She had no idea how much force it would take to drive the wooden bolt into JasperMax's heart. She just knew she was going to give it everything she had.

As she fell toward her target she saw Tommy coming in for another round from her right side. She feared he would get between them and ruin her plan, but at the last instant he stopped. And that proved to be the final distraction. As JasperMax reached a hand toward Tommy, he had no idea of the incoming threat that was Toni.

She fell towards JasperMax with just one thought. *I'm finally going to get the son of a bitch who killed George.*

Ignoring her shin as it whacked the hardwood back of Manny's chair, Toni fell into JasperMax and planted the wooden bolt between his shoulder blades with all her strength.

Time slowed down again as the bolt drove home with a SPLUCK!

Then, just as everything had been a blurred fury of action, it all stopped. Max's body slumped forward, pinning Bianca to the floor. Toni pushed herself to her knees while Manny pulled himself off the floor to her left. Then everyone stayed still, mesmerized by the scene that unfolded before them. Max's engineer hat had fallen off and covered Bianca's nose and mouth, but Toni could see she was back to reality. Her eyes shifted from the lustful, inviting gaze, to one of sheer horror.

Still, nobody moved. They all watched in amazement as the body that was Max started, what could only be described as melting. Not melting like an old witch with a bucket of water. It was more of a dry melt – as though every molecule or atom of Max's body slowly turned into ultra-fine specks of dust. Dust particles that were so fine they began to flow like a liquid, out through his sleeves and pants. Everywhere, little rivulets of Max gravy ran down in all directions over a petrified, frozen Bianca. And everywhere the dust rivers settled into pools on the floor, the air above the pools began to shimmer – like looking across a hot desert. Then the dust particles slowly disappeared – absorbed into the air like steam particles.

Nobody moved for what seemed like several minutes as they watched Max's body slowly vanish into thin air – an incredible display of inter-dimensional mumbo jumbo. Eventually, there was nothing left of Max. His clothes lay tight against Bianca. His shoes and belt lay where they were last. His gold railroad watch peeked out of its pocket and threatened to slide down Bianca's side.

And still, it seemed nobody dared to move.

Finally, Bianca brought them out of their daze. She reached

down with her left hand and pulled Max's hat off her face. She looked around and said, "Ewwww!"

That jolted them all back to action. Tommy quickly moved to help Toni to her feet. Then they grabbed Bianca's hands and pulled her up as Max's clothes and things fell to the floor. She pulled at the front of her shirt, as though it laying against her skin was uncomfortable. It was all too much and the three embraced in a tight hug. Tears flowed freely from the girls. Toni didn't look to see if Tommy was crying. She kept her face buried in his chest and Bianca's hair.

Meanwhile, Manny seemed rather businesslike. He immediately took up Max's jacket and went over to the upended coffee table where he worked the body of Little Whiskey free. He tossed the bloody bolt into the fireplace and wrapped Little Whiskey in Max's jacket with as much dignity as possible.

Tommy decided to help. As he and Manny righted the coffee table, Tommy gestured at the small puddle of blood left behind by poor Little Whiskey.

"No worries." Manny shrugged. "I'll make a call. By tomorrow there will be no evidence either Max or his dog were ever here."

Tommy shook his head in wonder and began picking up Max's things, placing them on the table near Manny, while the girls continued their hugging and crying. Manny gathered up the broken crossbow and put it into the duffel bag. Then he placed the rest of Max's belongings in there, starting with the wrapped-up Little Whiskey.

The girls finally separated and turned to watch. Manny tried zipping up the over-filled bag, but he stopped as the bill of Max's hat stuck out. As he began to stuff it inside, Bianca, still pulling at her shirt, moved forward and put her hand on his.

She said, softly. "Do you think I could . . . I mean . . . do you think Max would mind?"

Manny unzipped enough to pull the hat out. He turned and placed it on Bianca's head. It was a touch too small, so he had to leave it toward the back with the bill sticking almost straight up. Still, Bianca had that rare ability to look absolutely ridiculous and stunningly cute at the same time. She put her fist up next to her head and pumped it. "Woot! WOOT!"

They all burst out in much-needed laughter. They had been through a lot, and emotions were in full swing.

Manny went back to zipping up the bag. Then he stopped again and rummaged around inside for a moment. He pulled out Max's railroad watch and turned to Toni, placing it in her hand. "And I think he'd be glad for you to have this."

Laughter turned back to tears as Toni hugged first Manny, then Tommy and Bianca again. She flipped open the watch's cover to see a picture of a young Max in his Army uniform, along with his beautiful young bride in her wedding gown. Toni stopped Manny from zipping up while she fished out the picture.

"I'll cherish this watch forever," she said as he handed the picture to him. "But this belongs in Max's jacket pocket, next to Little Whiskey."

Manny nodded, placed the picture back inside, and finished zipping up the bag. Then he turned to the three and tried to speak, but struggled – a few tears appearing at the corner of his eyes. "I . . . I don't have the words to tell you all—"

"Can it, Manny." Bianca was firm but there was no malice. She smiled and added, "We're all glad it worked out. You can write a speech later."

Manny didn't seem to have a response. He stood there and smiled at them.

After a moment of silence Bianca, still pulling at her shirt, said, "Well I don't know about the rest of y'all, but I'm going to my room and get out of these clothes. Then I'm gonna take a long, hot shower. Then—" gesturing over her shoulder, she added, "I'm going over to Dirty Butt's and get drunk as an ever-loving skunk!"

Toni looked at Tommy, who was looking at her with agreement that it was exactly what they should do. After everything they had been through came to a screeching halt, nobody seemed to have a better idea. So that's what they did.

EPILOGUE

Sunday morning brought hangovers all around. Bianca, who was likely immune to morning-after effects – just like everything else – was true to her word and left early to go home.

With the previous night's tearful goodbyes just memories, Manny woke Toni and Tommy around 8:00 AM and insisted they get breakfast. After which, he disappeared for a few hours to give Max's effects and Little Whiskey a hero's burial at some secret Monkey Beans location.

Toni and Tommy spent the day relaxing and napping. Recovery from a drinking binge wasn't as easy as it used to be.

Later, when they all felt better, Manny insisted they get cleaned up and have a nice dinner together. He took them to a beautiful log cabin restaurant in Keene Valley that overlooked a wild section of a river. They sat on a patio while the sun set behind the mountains. They spared no expense, with surf and turf, appetizers, and plenty of champagne to celebrate their success.

Eventually, they found themselves back at the conference center sitting in comfortable Adirondack chairs – positioned in a semicircle around the coffee table, facing the fireplace. A large goblet of mostly untouched Patty Free Moose wine sat in front of each of them. It was a beautiful night. The garage door was open and the jukebox mix of classic rock and modern country filtered in from Dirty Butt's.

It was the end of an extraordinary few days, and the gang was in that end-of-vacation type mode where everybody knew they should go to bed. But they also knew that once they did, they would wake up in the morning and their time together would be over. So they took turns in between conversations pretending they weren't falling asleep. As nighttime wore on, conversation dwindled and the nodding off increased.

But they were steadfast, holding out as long as they could. Eventually, after a long silence that may very well have been the one that signaled the end, they were jolted awake when the soothing jukebox music gave way to an ear-splitting rendition of a Johnny Mathis song.

Apparently, Sunday was karaoke night at Dirty Butt's, and contestant number one was tone-deaf. They came to life and looked around, grimacing. Manny huffed a laugh, then got up and poked the fire back to life, adding some wood.

He sat back down. Attempting to ignore the awful serenade, he looked at the couple and asked, "So, what does the future hold for you two? Have we converted you into full-time peeno hunters? I can get you into Monkey Beans. In fact, you're both honorary members. Before we part I'll give you a card with a number in case you ever find yourself in any kind of jam. Just call, any time, day or night and tell them who you are. Our vast resources are at your disposal forever. This mission was huge, and you two are considered heroes in the eyes of Monkey Beans. You will also find a little bonus in your bank accounts every month."

That caught the couple off guard, but before they could say

anything Manny raised a hand and stopped them. "I don't want to hear it. You've earned it, and Monkey Beans can afford it. It will all be a legal dividend payment from Jackson Investments. Save your protests."

"But—"

"No. I won't hear it. That conversation is over. Now, I asked, will you be joining us? Are you converted to becoming full-time peeno hunters?" Manny gave them a warm smile.

Finally, Tommy said. "Well, no. Though we will be looking at the world differently from now on, we won't be joining you. Instead, we've had a long talk. Between my being a cop all the years and having rotating shifts, even after becoming investigator, and with Toni having run the diner seven days a week all this time, we realized we haven't taken a lot of vacations. That leisurely drive up here in the motorhome reminded us that we should take some time for ourselves. Hell, I've got a thirty-eight-year pension and I'm damned near old enough for social security. And although you wouldn't know it to look at her, Toni isn't far behind. And she has a long-time employee who's been asking for a chance to take over the diner on a lease-to-own basis."

"We've decided when we get home we're going to talk to the dealer where we rented the motorhome and see about buying it. Then call it quits on the careers, and hit the road for however long it takes to get it out of our system."

Manny beamed at them. "That sounds fabulous. I'm happy for both of you. Where will you go first? The mountains or the beach?"

Tommy said, "Mountains," while Toni said, "Beach."

They all laughed as the couple instinctively reached out between their chairs and locked their fingers together.

Toni added, "We'll figure it out. We always do."

Still beaming with happiness, Manny said softly, "It's wonderful to see a couple like yourselves, obviously deep in love after all this time together."

Tommy answered, "Well of course we've had some ups and downs. But overall we've been blessed, that's for sure." Then he gestured to Manny. "And what about you? You've been chasing a ghost for over half your life. This must be a huge shift for you. Do you have plans moving forward?"

Manny looked thoughtful. Smiled and almost laughed out loud. The offensive singing next door gave way to a much more enjoyable Patsy Cline imitation.

Finally, he said, "Well, my long-term plans involve joining a coalition to reach out to the peeno community. You see, we've been hunting them for centuries, trying to rid the world of them. And, quite frankly, we've failed miserably. But numerous Monkey Beans old-timers like myself are adopting the opinion that characters like Jasper aside, we can co-exist."

After a sip of wine, he kept on. "You see, most of the witches are good witches. And they do a fair enough job of policing their own – keeping the bad witches in check." Shrugging he added, "At least as good a job as we humans do with our bad apples. Take Jack the Oracle for example. There's no reason we can't get along with a guy like that, rather than try to hunt him and his kind to extinction."

"And then there's werewolves. They're all multi-generational. They own their own stock farms – cattle, sheep, goats, whatever, depending on where they live. And every month they go out to their back forty and do their thing – howling at the moon and feasting. And even if anyone finds the remains of their actions, they can blame it on regular wolves. Hell, there hasn't been an instance of a werewolf hurting a human in over thirty years. And even that was just a case of self-defense against a peeno hunter."

Toni and Tommy kept listening, interested.

"That leaves us with vampires. But the truth is, there aren't very many of them. They keep themselves spread out. Because of their daytime vulnerability, they keep a low profile as much as possible. They either live in isolated areas where their victims' bodies are devoured by animals before ever being discovered, or they live in crowded cities with millions of people and frequent murders. Like hiding a pebble on a beach."

Toni spoke up. "But you can't be okay with them killing people, even if it's on the down low."

Manny nodded. "That's the thing. Vampires are perfectly capable of living on animal blood. It's the life force they're after. They only keep after humans because it's been their tradition for centuries. Most of them are hundreds of years old. Maybe there's a preference – taste or something. But the thing is, we don't expect to change everything overnight. Still, change begins with the first step. We have a group – and the peenos have a group – who have agreed to meet and open discussions. That's where I'm headed."

Toni smiled and said, "That's very noble. You're a credit to the human race."

Before Manny could respond, Tommy added, "Yeah, you're not bad for a convicted felon, still wanted by the law."

There was a brief tense moment, but Tommy couldn't help but smile.

They laughed as he added, "I had to get that in there at least once more. No offense."

"None taken." Manny smiled.

Tommy continued. "You said that was your long-term plan. Do you have something different planned for the near future? A vacation or something?"

Manny assumed a sheepish look while he thought about his response. "It seems there's a matter of . . . uh . . . you remember I told you about Saavi, the powerful witch that cast the spell for us?"

The couple nodded.

"Well, our initial transaction was just a down payment. We agreed that if our mission was successful, I would return to the Catskills for . . . let's call it . . . further remuneration."

Manny started laughing, along with Toni and Tommy as it set in.

After a round of deep belly laughs, Tommy finally said, "Ahh, the things you do for your fellow man."

"I know! I know!"

Toni stopped giggling long enough to add, "You'd better refill that script, Manny. You ain't no spring chicken you know."

Through the laughs, all Manny could do was repeat himself. "I know! I know!"

When they finally subsided, Tommy leaned forward and raised his glass of Patty Free Moose.

"Here's to settling debts and new horizons." They grabbed their goblets and had a drink.

Then Manny added, "And here's to Max."

They nodded, and just before they drank, Toni added, "And to Little Whiskey."

Then Manny started over. He pulled himself out of the low Adirondack chair, with some considerable groaning. Not just because of his age, but also from the soreness of being tossed around like a rag doll the previous night. Tommy followed suit with similar physical and vocal protests. Toni rose and stood next to him.

Manny raised his glass and said, "Here's a toast to Maximilian Tiberius Beauregard, and his faithful companion, Little Whiskey."

They gave their goblets a triple clank and saluted with a proper sip. Then they sat down, slung low in their comfortable chairs, and went back to watching the fire as they took turns nodding off – feeling good about having made the world a better place.

* * * * *

On a lonesome stretch of highway in western Tennessee, a middle-aged woman drove southwest into the darkness.

The woman – whose conception was influenced by a bit of inter-dimensional mumbo jumbo thirty-seven years before – had no idea that deep inside her, a single cell she had always thought she couldn't produce, had been violated, and was rapidly dividing and multiplying with the miracle of life.

Feeling good about herself for helping rid the world of a monster, she sang along with Pearl Jam while looking forward to a nice rest in the next town. She let the warm wind blow through her wild, red hair as she drove – without a care in the world.

ABOUT THE AUTHOR

M. K. Danielson

M. K. Danielson is a retired operating engineer. He was born in Batavia, NY, and has lived most of his life in western New York, near the boundary of Genesee and Wyoming Counties. When he's not writing he likes to get in his truck and drive to places he's never been – just to see what's on the other side of the hill.

This is his second novel.

www.ingramcontent.com/pod-product-compliance
Lightning Source LLC
Chambersburg PA
CBHW020357110726
47899CB00006B/1754